OWL

||||| ||| ||| || | |||| ||| |||||| ||||| ||
D1615385

THE HIDDEN HARDY

Thomas Hardy, aged about 30.
Dorset County Museum

The Hidden Hardy

Joe Fisher

First published 1992 by
MACMILLAN ACADEMIC AND PROFESSIONAL LTD
Houndmills, Basingstoke, Hampshire RG21 2XS
and London
Companies and representatives
throughout the world

ISBN 0–333–52763–1

A catalogue record for this book is available
from the British Library.

Transferred to digital printing 1999

Printed in Great Britain by
Antony Rowe Ltd, Chippenham, Wiltshire

For Roy Fisher
and Barbara Venables Fisher

Contents

Textual References

With the exception of *The Mayor of Casterbridge* and *Tess of the d'Urbervilles*, where I use respectively Oxford and Penguin paperback editions, page references given in this text refer to Macmillan paperback editions of Hardy's work. Publication details of these are given in my bibliography.

Acknowledgements

I should like to thank a number of people for their generous help in the preparation of this book. Rhys Garnett, Peter Widdowson, Adrian Poole, Heather Glen, John Barrell and John Goode all read sections of early drafts of my manuscript and offered many valuable (and often salutary) comments and ideas. Beverley Skeggs and Pat Agar have both been unfailing sources of intellectual guidance, support and common sense throughout the project. An acknowledgement of one's parents is often merely a *devoir*; but in this case it represents my gratitude for the very active part they both played in developing the main arguments of this text. I am also grateful to Roger Ebbatson for permission to quote from unpublished material, and to Margaret Cannon, my editor at Macmillan, for her unflagging patience and support.

By far my greatest debt is to Tony Tanner, without whom this work would simply not have been done.

Errors and opinions are, of course, my own.

'Never speak disrespectfully of society, Algernon.
Only people who can't get into it do that.'

Lady Bracknell, in *The Importance of Being Earnest*

Introduction

My aim in this study is to identify, and establish the force of, partly concealed patterns in the fabric of Hardy's prose fiction, and to relate these to recent marxist and feminist critical writing on Hardy, especially to work done by Penny Boumelha (1982)[1], George Wotton (1985)[2], John Goode (1988)[3], Patricia Ingham (1989)[4] and Peter Widdowson (1989)[5].

As Widdowson's work shows with particular clarity, the 'Thomas Hardy' who has been produced by a century of criticism and interpretation is very much a culturally generated object, which might equally be described as an ideologically informed discourse placed in front of the texts, with the effect of disabling readings which may be regarded as perverse or dangerous by 'bourgeois liberalism'. As Wotton puts it:

> The ideological forms and institutional practices of English are, despite every attempt at concealment, profoundly political . . . English . . . is . . . not an immutable cultural object but the site of cultural struggle. It is a struggle in which there are no neutral positions and in the present situation every reading of Thomas Hardy is an act of political commitment.[6]

A Hardy criticism which calls these issues into question must in many ways begin, like the idealized future Hardy finds at the end of *A Laodicean*, with a process of demolition. In *A Laodicean* the raw materials of Castle de Stancy are to be used in the creation of a new house, and a similar reclamation of the raw materials of the texts themselves from ideologically informed interpretative structures is necessary here before rebuilding can begin. The first move I propose is an extension of Widdowson's exercise in his reading of *The Hand of Ethelberta*. The key to this novel is the relation between classes; between master and servant, property owner and artisan. The heroine is a storyteller, and her 'reserve' story is an account of her own life. Ethelberta's fiction is both the story of the novel and a definition of the novel itself. This is an extremely potent and subversive conceit. Widdowson argues that

1

[*The Hand of Ethelberta*] threatens the coterminous notions of 'the individual' and of 'character' which lie at the heart of bourgeois liberal-humanist ideology and its dominant literary form. 'Artificiality' parallels 'alienation', 'fiction' parallels 'class'; and the character 'Ethelberta' is no more than the amalgam of the discourses which structure her in the novel.[7]

He goes on to show how the minor novels, and specifically the Novels of Ingenuity, have become a '"neutralized" sub-group'[8] in the Hardy canon. To use *A Laodicean's* architectural metaphor, these are building materials which have never carried any structural weight in the project of critically rewriting an 'acceptable' Hardy; and their redundancy in this regard produces an area in which a new approach to Hardy's prose fiction can be formulated. As I shall show, patterns revealed by such an examination strongly suggest that the dangerous subversions of mode and ideology of the Novels of Ingenuity, which have been critically suppressed in favour of the 'acceptable' Novels of Character and Environment, in fact provide important clues to reading the Novels of Character and Environment, and demonstrate that such subversions are in many cases very important factors in the making of these fictions. The difference between the two groups of texts I define as the Myth of Wessex. Pierre Macherey's comments about Balzac's Paris might equally be applied to Hardy's Wessex:

the Paris of the *Comédie humaine* is a literary object only in so far as it is a product of an effort of writing; it has no prior existence. But the elements that comprise this object, the relationships that give them coherence, are reciprocally determined. They draw their 'truth' from one another and not from anything else. Balzac's Paris is not an expression of the real Paris, a concrete generality (whereas the concept would be an abstract generality). It is the product of a certain labour, dictated not by reality but by the work. It is not the reflection of a reality or an experience but of an artifice, which consists wholly in the establishment of a complex system of relations.[9]

In terms of the production of an 'acceptable' Hardy, the literary artifice of Wessex becomes, in its insistence on landscape and organic process, the apparently 'natural' context for 'natural' characters and dramas, work practices and power relations. An 1881 survey article in the *British Quarterly Review* shows clearly how Wessex becomes, for its consumers, a harmonizing discourse of class, of the ostensibly fixed system of rank and authority which *The Hand of Ethelberta* blatantly disrupts:

> If Mr Hardy has indeed drawn his characters on the whole favourably, in spite of their many shortcomings; if he has drawn true gentlemen in his village carpenter John Smith, the reddleman Diggory Venn, the tranter Dick Dewy, it is because these men and their prototypes are so in fact . . . we never expect to find in any rank or position truer or more high-minded gentlemen than some Dorset labourers we are proud to call friends.[10]

This Wessex is, as I shall show, very much an authorial strategy developed and exploited by Hardy as a means of achieving the cultural (and economic) power confirmed by the collection of laudatory survey articles which began to appear around 1880. Essentially these celebrate Hardy's success as a trader in bourgeois fictions. I believe that there is a clear distinction to be made between Hardy's trading strategies, in which the exploitation of Wessex is the principal device, and his narrative strategies, in which the subversive complexities of the Novels of Ingenuity are central. My contention is that the Novels of Character and Environment represent an inherently conflictual engagement of the two.

I want to look at Hardy's trade as a novelist first in terms of his relation to the Victorian fiction market's production process, and secondly in terms of his own manufacturing process in creating an object to be traded in this market. George Moore offers this provocative account of the literary production process in his introduction to the 1885 English translation of Zola's *Piping Hot*:

> We judge a pudding by its eating, and I judge Messrs Mudie and Smith by what they have produced; for they are the authors of our fiction . . . [they] have thrown English fiction into the abyss of nonsense in which it now lies.[11]

This is effectively an attack on Mudie and Smith's power, as the proprietors of circulating libraries, to use their position as the principal buyers of three-volume novels to determine the nature of 'publishable' fiction. A novel likely to be unacceptable to the libraries becomes unpublishable because it has no market; consequently

the risk to a publisher like Tinsley or Macmillan of printing such a
fiction becomes unacceptable. As Norman Feltes argues:

> The hegemonic system, based on a high initial price for a three-
> volume novel, generated large profits which were divided among
> publisher, library and author. But the very safety of this mode
> of petty-commodity book production precluded its achieving the
> profits available by the capitalist production, in part-issue, of
> commodity-texts. The surplus value of the commodity-text was
> made possible by capitalist control, to a greater extent, of the
> actual production process, a form of alienation which the writer,
> to some extent, might resist . . . To that extent, part-issue was,
> for the capitalist publisher, an imperfect form of commodity-text
> production; control of the production process was erratic, the
> process itself being potentially a disruptive moment of class
> struggle. The structures of magazine serial publication, on the
> other hand, allowed a far more subtle and effective form of con-
> trol of the production of commodity-texts . . . The writer's work
> was produced in a journal within relations of production ana-
> logous to those prevailing in a textile mill.[12]

It is romantic, however, to see Hardy as a worker in this process. He
is in no sense a wage-labourer in a textile mill, and he never offers
this definition of himself. Technically he is a small entrepreneur
selling his produce on to a larger one. (In the autobiography, which
Widdowson rightly defines as Hardy's last fiction,[13] the Hardy family become small entrepreneurs and craftsmen descended from the
gentry rather than the domestic servants, teachers and slightly el-
evated workfolk they really were.) He is also, in all the texts I
examine after *Desperate Remedies*, balancing the relative freedom of
three-decker publication against the strictures of serialization, effectively greater because the magazine publisher combined the functions of publisher and circulating library owner.
    I believe that Hardy identifies and exploits Feltes's 'disruptive
moment of class struggle', using his position as a small entrepreneur
to create a product which, until the sustained and open challenge to
sexual morality of *Tess of the d'Urbervilles* and *Jude the Obscure*, is
overtly acceptable to, and accepting of, the hegemonic authority of
library buyers and magazine editors and which covertly makes radical attacks on this authority. (It is significant that the attacks become
increasingly overt as the three-decker's hegemony is eroded: as

Guinevere Griest shows, *Jude the Obscure's* publication in 1895 comes at the point of a dramatic collapse, from 184 three-decker novels published in 1894 to four in 1897.[14]) As a trader Hardy effectively 'buys in' and 'sells on' the raw material of Wessex, adding value by the creative artifice of manufacture and synthesizing an observed 'reality' into an 'acceptable' unity by means of plotting and narration. This is intimately linked to a calculating attempt to gain cultural power and its accompanying political platform. Goode offers a comment on the self-comparison with Napoleon which eventually led Hardy to write *The Dynasts*, and which offers valuable clues to a driven, dangerous, over-reaching quality which runs through all the fictions I examine here:

> At various times during the seventies, Hardy planned to write a literary account of Napoleon which finally came to fruition a quarter of a century later as *The Dynasts*. The upstart who nearly ruled Europe clearly fascinated the *ariviste* who conquered by writing the culture which did not know him. It is not surprising that the first coherent response to this ambivalent hero is to repress him, to represent him, indeed, as an absence [in *The Trumpet-Major*].[15]

In this context each text becomes a struggle for power, a deliberately chosen battle in a steeply geared and self-conscious assault on 'greatness'. Hardy's use of subject matter is as ruthless as this exercise demands. Roger Ebbatson's reading of 'The Dorsetshire Labourer'[16] makes the nature of this process particularly clear. This apparently sympathetic text is ultimately a trader's attempt to disable and silence his sources. The agricultural labourer, the Shakespearian peasant of *Far From the Madding Crowd* and *The Return of the Native*, becomes the victim of circumstance, silenced in this essay by 'the seamless flow of Hardy's meditative prose' and silenced in the novels by the linguistic distance between the narrator's standard English and the trader's (mis)representation of dialect and vernacular speech patterns. As Ebbatson puts it, 'the novel [*The Return of the Native*] unconsciously mirrors and re-works issues of class-division and a history of appropriation and centralisation'. He also points out that Hardy ignores significantly changed work patterns in Dorset/Wessex in his own lifetime whereby larger and more irregular work-teams led to the emergence of a working class consciousness far more coherent than anything Hardy chooses to represent. The 1872

Revolt of the Field, for instance, is totally ignored in the novels, although Joseph Arch (certainly one of the most 'acceptable' Victorian trade union leaders) is mentioned in complimentary terms in 'The Dorsetshire Labourer'.[17] Hardy covers himself, as it were, by setting the Wessex novels back forty or fifty years, but this seems a very token gesture.

But this concealed corruption in the trader's 'buying in' process is in many ways cancelled out, even justified, by concealed corruptions of narrative and plot when Wessex is 'sold on'. Making a direct assault on the market requirements and breaking the rules would simply result in rejection and silence, as in the case of *The Poor Man and the Lady*. In *The Principles of Success in Literature*, published originally as a series of articles in 1865, two years before *The Poor Man and the Lady* was written, the critic and magazine editor G. H. Lewes offers this justification of bourgeois fiction's claim to hegemonic power:

> Literature is at once the cause and the effect of social progress. It deepens our natural sensibilities, and strengthens by exercise our intellectual capacities. It stores up the accumulated experience of the race, connecting Past and Present into a conscious unity; and with this store it feeds successive generations to be fed in turn by them. As its importance emerges into more general recognition, it necessarily draws after it a larger crowd of servitors, filling noble minds with a noble ambition . . . It is natural that numbers who have been thrilled with this delight should in turn aspire to the privilege of exciting it. Success in literature has thus become not only the ambition of the highest minds . . . Prime Ministers and emperors . . . have longed also for the nobler privilege of exercising a generous sway over the minds and hearts of their readers . . . Success in literature is, in truth, the blue ribbon of nobility.[18]

In the presence of so much nobility, and having in effect contracted to misrepresent the true position of agricultural workfolk and small traders, Hardy's own will to power over the real producers of his fictions consists in cheating them. The prescribed necessary length of a novel, and the amount of narrative padding necessary to fill it, provide Hardy with a potent area of reserved power between 'traded' and 'narrated' texts. Henry James senses this process, though not necessarily its contents, in his 1874 review of *Far From the Madding Crowd*. The novel is

> extended to its rather formidable dimensions by the infusion of a large amount of conversational and descriptive padding and the use of an ingeniously verbose and redundant style . . . *Far From the Madding Crowd* gives us an uncomfortable sense of being a simple 'tale', pulled and stretched to make the conventional three volumes.[19]

Hardy does not, at least in his crucial early development as a novelist between *Desperate Remedies* in 1871 and *A Laodicean* in 1881, offer the same head-on challenge as Moore. Instead he becomes a proficient 'trader' in the established fiction market. But he uses the gap between the trader who sells the story and the narrator who tells it to corrupt the traded object; and he does this in such a way that the traded text is still fit for its complementary tasks of producing surplus value and reproducing patterns of social deference in terms of class and gender. This self-subversion is not a matter of momentary disruption, or an uneasy problematization of the text's fictiveness: it is a sustained campaign of deception which runs through all Hardy's novels, creating hostile and part-visible patterns beneath what might generally be regarded as the 'surface' of the text. This is perhaps best explained in terms of painting.

In his incomplete novel *Work Suspended* (1943), Evelyn Waugh uses painting as a metaphor for the paternal shadow cast into the twentieth century by the Victorian novel. The relationship between underpainting and finished canvas becomes an image of its double standard, of the relationship between technique and product:

> My father made copious and elaborate studies for his pictures and worked quickly when he came to their final stage, painting over a monochrome sketch, methodically, in fine detail, left to right across the canvas as though he were lifting the backing of a child's 'transfer'. 'Do your thinking *first*,' he used to tell the Academy students. 'Don't muddle it out on the canvas. Have the whole composition clear in your head before you start,' and if anyone objected that this was seldom the method of the greatest masters, he would say, 'You're here to become Royal Academicians, not great masters. If you want to write books on Art, trot round

Europe studying the Rubenses. If you want to learn to paint,
watch me.' The four or five square feet of finished painting were
a monument of my father's art. There had been a time when I had
scant respect for it. Lately I had come to see that it was more than
a mere matter of dexterity and resolution.[20]

The 'hidden' texts I identify here are very much the Academician's
'monochrome sketches', cartoons imperfectly covered by the painting of the 'finished' canvas. If the artist knows that his audience will
not be looking for his underpainting, or if the narrator of a novel
knows that his publisher and editor will not be looking for its fictional equivalent, this creative process is open to potential corruption: providing you produce an 'acceptable' end product for 'selling
on', you can draw what you like underneath. My argument here is
that in all the prose fictions I examine Hardy draws a cartoon of
Swiftian brutality on his empty canvas, then covers it, I believe
deliberately imperfectly, with what has more usually been regarded
as the 'finished' text. The presence of this hidden Hardy, and the
sustained arguments to be found inside rather than outside the
Trojan Horse of the 'traded' text, do much to justify and develop
the suggestions made first by Roy Morrell[21] and then more recently
by Ingham[22] and Widdowson,[23] among others, that a new and more
subversive Hardy may be found through the mechanisms of his
novel-writing.

In all the texts I examine here, plot is pre-eminently a matter of
gender. Every love plot, every marriage plot, every divorce plot,
indeed every manifestation of sexuality, all these are wholly politicized by gender relations. Dorothy E. Smith argues for a very fundamental connection between femininity and a mass fiction market:

> The discourse of femininity originates with the emergence of a
> wholly new order of social relations resulting from the discovery
> of moveable type and from the organizational and commercial
> developments which brought about a mass market for books and
> magazines. The emergence of a public, textually-mediated dis-
> course marks a new form of social relation, transcending and
> organizing local settings and bringing about relations among them
> of a wholly different order.[24]

Making the text of a novel, and in a larger sense making stories
which present themselves as 'true' histories, is almost by definition

a device of patriarchal control in a patriarchally controlled society. Thackeray's dictum that the writer should 'have good manners, a good education and write in good English . . . We shall also suppose the ladies and children always present'[25] points in its last sentence to a consideration of, really a suppression of, the female and the impressionable. And tellingly it appeals to three patriarchally-controlled structures, 'manners', 'education', and writing as the means of carrying out this suppression. Ingham offers this account of the relationship between gender and market constraints in popular Victorian fiction.

> linguistic conventions . . . consisted centrally of a restricted set of 'feminine' signs clustered around 'the womanly' and 'womanhood' and the generic 'woman', a narrative syntax falling into limited patterns, cast resolutely in the indicative (the mood of assertion and definition) and a delimited semantic range that excluded the erotic.
>
> The internal safeguard and measure of these restraints was the required inscribed reader, much discussed in the reviews: young, female, aspiring to womanliness, ignorant, innocent of the physiological facts of sex, as well as being genteel, pious and intellectually unrobust. The required narrator was expected to collude with an implied (? parental) and hypocritical reader over this person's head so as 'not to bring a blush to her cheek', a much used criterion.[26]

Hardy's (often imperfectly) concealed transgression of these conventions and restraints is also a transgression of the basis on which his fiction, having been produced by the entrepreneurial processes of publication and marketing, is to be reproduced by the 'inscribed reader'.

The assumption of a feminine reader naturalizes the pressure on a reader to reproduce the text in a suitably deferential manner. As a woman, the reader is contracted to reproduce physically by bearing children, or at least to define her gender in terms of that paradigm; as a reader, she is then to reproduce ideologically. It is no coincidence that the processes are coterminate. Patricia Stubbs argues that the nature of the novel enforces and extends this invitation to be controlled:

The novel . . . is inherently bound up with the notion of a private
life which has its own autonomous moral standards and values.
At its best it explores private relationships and moral behaviour
as an expression of external social and economic realities, but its
central, its defining preoccupation, remains the elaboration of an
intensely personal world of individual experience, the moral structure of which is built up around carefully organized patterns of
social relationships.
But this is peculiarly damaging to women. For within bourgeois society women are confined to this private, largely domestic
world, and have become the focus of a powerful ideology which
celebrates private experience and relationships as potent sources
of human satisfaction.[27]

All of Hardy's novels seem at first sight to fit this pattern. And there
is an inherent connection in this transaction between the position of
women, constructed by an ideology which naturalizes alienation
and a novelistic convention which focuses on a covert world, and the
position of the workfolk and small traders whose alienation is also
naturalized and whose covert and detached world (think of the
titles: *Under the Greenwood Tree, Far From the Madding Crowd, The
Return of the Native*, the last suggesting, as John Lucas puts it ' a
work of sentimental anthropology[28]) is simultaneously marginal-
ized and fetishized for the reader. Paula Power, gendered first and
characterized second by the contents of her boudoir in *A Laodicean*,
is the victim of a very similar process. Both women and workers
are commodities presented as objects of consumption and control.
The essential difference between woman and worker lies, very
productively, in the area of sexuality, which also becomes a crucial
area of difference (and perhaps Hardy's key chosen 'site of conflict') in the conflictual relationship between 'traded' and 'narrated'
versions of the same fiction.
The sound practice of femininity should, at least in Victorian
bourgeois fiction, earn you a marriage contract. As Tony Tanner
puts it in *Adultery in the Novel*:

marriage is *the* central subject for the bourgeois novel; not marriage as a paradigm for the resolution of problems of bringing
unity out of difference, harmony out of opposition, concord out
of discord . . . but just marriage in all its social and domestic
ramifications in a demythologized society. Or rather a society in

which marriage *is* the mythology (at least the socially avowed one; it would be possible to say that money and profits made up a more secret mythology). Marriage, to put it at its simplest for the moment, is a means by which society attempts to put into harmonious alignment patterns of passion and patterns of property; in bourgeois society it is not only a matter of putting your Gods where your treasure is (as Ruskin accused his age of doing) but also of putting your libido, loyalty and all other possessions and products, including children, there as well. For bourgeois society marriage is the all-subsuming, all-organizing, all-containing contract. It is the structure that maintains the Structure.[29]

In this context, as the feminine (or more generally deferential) being who is to be constructed by novel-reading, you find out about sexuality only after you have been safely feminized and then contracted into patriarchy; and when your fertility has been contracted to the reproduction of the same process. In other words, usually after the novel has ended. Hardy's career as a novelist spans a critical period in terms of the status of this contract. Susan M. Blake cites the 1866 Hyde v. Hyde judgment as 'the classic English legal definition of marriage':

> Marriage has been well said to be something more than a contract, either religious or civil – to be an institution. It creates mutual rights and obligations as all contracts do, but beyond that it confers a status . . . I conceive that marriage as understood in Christendom may for this purpose be defined as the voluntary union for life of one man and one woman to the exclusion of all others.[30]

An appeal to this hegemony of Christendom was already tenuous in 1866. The 1857 Matrimonial Causes Act[31] made available limited grounds for civil divorce, and in doing so significantly eroded religious control of the marriage contract. It is not coincidental that the Obscene Publications Act, controlling the potentially dangerous power of fiction, was also passed in 1857. When Edmund Gosse said in 1892 that 'the Victorian has been peculiarly the age of the triumph of fiction',[32] he was (knowingly or not) more accurate than hyperbolic. The period between the 1857 acts and the 1890s marks a significant change in the treatment of marriage in popular fiction, and an equally significant change in fiction's importance in relation to the marriage contract. In fictions like Wilkie Collins's *The Woman in White* (1860), Mary Elizabeth Braddon's *Aurora Floyd* (1863) and *Lady Audley's Secret* (1864) and Hardy's *Desperate Remedies* (1871), bigamy, adultery and illegitimacy are dangerous adventures in fictions which can eventually be resolved in terms of the all-embracing contract. The treatment of marital relations in the fictions is dangerous precisley because the contract is assumed to be in some sense 'safe'.

Novels like William Hale White's *Clara Hopgood* (1896), Grant Allen's *The Woman Who Did* (1895) (not to mention the satiric riposte of 'Victoria Cross', *The Woman Who Didn't*), George Meredith's *Lord Ormont and his Aminta* (1894) and *The Amazing Marriage* (1895), George Gissing's *The Odd Women* (1892) and Hardy's *Tess of the d'Urbervilles* (1891) and *Jude the Obscure* (1895)[33] adopt a very different attitude. The contract, and all the larger contracts it implies, is at least theoretically negotiable. It becomes possible to argue that a woman can have identity and sexuality outside the male conception of marriage. Thus the period of Gosse's 'triumph of fiction' coincides with a period in which the marriage contract's authority and its christian justification seem to be eroded. The Hardy written by Hardy in the *Autobiography* parallels this process, in terms of christianity if not of marriage. His gradual loss of religious faith is well known, and Timothy Hands, having established Hardy's commitment to evangelical christianity in the early 1860s, argues persuasively for a correlation between the increasingly overt and polemical centrality, from the late 1880s, of religious and marital issues in the novels.[34]

The all-subverting, all-threatening act which can destroy the structure that maintains the Structure is the physical act of sexual intercourse. If a christian god can no longer maintain the marriage contract, a proposition dealt with overtly in *Jude the Obscure*, human sexuality, even if it is not breaking a formal marriage contract, takes on a huge transgressive function. So do words and images connected with it. Hardy exploits this in a sequence of part-concealed 'dares' (not dissimilar to the behaviour of the aptly-named Willy Dare, the Mephistophelean villain who corruptly manipulates photographs in *A Laodicean*). As Peter Stallybrass and Allon White argue centrally in *The Politics and Poetics of Transgression*,[35] sexuality is a sign of Victorian 'low' culture, just as femininity is a sign of 'high' culture. As I shall show, Hardy makes his attack on the 'high' cultural edifice of the novel as dangerous as possible by using the devices of the 'low' as the concealed devices of its creation. Covert and semi-covert images of sexual intercourse and female anatomy are central in the narrator's antithetical counter-texts, corrupting the fiction 'sold on' to publishers and magazine editors. This strategy is perhaps the principal source of a response exemplified by Lionel Johnson's comment in 1894, amplified and repeated many times since, that there is in Hardy's writing 'something unkind, an uncanny sort of pleased and sly malevolence . . . a somewhat mean unpleasantness'.[36]

Ebbatson makes the suggestion that in Hardy's fiction it is 'the woman's role to be inspected and studied in the throes of a sexual passion which threatens male hegemony, and this potent fantasy of erotic surveillance would seem to have its roots deep in Hardy's psyche'.[37] The concealed sexualization of the texts and their women characters by a male writer is somewhere between covert foreplay and Tess Durbeyfield's questionably unconscious rape in *Tess of the d'Urbervilles*. In one sense this is an extreme instance of a male writer making his dominance over a woman reader as nearly physical as it can be in a book. But this line of argument is only convincing if the narrator's project is merely to illustrate, and thus endorse, the traded and 'acceptable' text. The erotic surveillance has its roots deep in the genre (indeed, you might argue from Smith's points, it is *the* root of the genre).

The narrator of Hardy's novels is seen to carry out a desexualizing erotic surveillance, and in this sense the authorial 'psyche' really becomes the servant of its mode of production and reproduction, the author 'trading' his text. Sexuality, especially female sexuality, is removed and supplanted by a more 'acceptable' male voyeurism, suppressed into harmonious patterns of property and propriety by plots in which marriage is the essential integer. But this supplanting by the male-produced feminine of any alternative female-produced feminine is the 'official' policing process of the traded text. The insistent presence of sexuality and the self-consciousness of the erotic surveillance become an ever-present subversion.

If you accept that there is an inherent connection between the enforced deferences of gender and class, Hardy's use of a concealed sexual act also becomes an attack on the naturalized alienation and deference of the workfolk and small traders he uses to represent the 'natural' and 'organic' Wessex. The connection which lies beyond this, and which reinforces it, is the relationship between the workfolk and the land. Almost all the characters in the Novels of Character and Environment (with the striking exception of the characters in *Jude the Obscure*) work in some kind of organic or natural process. Something animal or vegetable is being planted, grown, harvested and traded. A novel which seems to describe this process would seem the perfect vehicle of naturalization: why look past the writer's connection of character and environment to suggest that the one is not as natural as the other? In fact neither is remotely natural in the Wessex novels. The characters who have been 'sold on' to become bourgeois role models for the reviewer in *British Quarterly Review* live and work in an environment which has been systematically defertilized for just that purpose.

This defertilization is essentially the same process as Hardy's unsexing of his female characters. It is equally, in terms of the relationship between trader and narrator, a corrupt process. The 'traded' Wessex is an anthropological travelogue, the picturesque and sometimes organically threatening background of bourgeois drama, ersatz tragedy and melodrama. Poverty is an honourable state; no one starves; no one rises up against his or her master. There is no hint that the real Blackmoor Vale was the site of the worst poverty and unrest in Dorset in the 1830 Swing Riots and hardly any sign of the poverty endemic in Dorset throughout the period Hardy writes about.[38] Egdon, Weatherbury and Blackmoor Vale are celebrated for their natural beauty, not for the work done there; and yet the beauty depends on the country Hardy describes being a working environment.

Just as Hardy the narrator writes a woman, so he writes a landscape. Just as Ethelberta is the sum of the narrative discourses which construct her in the text of *The Hand of Ethelberta*, so Egdon is the sum of the narrative discourses which construct it in *The Return of the Native*. Both are equally and transparently artificial. Hardy the trader has 'sold on' a bourgeois drama set in the fashionably quaint countryside, and his defertilization exercise means that the Novels of Character and Environment are set in an environment which has been robbed of its 'reality' (the work practices and class divisions which really make it) and rebuilt for the market. If Wessex contains 'eternal verities', they are the kind of verities acceptable to readers who would find it most comfortable to think of Dorset workfolk as 'gentlemen'. This gives the narrator a mandate to refertilize his own narrative, on his own terms if he conceals it. Hardy re-mythologizes Wessex on this basis, and the connection between the myths of a fertile land and a covert female sexuality allows him to secrete his own code of explanation for the woman in the land, and the land in the woman.

Hardy's use of myth and allusion is extensive and catholic. As Marlene Springer argues, this is used to retain an unusually high degree of narrative control.

That Hardy was a conscious artificer, eventually successful in his search for a stylistic mantle, becomes graphically apparent through a study of his allusive practices. For through his increasingly adroit manipulation of references he not only helps transform the prosaic into the complex, but also gains an unusually strong control over the total effect of his fiction.[39]

To some extent this is a matter of auto-didactic showing-off. In terms of the traded text this is correct: Hardy over-quotes and name-drops to show his references for the job of bourgeois novelist and the tactic succeeds. *Far From the Madding Crowd* and *Tess of the d'Urbervilles* are the most striking examples of this process being used as the entrepreneurial 'front' for a very different exercise. Both texts seem to be overloaded with allusions and external references. Both use an allusive base which is (relatively) popular, accessible and fashionable; *From From the Madding Crowd* refers extensively to a Greek Arcadia, and, as Gillian Beer[40] and J. B. Bullen[41] both show, *Tess of the d'Urbervilles* refers heavily to Friedrich Max Müller's work on solar myth. But in both cases, as I shall show, these are merely the fully visible and 'acceptable' 'surfaces' of the systematic allusions and extra-textual reference which create the machinery of a counter-text which subverts and contradicts its 'traded' and more easily visible narrative surface. The moments of disruption created when Hardy's use of allusion seems most pretentious or fatuous, as for instance in the characters' names in *Desperate Remedies*, are almost invariably points where the narrator risks sacrificing elegance in the traded text for continuity and structure in the antithetical counter-text. In this sense these moments of disruption are primarily wilful flourishes and dangerous 'dares'.

The dares to find the counter-text are offered in the historical context of the erosion of the christian contract of bonding individual to individual and, by implication, individual to Structure. Hardy principally builds his alternative fictions, or his anti-bourgeois bourgeois dramas, on foundations of anti-christian and pre-christian myth and ritual. *The Woodlanders* uses the allusive base of its traded sylvan setting to make a counter-text which transmutes Giles Winterborne into a Wild Man and Marty South into a dryad. Both were proscribed by the medieval christian church as subversive images of the Old Religion. The same point can be made about the Mummers, still vestigially active but greatly bowdlerized when *The Return of the Native* was written, and of course about witchcraft, used most extensively in *The Mayor of Casterbridge*. The means of destroying christianity are brought to bear on the 'sexual relationship' plots which provide the driving machinery of all these fictions; and so pre-capitalist myths, almost all in some sense linking fertility and female sexuality, are used as a destructive internal strategy against the contract which maintains and dictates the patterns of deference which are articulated in the 'traded' text. Very often this produces a complete change of polarity (two very striking examples of this come, as I shall demonstrate, in *The Woodlanders* and *Tess of the d'Urbervilles*, in which counter-texts completely contradict their 'received' surfaces).

Ultimately at issue in this intra-textual conflict is Structure, both as the analogue of socio-economic power and literally as the home of the individuals who represent the power, and the effects, of that Structure. In his introduction to the Macmillan New Wessex paperback of *Jude the Obscure* Terry Eagleton makes the point that in Christminster, 'a repressive rubble of crumbling masonry and dead creeds', 'Jude's labour-power is exploited literally to prop up the structures which excluded him' (*JO*, pp. 12–13). As J. Hillis Miller points out, Marcel Proust refers to Hardy's 'géométrie du tailleur'.[42] In *Desperate Remedies* almost all the male characters are architects. *A Laodicean* is a love story about a competition to rebuild a castle. Jude Fawley is a stonemason whose job is to restore buildings. Buildings are central indicators of wealth and power, poverty and powerlessness in all Hardy's novels. The Stoke-d'Urbervilles' new house at Trantridge contrasts with the Durbeyfields' cottage at Marlott; Giles Winterborne loses his house at Little Hintock and dies in a lean-to shelter in the woods while Felice Charmond lives in a great stone house; Gabriel Oak moves from his portable shed at Norcombe to a marital home with Bathsheba Everdene at Weatherbury; Michael Henchard moves from homelessness to a large house of his own at Casterbridge, then descends to lodging with Joshua Jopp and finally becomes homeless again. Superficially these follow the novelistic convention of the building a character lives in indicating his or her wealth or moral 'worth'. In Hardy's 'traded' texts, 'acceptable' to publishers and editors, the crucial area between wealth and moral worth is to be arbitrated by the events of the plot. But in his *narrated* version of the same text each building described is, like the protagonists and the landscape, the product of the narrative discourses which create it. Almost every description of a building is encoded with meaning, and again the meaning is part of the authorial strategy which makes the subversive counter-text.

Hardy's architectural descriptions thus become an ironic and corrupting alternative to, for example, Trollope's inverted description (in that he talks about the qualities and lets the reader imagine the architecture) of Greshambury Park in *Doctor Thorne*.

> But the old symbols remained, and may such symbols long remain among us; they are still lovely and fit to be loved. They tell us of the true and manly feelings of other times; and to him who can read aright, they explain more fully, more truly than any written history can do, how Englishmen have become what they are.[43]

Compare this with Hardy's description of the staircase at Enckworth Court in *The Hand of Ethelberta*:

> To the left of the door and vestibule which Ethelberta passed through rose the principal staircase, constructed of a freestone so milk-white and delicately moulded as to be easily conceived in the lamplight as of biscuit-ware. Who, unacquainted with the mysteries of geometrical construction, could imagine that, hanging so airily there, to all appearance supported on nothing, were twenty or more tons dead weight of stone, that would have made a prison for an elephant if so arranged? The art which produced this illusion was questionable, but its success was undoubted. 'How lovely!' said Ethelberta, as she looked at the fairy ascent. 'His staircase alone is worth my hand!' (*HE*, p. 304)

The disruptions of (even hypothetically) putting an elephant in an English country house and suggesting that a woman would marry a man for his staircase give some indication of the novel's overall project; but the point here is that nothing which has been built ever becomes a 'natural' or 'fixed' object. Where Trollope's country house

is a 'fixed' ideological and historical allegory, Hardy's only continues to stand because of 'the mysteries of geometrical construction'. And these are always clearly described by the narrator.
Hardy's houses have the same relation to history and Structure
as Greshambury Park, and in this sense they do what the genre
demands; but the narrator's insistence on the details of design,
building and decoration suggests that they have an explanation
which also insists on their artifice. Hardy's buildings are literally a
battlefield, characterised in terms of a competition for a woman's
hand in marriage in *A Laodicean*, the most architecturally explicit of
the novels I examine here. The struggle is between the owner and
the designer/builder, and by association also between the pub-
lisher/producer of a novel and its writer. Like the architect, the
writer is simply a notionally autonomous sub-contractor. Does the
building Hardy describes have the false meanings the property-
owning class who commission the work would like it to have, as an
object which somehow validates their position, or the contradictory
meanings generated by the process of building it? Does the history
written on the site of the house really belong to capital or labour?
This battle takes place in the historical context of a macaronic Victorian bourgeois architecture which is in many ways obsessed with
producing images of false historical continuity. An anonymous article in *The British Critic* in 1839 parallels George Somerset's eclectic
architectural knowledge in *A Laodicean*:

> The present age has no vernacular style of architecture . . . Archi-
> tecture is become a language. We learn a number of styles as we
> do a number of dead languages.
>   The exact scholar . . . though he trusts he can pass off his work
> on the present generation, knows full well that anyone to whom
> that style was natural would perceive a great uncouthness and
> probably detect some downright solecisms.[44]

A search for cultural identity (in other words, a search for public
images to naturalize dominance and deference) is focused on buildings because they are, apparently, the most permanent cultural
monument capital can 'create'. Architects are the one group who
understand the specific artifices involved in this process. They are in
this sense capital's most important artificers. An architect who has
become a novelist, like Hardy, is therefore doubly dangerous.

This may be an additional reason for the critical suppression of the Novels of Ingenuity. Apart from *Jude the Obscure*, which is as much the last Novel of Ingenuity as the last Novel of Character and Environment, these texts contain the fullest and most conclusive demonstration of Hardy's use of architecture as the analogue of historical and structural artifice. I deal later in more detail with Enckworth Court in *The Hand of Ethelberta*, with Knapwater House and the other buildings at Carriford in *Desperate Remedies*, and with the competition to rebuild Castle de Stancy in *A Laodicean*. There is nothing 'natural' or 'organic' in any of these structures. Nor is there anything irrelevant in Hardy's detailed, almost obsessive descriptions of them.

Louis Althusser argues that by reproducing ideology, the bourgeois realist novel must necessarily represent

not the system of the real relations which govern the existence of individuals, but the imaginary relation of those individuals to the real relations in which they live.[45]

Hardy's subversive strategies in the reserved area of power between trader and narrator mean that his 'dares' and counter-texts penetrate to the roots of the essential relationship between prose fiction and the reproduction of ideology. They also present what may be a unique case study of a 'writer''s text transcending, or attempting to transcend, the means of its production and reproduction. To show how this works in practice I want now to offer readings, in order of publication, of all nine texts Hardy chose to define as 'novels'.

1

Desperate Remedies (1871): A Trojan Horse

Desperate Remedies was first submitted to Macmillan. Macmillan's reader, John Morley, gave this reason for advising rejection:

> the story is ruined by the disgusting and absurd outrage which is the key to its mystery – The violation of a young lady at an evening party, and the subsequent birth of a child, is too abominable to be tolerated as a central incident from which the action of the story is to move.[1]

The novel was then submitted to Tinsley Bros. Tinsley's reader for *Desperate Remedies* was William Faux, manager of W. H. Smith's literary department. Tinsley's assistant, Edmund Downey, reported that Faux saw the novel 'almost as a joke'.[2] Widdowson makes the same point, with particular reference to the ludicrously specific chapter headings, suggesting that 'there is an insistent possibility that the novel is simultaneously mocking the conventions of the genre it is imitating'.[3]

Tinsley's agreement to publish *Desperate Remedies* was on the basis of £75 deposit from Hardy to cover anticipated losses (*LTH*, 83). This would now be seen as vanity publishing; in a buoyant market for fiction it would be regarded as a speculative sharing of risk and profit. The publication of the novel is thus, for both trader and narrator, an investment of financial and cultural capital created outside novel-writing in the production of fiction. The division between capitalistic trader and craftsman narrator is inherent but not necessarily apparent. The writer's perception of this division is a matter of class identification. In the 'natural' worlds of Greshambury Park and Barchester there is no division because there is no class conflict; and Trollope's *An Autobiography*[4] is in many ways a sustained boast at having never knowingly sold corrupt product to a publisher or his readership. But even with £75 out of his entire capital of £123 invested in *Desperate Remedies*, Hardy's narrated text constantly and wilfully disrupts the traded surface. It is built principally out of this conflict.

In many ways *Desperate Remedies* is a joke; a sustained, contrived jest by the narrator at the expense of the buyer. It exemplifies the process which offended T. S. Eliot, of Hardy writing 'as nearly for the sake of "self-expression" as a man well can'.[5] But the novel defines the genre it imitates rather than simply mocking it. The satiric disruptions are used to create a novel-within-a-novel which makes the whole enterprise of *Desperate Remedies* a Trojan Horse. Internal evidence suggests that this is entirely deliberate. The capitalistic investment Hardy the trader makes in his sensation novel follows the unpublished *The Poor Man and the Lady*, rejected by Macmillan after readings by Alexander Macmillan and John Morley, and then accepted by Chapman & Hall before George Meredith advised Hardy to withdraw it. Hardy's comments about the novel, and his meeting with Meredith, in his autobiography are worth quoting at some length.

> the firm were willing to publish the novel as agreed, but . . . [Meredith] strongly advised the author not to 'nail his colours to the mast' so definitely in a first book, if he wished to do anything practical in literature; for if he printed so pronounced a thing he would be attacked on all sides by the conventional reviewers, and his future injured. The story was, in fact, a sweeping dramatic satire of the squirearchy and nobility, London society, the vulgarity of the middle class, modern Christianity, church-restoration, and political and domestic morals in general, the author's views, in fact, being those of a young man with a passion for reforming the world – those of many a young man before and after him; the tendency of the writing being socialistic, not to say revolutionary; yet not argumentatively so, the style having the affected simplicity of Defoe's (which had long attracted Hardy, as it did Stevenson, years later, to imitation of it). This naive realism in circumstantial details that were pure inventions was so well assumed that both Macmillan and Morley had been perhaps a little, or more than a little, deceived by its seeming actuality; to Hardy's surprise, when he thought.
> The satire was obviously pushed too far – as sometimes in Swift and Defoe themselves – and portions of the book, appar-

ently taken in earnest by both his readers, had no foundation
either in Hardy's beliefs or his experience. (*LTH*, p. 61)

This is extremely contradictory. Hardy's revelation is effectively a
concealment and his attempted concealment is revelatory. Almost
every statement in this 'factual' account is a covert celebration of
Hardy's authorial power. Indeed he assumes the ultimate auto-
critical power of describing a text no one else can verify because it
has been destroyed. It is impossible to say whether the text described
here is the text submitted to Macmillan and Chapman & Hall.
Certainly the fragment published as 'An Indiscretion in the Life of
an Heiress' suggests rather less. But these idealized gestures of
dominance and control, concealed behind an old man's description
of a young man's effrontery, create patterns of disruption remarkably similar to those in *Desperate Remedies*. The illogic of Hardy's
fiction about himself (here describing, possibly fictionally, a further fiction) demands, and promises to reward, the ratiocinative
approach *Desperate Remedies* prescribes for reading the information
the narrator offers. How, for instance, can revolutionary sentiments
addressed to an anti-revolutionary bourgeois readership be anything but argumentative? Why affect modesty and invite comparison with Swift and Defoe (taking the trouble to snub Stevenson in
passing) at the same time? Why confess to the book's revolutionary
subversion when your reputation is built on the eternal verities of
Wessex? Why celebrate the deception of Macmillan in a book which,
quite apart from the layers of deception and artifice in its narrative,
was intended for publication by Macmillan, who were to be de-
ceived as to its authorship?

Every one of these disruptions courts (admittedly posthumous)
danger. Together they create a pattern of structured risk. Partly the
narrator of the autobiography seems to be testing the strength of the
cultural edifice Thomas Hardy by offering evidence which might be
used to break it; partly, by leaving clues like this behind, he is
inviting detection and creating a palimpsest which will stand as the
confession of the corrupt and subversive Hardy as well as the re-
miniscences of Hardy of Wessex. The 'traded' *Life of Thomas Hardy by
Florence Emily Hardy* is corrupted by the narrative strategies of an
ostensibly absent Thomas Hardy. A comparison with Aeneas
Manston's manipulations, deceptions and confessions in *Desperate
Remedies* is unavoidable, and in this sense it is clear that the sensation
novel, far from being a temporary expedient adopted in order to get

into print, informs Hardy's authorial project very deeply. Using the excuse that 'he took Meredith's advice too literally, and set about constructing the eminently "sensational" plot of *Desperate Remedies*' (*LTH*, p. 63) is again a diversionary tactic: blaming Meredith, however apologetically, for the mode of *Desperate Remedies* is to invite the reader not to look for any other reason. The narrator is protecting 'Hardy of Wessex' against the idealized subversive, who seems now to have mutated into a deferential follower of Meredith's advice. Again this device is so blatant as to court detection and interpretation.

The clue it reveals comes in Meredith's actual advice to Hardy to 'attempt a novel with a purely artistic purpose, giving it a more complicated "plot" than was attempted in *The Poor Man and the Lady*' (*LTH*, p. 62). According to the autobiography, the unpublished novel was originally subtitled 'A Story with no Plot' (*LTH*, p. 57). A story without a plot is simply meaningless; the obvious meaning which lies beyond is a novel without a narrative strategy. *Desperate Remedies* develops the missing strategy and conceals it where it will be hardest to find, in a genre characterized by complex narrative strategies. The socialistic and revolutionary tendencies are thus accommodated and their expression mutated by the process the narrator of the autobiography chooses to present as Meredith's advice. It is also worth pointing out one very striking parallel between the autobiographer's account of *The Poor Man and the Lady* and the final revelation of Manston's villainy, and hence the extent of the authorial devices, in *Desperate Remedies*. Referring to Macmillan (who also rejected *Desperate Remedies*), Morley and Meredith, the autobiography says that 'Except the writer himself, these three seem to have been the only ones whose eyes ever scanned the MS' (*LTH*, p. 62). When Manston tries to hide the dead body, three pairs of eyes are watching him.

Macherey's analysis of Ann Radcliffe's *Les Visions d'un Château des Pyrénées*, almost certainly a posthumous forgery, offers a productive model for reading *Desperate Remedies* as a similar exercise in self-conscious genre writing. It also suggests strong roots in the sensation novel for Hardy's use of architectural description.

In Mrs Radcliffe's version of the Gothic novel the protagonist confronts a vague diversity; he is pushed out beyond the comforts of dualism into a realm of endless transformations. The hero is not merely poised between misfortune and happiness, he is actually powerless to define his exact situation. Bewildered at the edge of the illusory, symbolised by the grounds of the château, he no longer knows who he is and cannot control his feelings. The enclosing château could be either a refuge or a prison. The one is frequently mistaken for the other, for it may be safe to shelter on the very threshold of danger except that the refuge may suddenly turn into a trap. The château is always changing, in a cycle of incessant novelty. The unfinished building and the inexhaustible scenery reflect the story played out in their midst . . . Every façade is hollow and deceptive, but never obviously so, as they come apart in self-contradictory ways. The only means of escape is to advance into the labyrinth, in the hope of eventually reaching the centre.[6]

Contrast Macherey's account with a passage Stubbs quotes from Ruskin's 1865 picture of the bourgeois home (where *Desperate Remedies* was presumably to be read) in 'Of Queen's Gardens': it is the 'place of peace; the shelter, not only from all injury, but from all terror, doubt and division. In so far as it is not this, it is not home'.[7] The buildings in *Desperate Remedies* do not change in ways which overtly challenge realism, but they are certainly mutable. The ostensible project of the novel is to create a Ruskinian harmony of home out of a series of quasi-Gothic buildings, and thus to allegorically tame the subversive potential of the genre. The Three Tranters, with all its images of organic continuity, can burn down; the outbuildings of Knapwater House can be 'half-buried beneath close-set shrubs and trees' (*DR*, p. 96) as the undergrowth reclaims the land; the original manor house can show an overt history of changed uses and status; and over all these images of changeable buildings at Carriford is laid the fact that the Houses of Parliament can burn down. Cytherea's father is an architect; her two lovers, Manston and Springrove, are architects, and being an architect is the most important qualification for the stewardship of Knapwater; Owen Graye works in an architect's office, and is later a Clerk of Works at Anglebury. The profession of making and remaking buildings unquestionably is the institution at the centre of the novel.

The action proper begins with Ambrose Graye's death: an architect falls off the structure he has been in charge of building before it is completed. This parallels his incomplete attempt to build his family's fortunes, and he dies bankrupt. The inherent connection with economic and contractual structure is therefore made overt from the start. On this basis, as Macherey prescribes, Cytherea enters the textual labyrinth and becomes the subject of whatever discourses narrative exigencies demand. This is announced with satirical self-consciousness as the narrator moves her into a position to see her father fall off the church spire:

> Why the particulars of a young lady's presence at a very mediocre performance were prevented from dropping into the oblivion which their intrinsic insignificance would naturally have involved – why they were remembered and individualized by herself and others through after years – was simply that she unknowingly stood, as it were, upon the extreme posterior edge of a tract in her life, in which the real meaning of Taking Thought had never been known. It was the last hour of experience she ever enjoyed with a mind entirely free from a knowledge of the labyrinth into which she stepped immediately afterwards – to continue a perplexed course along its mazes for the greater portion of twenty-nine subsequent months. (*DR*, p. 45)

As Ebbatson points out,[8] the plot of the twenty-nine month labyrinth is set in motion by two deaths. The second is the death of Miss Aldclyffe's father, whose death rattle Cytherea hears when she first arrives at Knapwater. Again this may be read as an essentially comic disruption; inflating and satirizing the devices of texts like Poe's 'William Wilson' or Wilkie Collins's *Armadale* (1866), Cytherea's employer shares her extremely unusual christian name. Having been forced to sell herself as a servant as a result of her father's death, Cytherea arrives at the house which becomes her Château des Pyrénées and immediately is present at the 'mediocre performance' of the narrator presenting her with the death of another Cytherea's father. The deaths of the two fathers liberate patrilinear inheritances, one of the property owner and the other of the property builder. These are encapsulated in the mistress/servant relationship of the two Cythereas.

The relationship begins with Cytherea Graye dressing Cytherea Aldclyffe for a party, and discovering that her new employer wears Ambrose Graye's picture in a locket around her neck. Later the same night Miss Aldclyffe comes to her room and gets into bed with her. While the two women are in bed together, Miss Aldclyffe's father dies and the Knapwater inheritance is freed. At this point, as the lesbian episode dangerously and prematurely implies, the full force of women holding patrilinear inheritances in a patriarchy is released. The narrative project of *Desperate Remedies* differs from Macherey's model in that its main protagonist is a woman, and in that the proprietor of the château is also a woman. At the same time, as Ingham demonstrates,[9] Cytherea is rewarded with Knapwater and marriage to Springrove only when she has become an acceptable chattel and practitioner of womanliness. She progresses towards this desirable state by means of the recurrent stock pattern of a woman seeming to choose from multiple options when the real choice is made by the man. This is the first example, chronologically, of Hardy's trade in feminizing parables. But the text is also a piece of satirical genre-writing. The narrator's insistence on the logical structures he prescribes is disruptively self-conscious. For instance:

> The comparative security from discovery that [Anne Seaway's] new position ensured resuscitated reason a little, and empowered her to form some logical inferences:-
> 1. The man who stood on the copper had taken advantage of the darkness to get there, as she had to enter.
> 2. The man must have hidden in the outhouse before she had reached the door.
> 3. He must be watching Manston with much calculation and system, and for purposes of his own. (*DR*, p. 385)

This constantly undermines the bourgeois parable of Cytherea's growth into womanhood. The bewilderment of the pseudo-active Victorian heroine is simultaneously the Gothic bewilderment of Macherey's hero. This bewilderment is amplified when Miss Aldclyffe, who is at once employer, gender model and surrogate mother, proposes herself as pseudo-male lover. This introduces the period of interregnum between the two deaths and the return of Knapwater to male ownership after Cytherea inherits it. While the mode of reading the genre prescribes is ratiocinative, and while *Desperate Remedies* draws heavily on Collins's *The Woman in White* (Morrell lists five key points of similarity: mistaken identity, a disastrous fire, a guilty secret, an illegitimate child and a confession clarifying earlier obscurities[10]) the dangers Cytherea faces are principally sexual and contractual. The sex, like Miss Aldclyffe's guilty secret and Manston's crime, is concealed, and specifically behind these two concealing characters. Both concealments are barely convincing, but it should be borne in mind that had they not convinced

Tinsley (not a notably fastidious publisher; only Newby and Reynolds had worse reputations[11]), the critics and the circulating librarians, Hardy would have risked prosecution and suppression under the Obscene Publications Act. Miss Aldclyffe's sexual approach to Cytherea is hidden by bourgeois femininity: no lady would make love to another lady, so the scene must mean what it says, not what it implies. Hardy thus tests the gullibility of the ideology he is expected to reinforce in the first sexual encounter he ever publishes, and the dare succeeds.

The sexual nature of Cytherea's first meeting with Manston is concealed by melodramatic imagery. The dare is again a test of the narrative power celebrated in the autobiographer's memory of deceiving Macmillan and Morley. Like the introduction of the labyrinth and the image of Mr Graye falling off the spire, it is a moment of satiric disruption of the genre novel. The encounter begins with the often-quoted passage in which the narrator sexualizes Cytherea's clothes:

At this moment, by reason of the narrowness of the porch, their clothing touched, and remained in contact.

His clothes are something exterior to every man; but to a woman her dress is part of her body. Its motions are all present to her intelligence if not to her eyes; no man knows how his coat-tails swing. By the slightest hyperbole it may be said that her dress has sensation. Crease but the very Ultima Thule of fringe or flounce, and it hurts her as much as pinching her. Delicate antennae, or feelers, bristle on every outlying frill. Go to the uppermost: she is there: treated on the lowest: the fair creature is there almost before you.

Thus the touch of clothes, which was nothing to Manston, sent a thrill through Cytherea, seeing, moreover, that he was of the nature of a mysterious stranger. (*DR*, p. 164)

This seems at first to be a conventionally essentialist view of femininity, which is capable of building to the extreme stage of Boldwood fetishizing a wardrobe full of women's clothes with Bathsheba's name on them in *Far From the Madding Crowd*. The nature of Boldwood's sexual fixation on Bathesheba offers a productive clue to Hardy's use of women's clothes here. In fact it is the first allegorical piece of foreplay in a sustained and mutually satisfying sexual encounter. What is significant is that the narrator extends the pseudo-

active mode of the woman seeming to choose her partner to a
genuinely active (although in no sense dominant) sexual arousal and
response. She is aroused by Manston's first touch, and, as Ebbatson
points out,[12] her 'parted lips' after the thunder and lightning are
almost certainly not the lips on her face. I want to give several
extracts from the passage that follows. The OED confirms that
'organ' was in regular use from at least 1836 as part of the phrase
'sexual organ'.

> 'Look, the rain is coming into the porch upon you,' he said.
> 'Step inside the door.'
> Cytherea hesitated,
> 'Perfectly safe, I assure you,' he added, laughing and holding
> the door open . . . 'You know the inside of the house, I dare say?'
> 'I have never been in.'
> '. . . The only piece of ornamental furniture yet unpacked is
> this one.'
> 'An organ?'
> 'Yes, an organ. I made it myself, except the pipes. I opened the
> case this afternoon to commence soothing myself at once. It is
> not a very large one, but quite big enough for a private house.
> You play, I dare say?'
> 'The piano, I am not at all used to an organ.'
> 'You would soon acquire the touch for an organ . . .'
> Cytherea all at once broke into a blush . . .
> 'I play for my own private amusement only,' he said. 'I have
> never learned scientifically. All I know is what I taught myself.'
> The thunder, lightning and rain had now increased to a terrific
> force. The clouds, from which darts, forks, zigzags, and balls of
> fire continually sprang, did not appear to be more than a hundred
> yards above their heads, and every now and then a flash and a
> peal made gaps in the steward's descriptions. He went towards
> the organ, in the midst of a volley which seemed to shake the
> aged house from foundations to chimney.
> 'You are not going to play now, are you?' said Cytherea un-
> easily.
> Without waiting to see whether she sat down or not, he turned
> to the organ and began extemporizing a harmony . . .
> The thunder pealed again, Cytherea, in spite of herself, was fright-
> ened, not only at the weather, but at the general unearthly
> weirdness which seemed to surround her there.

'I wish I – the lightning wasn't so bright. Do you think it will last long?' she said timidly.

'It can't last much longer,' he murmured, without turning, running his fingers again over the keys . . .

He now played more powerfully. Cytherea had never heard music in the completeness of full orchestral power, and the tones of the organ, which reverberated with considerable force in the comparatively small space of the room, heightened by the elemental strife of light and sound outside, moved her to a degree out of proportion to the actual power of the mere notes, practised as was the hand that produced them. The varying strains . . . shook and bent her to themselves, as a gushing brook shakes and bends a shadow cast across its surface . . .

She was swayed into emotional opinions concerning the strange man before her; new impulses of thought came with new harmonies, and entered into her with a gnawing thrill. A dreadful flash of lightning then, and the thunder close upon it. She found herself involuntarily shrinking up beside him, and looking with parted lips at his face . . .

He modulated into the Pastoral Symphony, still looking in her eyes. (*DR*, pp. 165–8)

Feminization into sexlessness thus becomes sexual initiation. Manston's auto-eroticism gives a pejorative and accurate introduction to his character; and so does his egotistical notion of foreplay, metaphorically turning the woman into an unwilling voyeur while he masturbates his 'organ'.

The 'normal' system of powerholding which *Desperate Remedies* presupposes is male ownership of land, and the twenty-nine month labyrinth is in this sense a period of interregnum. Manston is brought to Knapwater by Miss Aldclyffe's subterfuge, and his appointment as steward reasserts male ownership by a blood line. Because it is not a patrilinear inheritance, in the normalizing bourgeois fable of the traded text it becomes an interregnum within an interregnum, or a labyrinth within a labyrinth. Springer demonstrates a number of ways in which Manston's masculinity and power are eroded by biblical and christian allusion,[13] but in missing the allusive force of his name she fails to detect an alternative plot machinery which rewrites the bourgeois fable. The credibility of the main characters in *Desperate Remedies* is heavily disrupted by intimately connected processes of naming and allusion. Hardy places a significant clue to this, and to the motivation behind the strategies he employs in *Desperate Remedies*, in the autobiography: the narrator explains that Hardy was reading the *Aeneid* in the period between submitting *The Poor Man and the Lady* to Macmillan on 25 July 1868 and getting a reply on 12 August. (*LTH*, p. 58)

In the *Aeneid* Cytherea is a Venus/Aphrodite derivative and Aeneas's mother. At least three significant disruptions to the traded text follow from this. The lesbian encounter between the two Cythereas becomes a conceit based on their name; the nature of Miss Aldclyffe's relationship with Manston is known before it is revealed; and because of Cytherea Graye's name, Manston is accused of having a sexual relationship with his own mother. (This dual function of lover and mother is confirmed by another reference to the *Aeneid*. Dido, Aeneas's lover, dies spurting blood: Cytherea Graye is seriously ill with a haemorrhage, and Cytherea Aldclyffe dies of one.)

The last point is driven home further. Knapwater's village is Carriford; which becomes *carrefour*, as well as Carry-Forward (in the sense that it contains that part of the past which is to be carried forward; the village, as its buildings argue, is a consciously contrived account of the movement of past into future), so that it both echoes the four-square arrangement of Knapwater House itself, and suggests Oedipus's crossroads. The reference to Oedipus would be tenuous if it did not immediately serve as a satiric base, introducing a series of negatives which are used to subvert Aeneas's heroic status: there was no Laius to be killed, because the Oedipus is illegitimate, and was in the first place conceived semi-incestuously (his father having been Miss Aldclyffe's cousin); if the narrative is taken literally he fails to sleep with his mother's surrogate, being prevented at the last minute by Owen and Springrove's trip to Southampton; and instead of solving the riddle that has plagued the community he is himself the riddle; he is, indeed, the Sphinx, whose death liberates the community and allows it to go about its business again.

The *Aeneid* depends on the idea that it is possible to rename and reconstitute gods, and then to use the gods and their mythology to justify the control and conquest of a new land and a new people. Aeneas survives the burning of Troy. This parallels Manston's birth when the Houses of Parliament were burned in 1834. The connection is confirmed by the legend that London's former name, Troynovant, came from its foundation by another Trojan refugee, Brutus.[14] It is further amplified by the book's title, which (presumably) comes from Guy Fawkes's statement after the attempt to destroy the Houses of Parliament in 1605: 'desperate causes require desperate remedies'. Aeneas then founds Rome. Manston's unsought move to Knapwater is an ironic commentary on this. He is an illegitimate son unheroically brought to take over the stewardship of his natural mother's estate. He does not found a new order of old heroes: on the contrary, his past finds him, and the indigenous community witnesses his disgrace and death. Aeneas Manston brings three major contractual transgressions from Troy to Rome/Carriford: bigamy, adultery and illegitimacy. The clear implication, played out in the presentation of Manston and Springrove as choices of husband for Cytherea, is that the rebuilt Houses of Parliament (false Gothic) represent a similar usurpation of any justice and legitimacy not based on cash ownership.

This erosion of legitimate meaning and function by the disruptive counter-text (with Manston's illegitimate conception, in every sense, at its centre) is the most striking feature of *Desperate Remedies*. At times it makes the traded text, almost literally, into a Trojan Horse. Cytherea's other lover, Edward Springrove, is the representative of the good values of the land and its indigenous community and its defender against the invading Manston. This is undercut when Cytherea first comes to Carriford and sees her lover's initials marked in red on the buttocks of a herd of sheep. All this subversion of the traded text, especially as its action approaches the refuge or prison of Knapwater, would seem pointless if it were not anchored by the meanings Hardy gives to the main buildings at Carriford. Again erosion threatens all three, and again I want to quote at some length because of the architectural articulacy of the descriptions:

> [Knapwater House] was regularly and substantially built of clean grey freestone throughout, in that plainer fashion of classicism which prevailed at the latter end of the eighteenth century, when the copyists called designers had grown weary of fantastic variations in the Roman orders. The main block approximated to a square on the ground plan, having a projection in the centre of each side, surmounted by a pediment. From each angle of the inferior side ran a line of buildings lower than the rest, turning inwards again at their further end, and forming within them a spacious court, within which resounded an echo of astonishing clearness. These erections were in their turn backed by ivy-

covered ice-houses, laundries, and stables, the whole mass of
subsidiary buildings being half-buried beneath close-set shrubs
and trees. (*DR*, p. 96)

In front, detached from everything else, rose the most ancient
portion of the [original manor-house] – an old arched gateway,
flanked by the bases of two small towers, and nearly covered with
creepers, which had clambered over the eaves of the sinking roof,
and up the gable to the crest of the Aldclyffe family perched on
the apex. Behind this, at a distance of ten or twenty yards, came
the only portion of the main building that still existed – an Elizabethan fragment . . . fitted with cottage window-frames carelessly
inserted, to suit the purpose to which the old place was now
applied, it being partitioned into small rooms downstairs to form
cottages for two labourers and their families; the upper portion
was arranged as a storehouse for divers kinds of roots and
fruit. (*DR*, p. 133)

The Three Tranters Inn, a many-gabled, medieval building, constructed almost entirely of timber, plaster and thatch, stood close
to the line of the roadside, almost opposite the churchyard, and
was connected with a row of cottages on the left by thatched
outbuildings. It was an uncommonly characteristic and hand-
some specimen of the genuine roadside inn of bygone times; and
standing on one of the great highways in this part of England, had
in its time been the scene of as much of what is now looked upon
as the romantic and genial experience of stage-coach travelling
as any halting-place in the country. The railway had absorbed
the whole stream of traffic . . . Next to the general stillness pervading the spot, the long line of outbuildings adjoining the house
was the most striking and saddening witness to the passed-
away fortunes of the Three Tranters Inn. It was the bulk of the
original stabling, and . . . the line of roofs – once so straight – over
the decayed stalls, had sunk into vast hollows till they seemed
like the cheeks of toothless age, (*DR*, p. 153)

All three descriptions seem to conceive of the buildings in 'natural'
and 'organic' terms. These qualities actually refer to the process of
erosion which affects them all in different degrees. Knapwater, the
newest building, is being attacked by the wilderness, growing in-
wards from the working outbuildings. The process has gone much

further in the gateway and the remnants of the Elizabethan manor-house. The wilderness has taken over the gateway, its final target being the crest of the family which built the house. The manor-house had had its status and style eroded by proletarian use. These are the related threats hanging over the problematized Aldclyffe hegemony at Carriford. The oldest building, The Three Tranters, has been eroded by a change in the infrastructure and is now more use economically to its tenant as a farmhouse than an inn. The difference is that The Three Tranters is rented (from Knapwater), rather than owned, and its architectural meanings therefore refer to a history of eroded trade rather than eroded control. The power relations of ownership and tenancy are enacted when The Three Tranters suffers the most extreme erosion of being burned down, and is not rebuilt because it is not insured and no longer viable as a trading site.

The description of Knapwater House seems to contain a brisk analysis that defies further analysis. It is 'regularly and substantially built,' and its design belongs to a period in which 'the copyists called designers' have become bored with elaboration and returned to simple and derivative classicism. There seems no point in address-ing further questioning to Knapwater and its contents, just as there seems little point in addressing further questioning to the totally inaccurate verdict of the Coroner's Court after Eunice Manston's supposed death in the fire at The Three Tranters. Both seem at first sight self-evident statements of fact, which conceal nothing and require no further investigation. But just as the coroner's verdict must be overturned in order to reveal a 'truth' the narrator has planted further into the labyrinth, so must the idea that Knapwater's regular and substantial structure has no further revelations to offer.

The invasive undergrowth has been dealt with. 'Freestone' is technically correct, but intrinsically ironic, since the stone is any-thing but free, when applied to a building and its decorative front. The 'spacious court' is linked, by its four sides, to Carriford,[15] and thus to Manston and his satiric connection with the Oedipus legend. The traded story of transgression and suspense might be supposed to lead to court, trial and retribution if it is to be duly normalized (although the only court which actually appears, the Coroner's court, is demonstrably wrong; Manston does not come to trial and his retribution is self-administered). If the ratiocinative mode of the traded text does indeed offer a model for the reading of details as clues, the court at the house must therefore echo, or adumbrate, a court of law. There seems to be no other purpose for the information being given by the narrator. The 'echo of resounding clearness' tends to confirm the point. We are thus given a resonant (and on the evidence of the Coroner's Court, unreliable) court in a problematized structure, so the question of structure and its status is literally made to resound through the rest of the counter-text.

The meanings of the lesser houses define Cytherea's two lovers in terms of the competition for the stewardship of Knapwater. The tenancy of The Three Tranters is Springrove's lost inheritance; the original manor-house is rebuilt for Manston, and occupied by him. The rebuilding of the Elizabethan fragment is an attempt to reverse the historical processes which threaten Knapwater, and Manston's personal corruption (and his onanism) express the narrator's opinion of this imposture. Even before its rebuilding the narrator gives the house its later function. It is arranged as an apparently innocent and eminently organic 'storehouse for divers kinds of roots and fruit'. This is just the arrangement made when it is renovated: the roots are a history of Manston's illegitimate birth and Miss Aldclyffe's disgrace, and the fruit is its revelation. In a wider sense these are the roots and fruit of the Aldclyffe hegemony, and in a wider sense still of the power relations it represents.

Springrove's candidature for the stewardship of Knapwater (and for stewardship, or political-executive control, of a larger structure) represents an attempt to add acquired knowledge, in the form of architectural training, to a natural knowledge of the land and its indigenous community. This gives him Hardy's own potentially dangerous power base. But since Miss Aldclyffe seems to advertise the vacancy only in order to find a way of appointing Manston, Springrove's application never has any chance of success. It must therefore be regarded not as dramatically balancing Manston's, but as offering an ideal alternative which is impossible from the point of view of the property-owning class. They prefer to bring in their own bastards and then legitimate illegitimacy by the exercise of power. Springrove's lost inheritance at The Three Tranters describes the inadequacy of this position exactly. The property has never been owned by its occupier and could only ever have been a trading enterprise with rent levied by the owner. The resulting necessity of the leaseholder to speculate led to Springrove's grandfather taking on more extensive property on repairing and rebuilding leases at a time when business was good: at the time of the fire, due to Farmer Springrove's oversight, the whole property is uninsured and so the family's ruin is complete. The balance of power follows what seems to be its logical course in Manston's favour. His wife has, it seems, been killed in the fire so that he is free to marry Cytherea. And as steward of the estate he will be in charge of enforcing penalties (although these are commuted to a surrender of the leases) on the Springroves.

After the fire the balance of the conflict between the Springrove legitimacy and 'nature' and the Aldclyffe/Manston illegitimacy and artifice (with Cytherea's bringing to contract at its centre) shifts. Once Manston's wife is supposed dead and he confesses his desire for Cytherea, the knowledge that Miss Aldclyffe is his mother becomes overt, rather than covert, between them. Marriage with Manston becomes a virtually inevitable consequence for Cytherea.

This marriage answers the question implicit in the opening chapters of *Desperate Remedies*: what larger cause (apart from the narrator's genre requirement of peopling his labyrinth) can be found for the series of misfortunes which robbed Cytherea of security and status? Why was she forced to leave Hocbridge and float herself on the commodity market as material for labour or marriage? The original disasters are, by a narrative conceit, literally telegraphed from Hocbridge into the explanatory Carriford-Knapwater labyrinth by a strikingly connected pair of images.[16] When Ambrose Graye falls off his spire, the narrator observes:

> Emotions will attach themselves to scenes that are simultaneous – however foreign in essence these scenes may be – as chemical waters will crystallize on twigs and wires. Ever after that time any mental agony brought less vividly to Cytherea's mind the scene from the Town Hall than sunlight streaming into shaft-like lines. (*DR*, p. 47)

Chemical water travels along a telegraph wire, as the plot of *Desperate Remedies* travels, obsessively, by train and telegraph and post (even by the drunken foot-post to Anglebury). The images of infrastructure provide one of the narrator's principal means of controlling the pace of action and revelation. The chemical water crystallizes, as Cytherea's new mental agony takes her back to the image of her father's death, on the day of her wedding to Manston. This is greatly amplified as the fire at The Three Tranters turns to sudden, localized snow and ice; and while the village is thus crystallized, it is revealed that it would be possible for Cytherea to marry Edward Springrove after all because his fiancée has just married a rich farmer. Cytherea is not to be told about this; the freeze ends, and the wedding takes place. During the ceremony (which takes place, obviously, in a church; the structure Ambrose Graye was working on, and which metaphorically flung him to his death; a metaphorical accident which also befalls the maritally transgressive Jude Fawley), Cytherea sees Springrove, but goes ahead and marries Manston. Once the reprise of the novel's first premise has been made, she is faced with the fact that she has been driven into a miscontract by poverty. Partly she is the victim of the traded text's pseudo-active mode and partly she is the subject of the counter-text's allegorical explanation.

The telegraphic connection and the narrator's anti-realistic power to have images transmitted at will is confirmed after the thaw, in a passage which parallels Henchard's sight of himself in the river in *The Mayor of Casterbridge*:

> She hastily hid herself, in the lowest corner of the garden close to the river. A large dead tree, thickly robed in ivy, had been considerably depressed by its icy load of the morning, and hung low over the stream, which here ran slow and deep. The tree screened her from the eyes of any passer on the other side.
>
> She waited timidly and her timidity increased. She would not allow herself to see him – she would hear him pass, and then look to see if it had been Edward.
>
> But, before she heard anything, she became aware of an object reflected in the water from under the tree which hung over the river in such a way that, though hiding the actual path, and objects upon it, it permitted their reflected images to pass beneath its boughs. The reflected form was that of the man she had seen further off, but being inverted, she could not definitely characterize him . . . It was Edward Springrove. (*DR*, p. 274)

The image has been inverted, reflected, seen as if her lover is a ghost; some trouble has been taken to make it seem imperceptible. But Springrove must return if the non-patrilinear interregnum at Knapwater is to be resolved in terms of the debate between nature and artifice. Indeed, the image in the river and the whole sudden freeze before the wedding represent nature's artifice rebelling against artifice naturalizing itself in Manston's bigamous marriage to Cytherea.

Miss Aldclyffe and Manston both die, and the non-legitimate, non-patrilinear blood line dies with them. The fact that the estate is left to Cytherea ('*the wife of Aeneas Manston*' (*DR*, p. 418) specified in Miss Aldclyffe's will) is a final disruptive paradox of contract. Her means of escape from the château is to own it: then she can dispose of it to Parson Raunham, and without the burden of ownership live at Knapwater with her new husband, Springrove, who will act as agent and steward. And because Cytherea is now a dutiful wife, brought into the structure that maintains the structure, the settlement of the estate will pass to the children of her marriage to Springrove. Her ordeal in the labyrinth has therefore produced the 'natural' stewardship of Knapwater which the corrupt Aldclyffe hegemony prevented, and because she has repudiated her own inheritance of the estate, she has removed the threat of a matrilinear succession. The structure will not be left in the hands of women and bastards again; and to be completely on the safe side it is being exorcised by a generation of ownership by a clergyman. In this sense the traded text provides the ideologically-weighted conclusion the bourgeois parable demands.

But the tortuous and satiric detail of this ending is, like the narrative that precedes it, profoundly disruptive. The traded text arrives at its conclusion only on the basis that it has been heavily undermined by the process of its narration. Beyond this, the narration has offered a subversive counter-fiction in which the threats to the contractual state of sexual relations (bigamy, adultery, illegitimacy) which are the staples of the mystery novel have been turned to outrageously sexual dares, and in which a systematic Virgilian allusion has turned the characterization of local property owners into a larger and unequivocally hostile critique of a state serving the interests of a property-owning class. Above all *Desperate Remedies* is a flamboyant display of the power celebrated in the autobiographical account of *The Poor Man and the Lady*, the power of the narrator to disrupt the traded text at the expense of its readers. The difference here is that the readers are now part, albeit a small one, of a mass readership.

2

Far From the Madding Crowd (1874): Priapus in Arcadia

Society is founded not on the union of the sexes but on what is a widely different thing, its prohibition, its limitation. The herd says to primitive man not 'thou shalt marry', but, save under the strictest limitations for the common good, 'thou shalt *not* marry'.

(Jane Harrison, *'Homo Sum'; being a letter to an Anti-Suffragist from an Anthropologist* (1913)[1]

The text of *Far From the Madding Crowd* seems both accessible and 'acceptable': a pastoral which, although its tone is chidingly ironic, does little to disenchant the reader in search of a lost and picturesque organic world where prosaic events may become mildly mythic; a love story which rewards continence, persistence, selflessness and good-heartedness in a man, and the acceptance of objectification and patriarchal structures in a woman. Spontaneous desire, libertinism, importunity, deception, obsessional behaviour and melancholia are admitted as human failings, but are not to be encouraged. The surviving lovers, discovering their true love only after these dangerous elements have been played out by other characters (who have conveniently been removed from the scene, one dead and the other locked away), achieve a resolution of property and propriety which is, particularly from the man's point of view, unusually generous in the matter of property. The woman, of course, is given her resolution in the form of marriage to a 'good' man.

The 'old' Hardy criticism regarded texts like *Desperate Remedies* and *A Laodicean* as, at best, points along an authorial route to texts like *Far From the Madding Crowd* and *The Mayor of Casterbridge*. But it is equally accurate to say that *Far From the Madding Crowd* is a point along the route from *Desperate Remedies* to *The Hand of Ethelberta*, or that *The Return of the Native* is a point along the route from *The Hand of Ethelberta* to *A Laodicean*. The narrative and structure of *Far From the Madding Crowd* amplify and extend the schematic control of *Desperate Remedies*. There is more artifice here, not less. Hardy's division in the 1912 General Preface of Novels of Ingenuity and Novels of Character and Environment is, as Widdowson points out, 'basically factitious'.[2] This factitiousness is another revealing concealment. 'Ingenuity' apologises for the presence of artifice in texts which are of necessity about characters and set in an environment. 'Character and Environment' celebrates a success in convincing readers and critics of the texts' 'naturalness'. As Eagleton puts it, 'Hegemonic in Hardy's own lifetime was the image of him as the anthropologist of Wessex'[3]; and what Hardy is really celebrating when he categorizes his novels is the success of authorial artifice in accomplishing this. And in doing this Hardy points to his crucial areas of manipulation and control in the 'major' fiction: the *ingenuity* of his creation of character and environment. This is where points of entry to the counter-text are to be found, and this is the source of T. S. Eliot's pained response (indicating the success of Hardy's attack on christian humanism) that

> . . . the author seems to be deliberately relieving some emotion of his own at the expense of the reader. It is a refined form of torture on the part of the writer.[4]

The presence of Wessex at the centre of the traded text has, because of its unexploded and critically sanctified myths of an organic past, hidden disruptions greater than those Hardy deploys in *Desperate Remedies*. And quite apart from the myths, almost all Hardy's readers, then and now, will have been almost totally ignorant of the production processes, economics and labour relations of a farm in Dorset/Wessex. The necessary credulousness of the reader in this situation, able to judge only the veracity of the bourgeois parable the characters play out, gives Hardy further power over his text and its reproduction. There is a sustained anthroplogical project in *Far From the Madding Crowd*, but it is founded in the concealed counter-text.

The plot device of a woman making a pseudo-active choice of lover is repeated. So is the device of making her fatherless, a situation which, as Boumelha shows, Hardy makes pervasive for his women characters. In the texts I examine, Cytherea Graye, Bathsheba

Everdene, Eustacia Vye, Thomasin Yeobright, Paula Power and Sue Bridehead lack fathers; Ethelberta Chickerel's father is alive, but in a class position which leaves her culturally and economically orphaned in smart London society; Elizabeth-Jane Henchard's paternity is crucially problematic and from her point of view crucially destabilizing; Grace Melbury's father has tried to project her into a class position of which he has no experience, and Marty South's moribund father dies; Tess Durbeyfield's father, who also dies after being moribund from the start, is strikingly incompetent. Also notable is the absence of brothers to relieve the women of the burden of an inheritance which might be expected to be patrilinear. Cytherea Graye and Ethelberta Chickerel have adult brothers but no inheritance; Tess Durbeyfield has siblings but all of them are infants. In terms of the traded text this makes it easier to write feminizing bourgeois parables, since none of the leading women characters has any man-defined status to retreat into if she fails to become sufficiently womanly to be marriageable. In terms of the corrupting narration it problematizes the whole notion of patriarchy. As Boumelha puts it

These [fatherless] women are freed to negotiate their own re-entry into the family through their choice of a marital or sexual partner – a choice which equally marks their assimilation into class structure. The effect of this is to highlight the modes of oppression specific to their gender; all the privileges of economic power are undercut by the marginality of women to the processes of production. The only freedom granted them by the absence of the father is the freedom to choose a man: it is only by a voluntary re-subjection to the patriarchal structures of kin that women find any point of anchorage in the social structure at all.[5]

Far From the Madding Crowd adds to this the setting of a working mixed farm run by a woman. In the 'traded' text Bathsheba's tenancy of the farm at Weatherbury naturalizes the ideology of femininity. The challenge set her is to learn the correct management of a fertile holding, of which she has become tenant by inheritance. In other words she has to manage a fertile body and marry the man who will make the best job of propagating her and tending the results. Her fertility cannot become active without a man to plant the seed, and this is the function she is being prepared for. The farm, like the woman, is in a state of interregnum because of a gap in male proprietorship. But this 'naturalization' is the site of serious narrative disruption. *Desperate Remedies* uses a genre pastiche of the sensation novel as the nurturing site of a necessarily parasitic counter-text, and *Far From the Madding Crowd* uses the equally fashionable Arcadian novel in the same way. Widdowson rightly points out that 'Hardy seems to have accepted almost all of [Leslie] Stephen's suggestions for revision and improvement'[6] for the serial version of the novel, which originally appeared in the *Cornhill*. This apparent deference to editorial requirements is made possible by Hardy's deployment of an subversive strategy not visible to an editor, and not threatened by changes on small issues of detail and taste.

Bathsheba Everdene and Fanny Robin are both physically invaded by Troy (which suggests a deliberate reference to *Desperate Remedies*; and between these two novels Elfride fires 'a small Troy' into Smith's heart in *A Pair of Blue Eyes*[7]) after displaying their fertility. The difference between their fates is the class difference between farmer and servant. According to what is stated rather than implied in the text, Bathsheba and Troy do not make love until they are legally married. Even without Boldwood's bribe there is a strong economic incentive for Troy to make a marital contract with Bathsheba. Troy impregnates Fanny without a contract and she and her baby die in Casterbridge workhouse. Again illegitimacy is forced into the dramatic centre of the narrative, here using the vehicle, in contrast to Miss Aldclyffe, of a patently uncorrupted character. Troy tries to marry Fanny, but she has gone to the wrong church; then the narrator's plotting machinery takes over and the class and power relations proceed to their logical conclusion. This is presaged by a narrative dare rehearsing this exact process of authorial determination, while Troy is waiting for Fanny to marry him (inverting the larger and socially more 'threatening' situation of Fanny waiting for Troy to marry her):

There was a creaking of machinery behind, and some of the young ones turned their heads. From the interior face of the west wall of the tower projected a little canopy with a quarter-jack and small bell beneath it, the automation being driven by the same clock machinery that struck the large bell in the tower. Between the tower and the church was a close screen, the door of which was kept shut during services, hiding this grotesque clockwork from sight. At present, however, the door was open, and the egress of the jack, the blows on the bell, and the mannikin's retreat into the nook again, were visible to many, and audible throughout the church, (*FFMC*, pp. 131–2)

As Christina Hole points out,[8] the idea that clocks are capable of foreknowledge is widespread in English folklore, and so is the idea that they are empathic as well as automatic. The point here is that the features which distinguish this clock are its implausibly humanized, perfectly regulated display and its revealed machinery. The image points clearly to the enactment of the narrative on authorially animated characters. We are not shown what will become of Troy and Fanny; we are shown instead what the author is capable of doing to them.

Both women's names are sexualized disruptions, and again run a calculated danger of bringing a blush to a feminine cheek. Bathsheba is a notorious biblical adulteress and Fanny is named after the female pudenda (Partridge confirms this as a current usage from 1860, with the suggestion that it may be much earlier; John Cleland's *Fanny Hill* (1749) seems to corroborate this. And by adding her surname and altering the spelling to match a pronunciation the character's name reproduces Troy's act of seduction, Fanny Robbing. 'Low' sexual culture, not inappropriately if you take Arcadia literally, is thus introduced into the 'high' culture of an Arcadia rewritten as a setting for a Victorian novel. As Merryn Williams notes,[9] this kind of Arcadian setting was usually the vehicle of naive idealism rather then sexual titilation. Hardy's landscape is also sexualized and gendered female. The men are incursions and are to be experienced sexually. Again the pseudo-activity of the traded parable is compromised by (barely) covert description. Goode offers this reading of Troy's sword exercise with Bathsheba.

> The landscape is, even more than the fir plantation, so obviously reminiscent of female genitalia that it is impossible to read the episode as anything other than symbolic of Bathsheba's sexual 'experience'. It takes place in a hollow amid ferns whose soft feathery arms absorb her. She sees a dim spot of artificial red moving around the shoulder of the rise (emulating the bristling ball of gold in the West which still sweeps the tips of the ferns with its long luxuriant rays). At the bottom of the pit, Troy looks up at her. Here the fern *abruptly* stops, and is replaced by a

yielding 'thick mossy carpet'. The sword gleams 'like a living thing' and seems to pass through her body, emerging 'free from blood' held vertically in Troy's hand. Later she is enclosed in a firmament of light, and of sharp hisses resembling a sky full of meteors close at hand. At the end, after a mere kiss, and the theft of a lock of hair (which has clear echoes) the blood comes beating into her face:

set her stinging as if aflame to the very hollows of her feet, and *enlarged* emotion to a compass which quite *swamped* thought. It had brought upon her a stroke resulting as it did Moses in Horeb, in a *liquid stream* – here a stream of tears. She felt like one who has sinned a great sin, (*FFMC*, p. 210; Goode's italics)[10]

This is really a more sophisticated version of Manston and his organ in *Desperate Remedies*, with the extra blasphemous 'dare' of Moses appearing conveniently at the moment of orgasm. The concealment is more effective because the tendency of this Arcadian genre is to naturalize rather than melodramatize.

Bathsheba's femininity is constructed, monitored and policed by the male gaze of her three suitors. As Bullen puts it, 'Hardy's characters are literally obsessed with watching each other, and almost all the events of [*Far From the Madding Crowd*] develop immediately out of the act of visual perception'.[11] On the face of it this 'primacy of the eye' represents Hardy adopting a fashionably Ruskinian position. But it is part of a deeper and more subversive pattern of structuring and gendering the text. Wotton describes this process as it is used in *Desperate Remedies*:

What the writing 'cannot see' is that when Cytherea, or any other woman, 'fetichises' her appearance she acts not instinctively but ideologically, surveying in her appearance the image men have of her. As an ideological object, Cytherea is subjected to and dominated by the masculine gaze, a subjection and domination which she experiences as guilt.[12]

Boldwood's evaluation of Bathsheba (at the Casterbridge market-house, where other naturally fertile objects are also valued for trading purposes) fits this model precisely. In his own trading process Hardy individualizes a general process of perception but then decorously exonerates the individual of any impulse of calculation:

Boldwood looked at her – not slily, critically, or understand-
ingly, but blankly at gaze, in the way a reaper looks up at a
passing train – . . .
   He saw her black hair, her correct facial curves and profile, and
the roundness of her chin and throat. He saw then the side of her
eyelids, eyes and lashes, and the shape of her ear. Next he noticed
her figure, her skirt, and the very soles of her shoes.
   Boldwood thought her beautiful . . . (*FFMC*, p. 134)

But the characterization of all three male suitors turns them into sites
of intense conflict and contradition. This is principally sexual. The
central dialectic of the text/counter-text relationship is thus located
within a deeply flawed and problematized masculinity. In a novel
which ostensibly deals with feminization and the restoration of patriarchal government this has great subversive potential. Gabriel
Oak's case, which sets a psychological-realist characterization against
contradictory allusive discourses, is the most striking and unexpected. This is also part of Hardy's covert sexualization of his
text. Oak is first described (and later first describes himself) in terms
of everyday normality; as

upon the whole, one who felt himself to occupy morally that
vast middle space of Laodicean neutrality which lay between the
Communion people of the parish and the drunken section, – that
is, he went to church, but yawned privately by the time the
congregation reached the Nicene creed, and thought of what there
would be for dinner when he meant to be listening to the sermon.
(*FFMC*, p. 9)

In fact this neutrality represents an insupportable mid-point.
The allusions which frame Oak's characterization dramatize what
is said about Boldwood:

The phases of Boldwood's life were ordinary enough, but his
was not an ordinary nature. That stillness, which struck casual
observers more than anything else in his character and habit, and
seemed so precisely like the rest of inanition, may have been the
perfect balance of enormous antagonistic forces – positives and
negatives in fine adjustments. (*FFMC*, p. 138)

The allusive context also creates a conflict between priapic Greeks and prudish Victorians in a text which is designed to please the Victorians while it allows the Greeks to triumph, Hardy's use of the Nicene creed, in its origins a Greek profession of christian belief, is a significant first clue, Oak is Pan, the god of Arcadia: lazy, dissolute, promiscuous, a shepherd with half the body of a goat. He plays his pipes, guards his flocks and exercises authority and government over the notoriously old-fashioned and slow-witted Arcadian peasantry. As Pan, Oak also tends bees at Weatherbury and nearly dies of his tendency to sleep when he is overcome by fumes in his hut. Oak's ability to read stars is also part of this pattern: it derives from Hermes, who stole Pan's pipes. It is also appropriate, as it is in *Desperate Remedies* (Sergeant Troy is plainly another Trojan invasion) to identify the sheep-farming country with Alba Longa, Aeneas's first area of influence in Italy. Every one of Oak's attributes is negative in Judaeo-Christian terms. The space between the Communion people and the 'drunken section' becomes, in the concealed countertext, the site of major historical and ideological struggle. The goat is a diabolic image, and the idea of a goat set to guard sheep is as dangerous, in christian allegory, as a devil set to look after a flock of christians. It is thus no surprise that the sheep in Oak's care at Norcombe are killed. The fact that they are driven to death by one of Gabriel's dogs is also to the point, since in English legend Gabriel's Hounds are the harbingers of death and destruction, chasing the souls of the damned to hell. Edward Waring cites several instances of this on Dartmoor and Exmoor, and the legend is associated in Dorset with King John, who had a hunting lodge at Purse Caundle.[13] The fact that the sheep fall into a pit seems to further confirm the purpose of the allusion.

Hardy points out in the second paragraph of the novel, innocently enough, that Oak's first name is a *Christian* name. (Like the three pairs of eyes watching the body in *Desperate Remedies*, this may have a specific source: the abusive *Spectator* review of *Desperate Remedies*, which arrested sales and damaged Hardy's cash investment, referred to the author's anonymity saving the novelist's family name 'and still more [his] Christian name' (*LTH*, p. 84) from disgrace because of the novel's obscenity. The review goes on to suggest that he bury the secret; if the secret is Miss Aldclyffe's non-marital sex and Manston's bastardy then both are specifically buried here with Fanny Robin and her baby.) As Gabriel, Oak is made to double as

Greek god and christian archangel: and being a goat makes him a
devil in the guise of an angel in christian mythology. As Gabriel, Oak
is the archangel of prophecy and destruction, functions which are
articulated in the early events at Norcombe. As Oak he is, in Virgilian
terms, mankind's first oracle ('quercus, oracula prima': *Amores*, 3, 7).
Gabriel's two forms of heavenly vengeance are fire and thunder:
these are the sources of the two crises which threaten Bathsheba's
ricks at Weatherbury, and which Gabriel Oak singlehandedly averts.
This is unequivocally disruptive: the dramatic incidents which
indicate Oak's 'character' to Bathsheba are inherent in the allusive
discourses which created him at Norcombe.

If Oak is Pan he is also Silenus, and this connection makes him
part of another anti-christian, anti-realist mode of characterization in
Far From the Madding Crowd. Both Oak and Troy draw significantly
on traditional mummers' characters. Mumming has been taken largely
for granted as a piece of authentic Wessex colour, but it offers important explanations for a number of Hardy's characterisations and plot
devices. Alex Helm gives this short definition of mumming:

> A men's seasonal ritual intended to promote fertility, expressed
> basically in terms of an action of revitalisation, in which the
> performers must be disguised to prevent recognition.[14]

In other words it is the celebration of a male invasion/propagation
of a female landscape. Helm makes the connection between Silenus
and the mummers' character of the Wild Man, who traditionally
carries a tree to confirm his association with the woods. Plainly
Oak's surname confirms this. His portable wooden shed at Norcombe,
in conjunction with the name, may take the association further: the
name of the English Wild Man moves from the Anglo-Saxon
'Wudewasa' to the late medieval 'Woodehouse'.[15] The Wild Man
was a widespread archetype in an area bounded by the old limits of
the Roman Empire, traditionally either leafy (Oak) or hairy (Pan); as
late as 1800 the Bavarian government legally prohibited quack doc-
tors from exhibiting Wild Men to substantiate their wisdom. The
legend was certainly active in Dorset until late in the nineteenth
century. A. S. Parke cites the case of a pregnant unmarried woman
saying to Dorchester magistrates: 'Please your worshipfuls, 'twere
the Wild Man of Yal'ham'.[16] Most importantly in this context, the
Wild Man is perhaps the strongest instance of a figure of resistance

to christian hegemony who survives all attempts at suppression with his pre-christian roots intact. Hence Hardy's decision to re-animate him in the counter-text of *Far From the Madding Crowd* as that hegemony begins to collapse. Richard Bernheimer offers this general account of the eclectic medieval Wild Man figure who abducts Dürer's Prosperpina:

> The Wild Man's wildness is . . . not a simple concept; it has sociological, biological, psychological, and even metaphysical connotations. Wildness meant more in the Middle Ages than the shrunken significance of the term would indicate today. The word implied everything that eluded Christian norms and the established framework of Christian society, referring to what was uncanny, unruly, raw, unpredictable, foreign, uncultured and uncultivated. It included the unfamiliar as well as the unintelligible. Just as the wilderness is the background against which medieval society is delineated, so wildness in the widest sense is the background of God's lucid order of creation. Man in his unreconstructed state,. faraway nations, and savage creatures at home thus came to share the same essential quality.[17]

This further emphasises the link between Boldwood's hysterical calm and Oak's Laodicean ordinariness. The obsessional behaviour which turns to madness gives, in effect, a psychologized account of a Wild Man, so that Boldwood's alienated wildness comes in a form acceptable to readers of the traded bourgeois fable.

The Mummers' Play is the vernacular narrative structure which kept the Wild Man alive in 'low' culture until the late nineteenth century. By the 1870s mumming was moribund and heavily bowdlerized, partly through the uprooting of agricultural communities as a result of the change to annual hirings and partly through 'high' cultural opposition. Helm gives the example of the vicar of Wispington and his wife withdrawing from a Mummers' Play in their kitchen in 1889 because they were so disgusted by its contents.[18] The threats posed by the mummers are exactly those which eroded the Elizabethan buildings at Knapwater: working-class culture and the threat of the returning wilderness.

The most distinctive borrowing from the Mummers' Play in *Far From the Madding Crowd* is Sergeant Troy. In a 1901 interview with William Archer (who ends with the prophetic suggestion that 'Perhaps the superstition of Wessex is one day going to have the laugh of the scepticism of Middlesex'), Hardy offers an evasive half-recollection of the play's action.

W.A.   And what was the action of the play?

Mr Hardy   I really don't know, except that it ended in a series of mortal combats in which all the characters except St George were killed. And then the curious thing was that they were invariably brought back to life again. A personage was introduced for the purpose – the Doctor of Physic, wearing a cloak and a broad-brimmed beaver.[19]

Hardy also refers to a character who seems in many ways to be Troy's specific source, the Valiant Soldier, who nicks a wooden sword against a staff ('Here come I, the Valiant Soldier (nick), Slasher is my name (nick)'). The Dorchester Mummers' play is typical of hero-combat plays, with one exception which refers directly to Troy's reappearance as the suitably priapic *Dick* Turpin at Greenhill Fair (fairground booths were regularly used by mummers): apart from the human characters, Tommy the pony also dies and comes back to life, just as Troy's Black Bess does. Troy's half-blacked-out face at the fair parallels the traditional presentation of the Turkish Knight. Mummers in Cornwall and elsewhere were known as 'guisers', and it was considered extremely unlucky for any mummer to be recognized through his disguise. Troy appears at Greenhill in disguise and is recognized; then he appears at Boldwood's party in disguise and is recognized; then he is killed; then the Doctor of Physic from Casterbridge arrives but fails to save him. Only at this point do the requirements of the 'traded' text begin to take precedence over the sustained conceit of the counter-text. The psychologized, overtly Wild Man (Boldwood) kills the Valiant Soldier (Troy) and is imprisoned: the dramatized, covertly Wild Man (Oak) gets his land, is fused with St George and marries the Fair Sabra (Bathsheba).

In this anti-realistic context Oak's first sight of Bathsheba, sitting on top of her furniture looking at herself in the mirror (a working-class household god also commented on in 'The Dorsetshire Labourer') is an elaborated, allegorically detailed version of Boldwood's psychologized gaze at the market-house. The description begins with Bathsheba's 'deviant' narcissism, which she will overcome on the way to ideal womanliness, and with the same ambiguous sexual invitation Cytherea Graye offers Manston.

she drew the article into her lap, and untied the paper covering; a small swing looking-glass was disclosed, in which she proceeded to survey herself attentively. She parted her lips and smiled.

It was a fine morning, and the sun lighted up to a scarlet glow the crimson jacket she wore, and painted a soft lustre on her bright face and dark hair. The myrtles, geraniums and cactuses packed around her were fresh and green, and at such a leafless season they invested the whole concern of horses, waggon, furniture, and girl with a peculiar vernal charm . . .

The change from the customary spot and necessary occasion of such an act – from the dressing hour in a bedroom to a time of travelling out of doors – lent to the idle deed a novelty it did not intrinsically possess. The picture was a delicate one. Woman's prescriptive infirmity had stalked into the sunlight, which had clothed it in the freshness of originality. A cynical inference was irresistible by Gabriel Oak as he regarded the scene, generous as he fain would have been. There was no necessity whatever for her looking in the glass. She did not adjust her hat, or pat her hair, or press a dimple into shape, or do one thing to signify that any such intention had been her motive in taking up the glass. She simply observed herself as a fair product of Nature in the feminine kind, her thoughts seeming to glide into far-off though likely dramas in which men would play a part – vistas of probable triumphs – the smiles being of a phase suggesting that hearts were imagined as lost and won. Still, this was but conjecture, and the whole series of actions was so idly put forth as to make it rash to assert that intention had any part in them at all. (*FFMC*, pp. 12–13)

A sexually desirable woman is thus constructed out of discourses of household (the load of furniture), vanity (the mirror), a male perception of suitably non-sexual attributes (her face and hair), and nature (the scene's vernal charm). But this is presented disruptively. The self-conscious narrator's comment on the artificiality of the scene's charm and its transposition of a (potentially sexual) bedroom scene to an outdoor setting both undermines his naturalization process and lays a clue to its unambiguously sexual use in the counter-text.

The first vision of Bathsheba is equally a self-conscious statement of the narrator's position in relation to his own story and to the reader's (re)production of it. Bathsheba makes a conscious choice

to unwrap the mirror, take it out, and look into it to see herself,
just as the feminine reader has chosen to borrow or buy the book
(or magazine), unwrap it, and read it. The passage I have quoted
exploits this identification, actively taunting the reader about the
nature of authorial self-erasure. If there is no validity in suggesting
Bathsheba's thoughts, what point is there in imagining the conjecture so fully? If the actions which make up the novel are put forward
so idly, what validity will they have? In this sense the mirror is also
a challenge to the reader to assume (unless she accepts the author's
invitation to mistrust him) that she is watching herself.

The sexual-erotic aspect of this narcissism is developed further
when Oak (who, as a tree and a satyr, is in a state of perpetual sexual
arousal in the counter-text) watches Bathsheba riding through the
trees.

Gabriel was about to advance and restore the missing article,
when an unexpected performance induced him to suspend the
action for the present. The path, after passing the cowshed,
bisected the plantation. It was not a bridle-path – merely a pedestrian's track, and the boughs spread horizontally at a height
not greater than seven feet above the ground, which made it
impossible to ride erect beneath them. The girl, who wore no
riding-habit, looked around for a moment, as if to assure herself
that all humanity was out of view, then dexterously dropped
backwards flat upon the pony's back, her head over its tail, her
feet against its shoulders, and her eyes to the sky. The rapidity
of her glide into this position was that of a kingfisher – its noise-
lessness that of a hawk. Gabriel's eyes had scarcely been able to
follow her. The tall lank pony seemed used to such doings, and
ambled along unconcerned. Thus she passed under the level
boughs.

The performer seemed quite at home anywhere between a
horse's head and its tail, and the necessity for this abnormal
attitude having ceased with the passage of the plantation, she
began to adopt another, even more obviously convenient than
the first. She had no side-saddle, and it was very apparent that a
firm seat upon the smooth leather beneath her was unattainable
sideways. Springing to her accustomed perpendicular like a
bowed sapling, and satisfying herself that nobody was in sight,
she seated herself in the manner demanded by the saddle, though

hardly expected of the woman, and trotted off in the direction of Tewnell Mill. (*FFMC*, pp. 24–5)

Again the description works on two disruptive levels, one sexual and the other a dramatic adumbration. Riding is a sexual metaphor throughout *Far From the Madding Crowd*. Troy's display of bravura riding as Dick Turpin (making the statement that sexual performance is all anyone will pay him for) has already been mentioned; he also gambles away Bathsheba's profits betting on horse races; and Oak rides wildly after Bathsheba in a state of unstated sexual jealousy when she goes to Bath to join Troy. Significantly he makes this ride on one of Boldwood's horses. Here Bathsheba's unobserved supine riding suggests auto-eroticism, and re-mounting herself astride is a decisive gesture of sexual assertiveness. The practice of women riding side-saddle has a great deal to do with the denial of covert sexual pleasure, and the fact that Bathsheba wears no riding habit means that the 'decorous' sartorial explanation for this suppression is also removed. The formula developed in *Desperate Remedies* of a pseudo-active marital text transformed into a real-active sexual text is once more absolutely central.

The passage under the boughs at Norcombe also anticipates and defines Bathsheba's dramatic passage at Weatherbury. As the active rider, unexpectedly riding astride, she renders herself supine; and for the period of her passage under the boughs, has no control over her progress. This is just the personal-emotional control she loses when she takes over control of her uncle's farm. The thesis of the traded text is that she is placed in control of agricultural fertility when she has not yet gained control of her own; but this apparent fusion is also, in *Far From the Madding Crowd's* concealed narrative strategy, an important change of polarity between the pre-text at Norcombe and the main text at Weatherbury. This is represented most clearly by buildings; or rather, at Norcombe, by the lack of them.

Oak has leased land at Norcombe, obtained a flock of sheep on credit, and paid ten pounds for a portable house. In this he can keep his shepherd's tools, his books, his food, his drink and a bed; it is, in effect, a mock farm, a home-made, miniature and therefore transparent collection of propositions. The fact that all this is on the side of a hill emphasizes its transitory nature. We first see Bathsheba in a similarly transparent situation, sitting at the front of a wagon. She is on top of the load: the load consists of table, chairs, a settle, house-plants, a canary and a cat. The wagon is, in other words, a house in transit. Bathsheba comes back to visit Norcombe in order to milk her cow: again it is a miniature and portable agriculture. Oak is the male farmer and Bathsheba the landless female. Bathsheba saves Oak's life on a milking visit, and his Arcadian idyll and his hopes of winning Bathsheba last as long as her (female) cow is still in milk. Once this state of affairs changes, so does Oak's economic and social status. Even his portable home is taken away after the contradictions of his name are played out and he loses his stock and his land.

The first encounter between Oak and Bathsheba is concerned with money and passage. If Bathsheba and her load are to proceed to the next stage of the turnpike road, a price must be agreed and paid. The hypothetical house on the wagon can only become a real house if this is done. By implication this also applies to the narrative, which will also eventually deposit its load in an appropriate synthesis of property and propriety. What does it cost to proceed to the next stage of the story? Having traded his story to the market-makers, this is one point over which Hardy the narrator has absolute control. Bathsheba haggles: why should she, the unobserved reader admiring herself in a mirror, pay more than she thinks is a fair price in order to proceed?

The observer, unthanked, pays the balance: Bathsheba and her portable house proceed therefore on terms which depend on a joint purchase of passage. The watcher (whose perception may be as erratic and untrustworthy as his old silver watch) has subsidized the watched. This defines the contract of narrative structure which follows. The purchase price is defined by the narrator, who is keeper of the turnpike-route.

Oak's passage to Weatherbury (like Cytherea's passage to Knapwater) is similarly a matter of value, specifically of market-valuation overturning self-valuation. At the Casterbridge hiring-fair Oak describes, in reverse, the moves which made him Farmer Oak of Norcombe; farmer to bailiff and bailiff to shepherd. Having failed to find an employer at Casterbridge he makes for Shottsford and arrives at Weatherbury, as Bathsheba arrived at Norcombe, in a wagon; where she has sat, and driven, on top of a houseful of furniture, he sleeps, and is driven, on top of a small stack of hay.

After his allusively contradictory arrival at Weatherbury (in that he brings Gabriel's fire with him in the counter-text and puts it out in the traded text), the farmhouse he finds is equally contradictory, emphasising the change in polarity very directly because it is the wrong way round:

> By daylight, the bower of Oak's new-found mistress, Bathsheba Everdene, presented itself as a hoary building, of the early stage of Classic Renaissance as regards its architecture, and of a proportion which told at a glance that, as is so frequently the case, it had once been the manorial hall upon a small estate around it, now altogether effaced as a distinct property, and merged in the vast tract of a non-resident landlord, which comprised several such modest demesnes.
>
> Fluted pilasters, worked from the solid stone, decorated its front, and above the roof the chimneys were panelled or columnar, some coped gables with finials and like features still retaining traces of their Gothic extraction. Soft brown mosses, like faded velveteen, formed cushions upon the stone tiling, and tufts of the houseleek or sengreen sprouted from the eaves of low surrounding buildings. A gravel walk leading from the door to the road in front was encrusted at the sides with more moss – here it was a silver-green variety, the nut-brown of the gravel being visible to the width of only a foot or two in the centre. This circumstance, and the generally sleepy air of the whole prospect here, together with the animated and contrasting state of the reverse facade, suggested to the imagination that on the adaptation of the building for farming purposes the vital principle of the house had turned round inside its body to face the other way. Reversals of this kind, strange deformities, tremendous paralyses, are often seen to be inflicted by trade upon edifices – either individual or in the aggregate as streets and towns – which were originally planned for pleasure alone. (*FFMC*, p. 84)

Again none of this detail is pointless. Even the natural overgrowth cannot conceal the building's Gothic origins, and this novel's similarity in method to *Desperate Remedies*: the farmhouse becomes a château for Bathsheba, though less sensationally than Knapwater does for Cytherea, until she too finds the right male steward to defuse its frights. Having refused to become Oak's wife, Bathsheba has become, by a careful irony, his mistress. Since mistress in this context defines a possessor rather than a possessed, there is further sexual irony in the fact that something (a woman) planned for pleasure alone has been turned around to face in the other direction by trade, the trade in this case being in fertility and its products. This suddenly altered state is naturalized by the narrative conceit of saying that the new power relations facing Gabriel have a history as long and immovable as the building he now sees, in contrast with the old power relations at Norcombe, which were precisely as permanent as his repossessed hut. This alienating device (in the counter-text; in the 'traded' and 'acceptable' text a house has simply been described at some length) introduces more self-conscious commentary which contextualizes Weatherbury and the narrator's construction of it.

If you approach Bathsheba's house, and hence Weatherbury, from the obvious, imposing, picturesquely decayed side, the path you are offered is partly-obscured and overgrown. This path may be ignored; but if it is ignored, you cannot expect to pass from the distant focus of the house seen from the road to a fuller understanding of what lies inside it. Again you are being offered the chance to buy a passage. If you choose not to buy the passage represented by an interior explanation of this exterior complexity you will continue to see pointless, if picturesque, detail. You will not therefore register the significance of this house as the successor of the wheeled shepherd's hut and the furniture wagon, or the structural significance of the change in scene from Norcombe to Weatherbury.

The history Hardy gives of the old manor house having literally turned into a working farm specifies the way in which Bathsheba's (sexual?) bower has a precise economic location.

> There were five wheat-ricks in this yard, and three stacks of barley. The wheat when threshed would average about thirty quarters to each stack; the barley, at least forty. Their value to Bathsheba, and indeed to anybody, Oak mentally estimated by the following simple calculation:-

$$5 \times 30 = 150 \text{ quarters} = 500 \text{ l.}$$
$$3 \times 40 = 120 \text{ quarters} = 250 \text{ l.}$$
$$\text{Total} \ldots 750 \text{ l.}$$

> Seven hundred and fifty pounds in the divinest form that money can wear – that of necessary food for man and beast: should the risk be run of deteriorating this bulk of corn to less than half its value, because of the instability of a woman? (*FFMC*, pp. 272–3)

The money is the harvest; the harvest is the farm; the farm is the woman; and so the ricks become money dressed up as a woman. In the traded text the naturalization process has now been extended to add the economics of farming to the fusion of a fertile woman and the land. In the counter-text the backward-facing farm at Weatherbury, backward also in its peasantry and its adherence to tradition, is backward more fundamentally in that, in a post-Hellenic patriarchy, it is farmed as if it were part of a pre-Hellenic agrarian matriarchy. Weatherbury even has its own Maenads (whom Pan boasted as his sexual conquests), the ironically named 'yielding women', Temperance and Soberness Miller. It is important therefore that female cultivation of the land has been established not just by inheritance, but by the removal of a dishonest bailiff.

Pennyways' dismissal draws on a widespread nineteenth century tradition of real and fictional dishonest bailiffs; its immediate Dorset source is almost certainly the unsuccessful case brought in Chancery by the Seventh Earl of Shaftesbury against the bailiff of his estates at Wimborne, Robert Short Waters, in the 1860s. This case is revealing as a model because, as Barbara Kerr shows,[20] it drew considerable public attention not only to Waters's success in making money at his employer's expense, but also the Ashley Cooper family's high-minded naivety in the conduct of their estates. The bailiff holds an important position. He is the link between the feudal fantasy world of Tennyson or the Eglinton Tournament or Trollope's Greshambury Park and the economic realities which produced the Swing Riots and the Revolt of the Field, starvation and rural depopulation. In this sense, as the economic functionary of a property-owning class who substituted myths of 'natural' hierarchy for real power relations, his position is inherently corrupt. In the real world he is the agency of Eustace Lyle's concept of property as 'protector and friend' in Disraeli's *Coningsby*.

Pennyways' minor financial irregularities thus become the unacknowledged emblem of the major structural exploitations and cultural deceptions he keeps in place. This is the position Victorian hypocrisy and economic imperatives have pushed Gabriel/Pan into applying for. Pennyways' (an unambiguous type-name) agency is in every sense crucial in anchoring the counter-text played out at Weatherbury. First he is the farmer's agent, having also been her predecessor's agent; then by his dismissal he is the agent of creating the period of interregnum and female government which instigates *Far From the Madding Crowd*'s main drama; then he is the agent of

Troy's discovery at Greenhill Fair, his return to Weatherbury at Boldwood's party, the removal of the two suitors who threaten Oak and so ultimately the agent of the novel's resolution.

The main drama at Weatherbury is superficially a break in patrilinear inheritance, but it is really a period in which, until Oak takes on the job and restores order, there is no bailiff. This means that the conflictual relationship between feudal-Arcadian myth and economic reality is presented in its raw state. The misrule which follows Pennyways' dismissal thus takes its meaning from this absence. This is presented in terms of the allusive allegory created at Norcombe.

But this mythic farm, disruptively dismantled in order to fit the Victorian-Arcadian ideal, still has to trade, and its produce is taken to a male market to be valued and purchased; Oak's rough valuation of the ricks is a male valuation; and unless the crops are sold there will be no money to buy seed (appropriately in sexual/reproductive terms) for next season's crop. This is why Bathsheba's sexual evaluation must take place at the Casterbridge market-house, and why 'Queen of the Corn-Market' must be an ironic title; if she is queen in Arcadia, the most backward territory in the ancient world, she is also the newest farmer in the area, forced to prove herself in spite of the oddity of her sex.

The conflictual relationship between extreme modernity and extreme atavism, in having a woman farmer rather than a woman farmed, gives rise to a state of preternatural fertility. The lambing is slow, and may not be finished by Lady Day (when else?) because of the very high incidence of twinning. Oak, overseeing this process as he oversees the heightened state of human fertility (he carries Fanny's note before he knows who she is, thus becoming involved in her story as well as Bathsheba's), is suitably prophetic:

> Mr Oak appeared in the entry with a steaming face, hay-bands wound around his ankles to keep out the snow, a leather strap round his waist outside the smock-frock, and looking altogether an epitome of the world's health and vigour. Four lambs hung in various embarrassing attitudes over his shoulders, and the dog George, whom Gabriel had contrived to fetch from Norcombe, walked solemnly behind.
> . . . Oak lowered the lambs from their unnatural elevation, wrapped them in hay, and placed them round the fire. (*FFMC*, p. 123)

Wrapped in the hay which also enclosed Oak when he arrived at Weatherbury, the lambs are shown their ultimate fate: having provided the raw materials of clothing to wrap people in, they will eventually become roast lamb. Into this dramatically and analytically fecund situation comes another illegitimate, aristocratically-descended Trojan invader, Sergeant Troy. Troy characterizes misrule, and he is also the representative of the Hellenes, bringing (initially putative) male government to a matrilinear Greek world. Troy is *Far From the Madding Crowd's* principal agent of dramatic development and he has already impregnated Fanny Robin, thus announcing his function unequivocally. Where Boldwood makes sexual conquest a (presumably) distasteful sequel to the contractual ownership of a woman, Troy offers and inspires desire as a preliminary, if not as an end in itself. It is appropriate in this sense that his function, or his identity, is military. As the representative of the Hellenic invaders, he occupies a rank in a hierarchy which is male by definition, and which is at present a potential invasion force occupying and invading its own country. As a soldier (dressed in a red tunic to match the crimson jacket Bathsheba wears on her first appearance) his conquest of Bathsheba is made, emblematically at least, by his obviously phallic, glamorous and hypnotic swordplay. This has a comic but important counterpoint in Oak's rescue of the bloated sheep. Both Troy and Oak are invited by Bathsheba, in a piece of unambiguous sexual allegory, to bring out their swords (Boldwood, impotent in all but name, has a sword for relieving bloated sheep, but does not know how to use it) so that their display and performance may be evaluated. Oak's performance with his sword is a genuine matter of life and death; Troy's performance is really only a display; he merely plays with his mastery of the techniques of administering death. Troy cuts at the air, touching nothing; Oak save the lives of the animals in his care by puncturing what have become, effectively (like the Arcadian 'traded' text?), bags of wind.

Troy's surname, which is subject to the contradictory qualifier 'Frank', has (appropriately for a character described as a 'palimpsest') three principal meanings. The first describes Troy's own psychological state, and the psychological state he engenders in his lovers: according to the West-country expression used by Arthur Quiller-Couch in disguising his writing about Fowey, a Troy is a scene of disorder or confusion, or in the larger sense a labyrinth or maze (an allusion which is thus equally pertinent to the arrival of Aeneas in *Desperate Remedies*). The second describes Troy's function in disrupting the measure of the text already (subversively) defined by Oak's unsteady silver watch: Troy weight is used to weigh gems and precious metals, a suitably aristocratic application. Troy weight always gives short measure, since a Troy pound requires only 5760 grains, as opposed to the 7000 grains required to make an avoirdupois pound.[21] Sergeant Troy always, in some sense, gives short measure. The third meaning is the allusion to *Desperate Remedies*, the re-allusion to Troy and the re-invasion of England (or Rome, or Alba Longa). But the land Troy invades here is not Rome but Arcadia, the oldest and most old-fashioned part of Greece. Like the farmhouse, he seems to be going in the wrong direction. And Troy's name is also purely ironic: Virgil and Homer both describe their Trojans as truthful, brave, patriotic and confiding.

Oak is still part of Weatherbury after Troy's arrival, but his role is limited to shepherd. His sexual frustration is played out as he supervises the shearing and cuts a ewe in the crotch and makes her bleed while he is distracted by Bathsheba. But Troy's presence takes over from the moment of his arrival. Having learned to say one thing and mean another (and having thus become, as if by necromancy, the personification of Bathsheba's valentine card to Boldwood, even delivering the passion Boldwood lacks). Troy gives Bathsheba his watch. The relationship between Oak's erratic watch and its owner's patient stability is repeated, equally ironically, in the relationship between Troy and his watch. He is 'the erratic child of impulse' (*FFMC*, p. 198): his accurate watch has been designed to regulate the equally stable interests of the rich and powerful.

The valentine card, like the traded/narrated text, says one thing and means another. It is essentially a palimpsest, originally a manuscript in which one document has been written on top of another. As with anything brought to the market, the card, or the palimpsest novel, is to be valued in terms of its perceived utility. Boldwood only sees its mock meaning. As the representative of the Casterbridge market-house (which misvalued and rejected Oak), Boldwood grows desperate and mad in his attempt to execute a sexless and passionless purchase of his neighbour; she has also reserved the (pseudo-active) right to value him, and she is rightly suspicious of the token of exchange he offers. But Boldwood has his own form of sub-authorial pseudo-activity in the fetishistic creation of 'Bathsheba Boldwood'. In his internalized wildness, totally lacking Troy's potential for physical passion, he tries to sell Bathsheba's fertility to Troy, who has already assumed physical and contractual ownership. The force of cash power is cancelled out in the state of economic misrule created by the removal of the bailiff.

Troy's patriarchal government of Weatherbury thus becomes another interregnum. The new patriarch has a capacity for planting seed but none for husbandry. This is made very clear by his failure to protect the ricks because he and all of the men except Oak are too drunk to foresee the storm (again brought allusively by Gabriel) which breaks after the wedding celebrations. The disasters presaged by the storm are in turn presaged by the fact that Troy has, it seems innocently, ordered *hot water* to go with the brandy none of the men really wants to drink. The former matriarch disapproves, but no longer has the power to forbid; and this last drink is the one which sends them all to sleep (like Pan; but Pan is the one person who does not fall asleep). Water, naturally enough, falls during the storm. It falls on the part-protected ricks, which represent money as a fertile woman who may now be legally impregnated by the Hellenic invader. The paradox is that the storm threatens to destroy crops which have already been produced during the period of matriarchal tenure. Troy, after all, originally pursues Bathsheba by coming to help with her harvest. This suggests, or indeed proves, that patriarchal structures are not necessary to agriculture in either the literal or the larger sense.

This fall of water is repeated, with similar reference to Troy's blighted husbandry, when rain falls again on Weatherbury and the gargoyle spits all night on the garden Troy has planted on Fanny's grave. At the head of the grave is a stone 'Erected by Francis Troy in Beloved Memory of Fanny Robin' (*FFMC*, p. 356), which, if you accept that there is the same conscious choice in the author using 'erected' rather than 'placed here' as there is in his using the name 'Fanny,' sets erect male desire eternally in stone on top of the fanny he has 'robbed'. Passion has become ossified, just as it now has for the original sexual relationship proposed between Oak and Bathsheba. If you also accept the proposition that the gods, or the fates, have caused the rain to fall, you could also argue that the fall of water, thus angled, is also phallic; the gods are urinating on Troy. It is doubly appropriate therefore that, having disappeared from Weatherbury, Troy apparently dies by drowning, having left his clothes on the shore and deliberately entered the water; and since the stepfather who oversaw his growing up was a doctor, it is equally and ironically appropriate that a young doctor observes and testifies to his presumed death.

Eroticism (literally Fanny) is hidden, in another dare which challenges the reader to see Hardy's self-bowdlerization, under the acceptable allegory of Troy's headstone and his flower-garden. The ossified consummation takes place in a churchyard, albeit in the reprobates' quarter, and its image of sexual love and passion frozen into stone, and ecclesiastical structure, obviously anticipates *Jude the Obscure*. The god represented in the christian church is, through its gargoyle, making water on Fanny and her baby in the hope of washing them into oblivion because they represent sex and reproduction without its contract. The point made about the relation of a woman's fertility to the law in a patriarchy is unequivocal, and it restates exactly the points made about Bathsheba's farm, its trading of fertility and the nature of its ownership.

This thin earth outside a church also refers to the previous scene of revelation inside a church, as Troy sees the grotesque clockwork, the creaking machinery and the exposed mannikin of the novelist's automation while he waits in vain for Fanny to arrive and marry him. The workings are potentially visible in the gap between the belief that it is possible to convert a natural passion, or a natural marriage, into a contractual one, and the demonstration that it is not. The whole of *Far From the Madding Crowd* takes place in a larger version of this gap. The passage of time measured by the clock, and by Fanny's pregnancy (a season's fertility, as it is for the farm), converts the grotesque imitation of life in a church to a grotesque memorial of life outside one.

The revelation of the clock is also an indication that the relationship between Troy and Fanny has a revelatory purpose in terms of Oak's deferred love for Bathsheba. It is as if the innards of this clock may explain the oddities and inaccuracies of the early image of Oak's silver watch; and the innards of this clock lead us to the conclusion of Troy and Fanny's story in the wash-out grave. Oak and Bathsheba meet in the churchyard the morning after the destruction of the little garden (another emblematic statement; the garden destroyed is also, in effect, the garden planted to celebrate Bathsheba's passion for Troy).

Fanny is really dead and Troy seems to be dead. Bathsheba is now in a state of impossible matriarchy, since her ownership of her own farm depends on the question of whether Troy is dead or not. So does the question of whether Boldwood may court her again, and whether or not she has grounds for rejecting him. Her contractual state is both ossified and hypothetical. In this situation, Oak at last becomes bailiff, and eventually bailiff also of Boldwood's farm; the corn market's misvaluations are being reversed as Boldwood's reason continues to collapse. Pan's assimilation into the temporal life of Victorian Weatherbury is equally, and ironically, progressing. The licentious Greek god has abandoned his pipes and become a bass singer in the church choir instead.

When Troy returns, reduced to his crudest function in the riding exhibition, the crisis comes to a head. Troy reappears at Greenhill Fair, which has been introduced by the description of beasts being driven there for valuation, sale and ultimately for slaughter. It is no accident that all the significant residents of Weatherbury are at the fair; neither is it any accident that Troy's rencounter with the Weatherbury people at the fair, and then at Boldwood's Christmas party, are managed by the agency of Pennyways.

Boldwood kills Troy at the party given in Bathsheba's honour. Then he walks into Casterbridge to give himself up. Casterbridge is the trading centre where corn and seed and men and women are valued and bought and sold, and then dispersed to the farms to come to fruition or die. Everything in the agricultural process must pass through Casterbridge in order to be valued and sold; it leaves as seed and returns as harvest. The seed planted in Fanny comes back to the union workhouse in Casterbridge to die, with its mother, at the point of coming to fruition. The Hellenic invader, Troy dies in Weatherbury, but a Casterbridge surgeon has to be sent for so that his death, and the end of the patriarchy his marriage to Bathsheba represented, can be certified. Boldwood goes to Casterbridge for judgement and a (commuted) death sentence. In the traded text the trading centre, in a sense 'naturally' in the myth of naturalization, demonstrates its secure hegemonic control over the results of the non-patrilinear interregnum at Weatherbury. Boldwood's mad patriarchy and Troy's irresponsible patriarchy have cancelled each other out and it is now possible for Oak to marry Bathsheba, and for a mature, benign, sympathetic patriarchy to govern both farms at Weatherbury. A good and virile bailiff has finally subordinated his mistress by marriage, and has therefore now, appropriately, been given his own horse to ride. Now Bathsheba is properly feminized she is horse instead of rider.

But the conclusion of the counter-text, accommodated in the traded text's ideal conclusion to a bourgeois parable, is a celebration of a position which radically opposes this. The Greeks have defeated the Victorians without letting them know, and the old gods and their matrilinear inheritance have defeated the Hellenes. Bathsheba and Oak marry, but in the counter-text it is not a conventional marriage between woman and man. Marriage to a man would mean an end to matriarchal government on Bathsheba's farm. But by marrying Pan, formerly her faithful shepherd, Bathsheba has married the god of Arcadia. Their marriage has been legitimated by the christian church, which has thus been fooled into blessing a priapic celebration of sexuality. Because the narrator's corrupting strategies have made Oak and Bathsheba look like an ideal Victorian pastoral couple, matured by experience and at the start of their reproductive career, the potential for future subversion is tremendous. This establishes the position Hardy now tries to exploit in *The Hand of Ethelberta* where, as Ingham puts it, he 'turns pseudo-active into real active and so undermines the assertiveness of the text'[22] by taking the dangerous decision to adopt a mode which foregrounds a counter-text and for the moment abandons the strategy of concealment.

3

The Hand of Ethelberta (1876): Fanny Rampant

Life, says Ethelberta, is a battle, but only in the sense that a game of chess is a battle. The comedy proves her point. The novel, however, makes it clear that life is not a comedy, that in the last resort, the only loser is Ethelberta herself . . .

Battle and game are thus dramatized as a complex dialectic mirroring and yet limiting each other. The game not only provides Ethelberta with a career but also establishes a scenario which brings together a range of issues which add up to nothing less than the state of English society, the sexual and class power relations of its institutions, the effect of increasing urbanization, the state of the arts and the role of the estranged consciousness in the individual's negotiation of the social world. The novel takes on too much too soon.[1]

Imaginary circumstances that on its first publication were deemed eccentric and almost impossible are now paralleled on the stage and in novels, and accepted as reasonable and interesting pictures of life; which suggests that the comedy (or, more accurately, satire) – issued in April 1876 – appeared thirty-five years too soon. The artificial treatment perceptible in many of its pages was adopted for reasons that seemed good at the date of writing for a story of that class, and has not been changed.

August 1912   T.H. (*HE*, pp. 31–2)

Hardy's own re-introduction to *The Hand of Ethelberta* is to a large extent part of the autobiography's tactic of revelatory concealment. He seems to justify his text in terms of the 'classic realist' fictional project: it presents 'reasonable and interesting pictures of life'. He seems to argue that his sense of plausibility and fidelity to life was thirty-five years ahead of his critics', and that he had a better idea of realism than they did. At the same time he apologises for artificiality on the grounds of the 'class' of the story. 'Class' can have three distinct meanings here and Hardy does nothing to prioritize any of them. 'Class' may refer to the genre of satirical comedy; it may refer to the haute-bourgeoisie among whom Ethelberta moves; or it may refer to the servants and artisans in her family. Only the first of these would be an 'acceptable' disruption of classic realism, in the sense that modal artifice is somehow 'acceptable' if it has no other purpose; yet the other two meanings are still offered, leaving the far more disturbing possibility that this one justification for reproducing class as artifice is a general principle which should be applied to the other two possible 'classes' and perhaps to the notion of class in general.

Goode's criticism of *The Hand of Ethelberta* taking on 'too much too soon' is, oddly enough, something of an appeal to the Myth of Wessex. The text is read as part of an argument that 'another twelve years will pass before [Hardy] publishes a text, *The Mayor of Casterbridge*, which is a satisfactory advance on *Far From the Madding Crowd*',[2] that a form has to be found which will allow Ethelberta's perception 'that the social fight is matched against "the attenuating effects of time"' and that in order to do this 'a break has to be made with the ideology of submission. That break begins to be made by *The Return of the Native* but *The Hand of Ethelberta* takes us to the edge.'[3] Leaving aside the difficulties presented by the idea of prescriptive imperatives and 'satisfactory' advances, I believe that this position in many ways represents all you can see of Hardy's development without accepting the presence and importance of the counter-texts.

In fact *The Hand of Ethelberta* is 'too much too soon' principally because it is a trading error. This is all Hardy actually admits to in his 1912 re-introduction to the novel. As a trader running a business in fictions, I believe that Hardy never really does more (except in *Jude the Obscure*, when he moves beyond trading considerations for the first and only time) than buy in information and sell it on in acceptable form at a profit. It is simply not acceptable for criticism to demand that 'artistic' (or for that matter subversive and developmental) considerations should ever overturn the primacy of this process. The narrator's 'dares' and subversions are not, in general, part of an overall fabric of the text, which would be economically suicidal: they are part of his own alternative fabric. They become partly visible so often, like the Roman remains revealed at Casterbridge, because Hardy chooses to court exposure as nearly as possible and as often as possible. In doing this he overturns the capitalist/individualist paradigm of private risk for public reward and wealth and substitutes an authorial paradigm of maximum public risk for maximum private reward, still managing to generate wealth in the process. The success of the 'Trojan Horse' strategy in *Far From the Madding Crowd* leads to the trading megalomania which leads to Henchard's self-destruction in *The Mayor of Casterbridge*. In *The Hand of Ethelberta* Hardy goes too far and tries to 'trade' what is primarily a counter-text. This gives it, in common with all the other counter-texts, the scale of engagement with major structural issues which Goode rightly identifies. *The Hand of Ethelberta* is Hardy without the Myth of Wessex, without the mis-represented workfolk and small traders to provide bourgeois para-bles and an anthropological travelogue (none of which is remotely amenable to reinterpretation as socialist parable, which has been a key weakness in many marxist and pseudo-marxist attempts to re-write Hardy). For Hardy to explain an exposed counter-text away on the grounds of modal irregularity and prematurity, as he does in his re-introduction, is proof of Wessex's huge potential for intellectual stultification and of a 'great' writer's power in a critical climate which came to worship 'great' writers.

Hardy threatens to overtly explode his own pastoral mode in the description of Farnfield. This extraordinary passage is worth quot-ing at some length.

where there should have been the front door of a mansion was simply a rough rail fence, about four feet high. [Ethelberta and Picotee] drew near and looked over.

In the enclosure, and on the site of the imaginary house, was an extraordinary group. It consisted of numerous horses in the last stage of decrepitude, the animals being such mere skeletons that at first Ethelberta hardly recognised them to be horses at all; they seemed rather to be specimens of some attenuated heraldic ani-mal, scarcely thick enough through the body to cast a shadow: or enlarged castings of the fire-dog of past times. These poor crea-tures were endeavouring to make a meal from herbage so trodden and thin that scarcely a wholesome blade remained . . .

Adjoining this enclosure was another and smaller one, formed of high boarding, within which appeared to be some sheds and outhouses. Ethelberta looked through the crevices, and saw that in the midst of the yard stood trunks of trees as if they were

growing, with branches also extending, but these were sawn off
at the points where they began to be flexible, no twigs or boughs
remaining. Each torso was not unlike a huge hat-stand, and suspended to the pegs and prongs were lumps of some substance
which at first she did not recognise; they proved to be a chrono-
logical sequel to the previous scene. Horses' skulls, ribs, quarters,
legs, and other joints were hung thereon, the whole forming a
huge open-air larder emitting not too sweet a smell.

But what Stygian sound was this? There had arisen at the
moment upon the mute and sleepy air a varied howling from a
hundred tongues. It had burst from a spot close at hand – a low
wooden building by a stream which fed the lake – and reverberated for miles. No further explanation was required.

'We are close to a kennel of hounds,' said Ethelberta, as Picottee
held tightly to her arm . . .' Those poor horses are waiting to be
killed for their food.'. . .

'The man owning that is one of the name of Neigh,' said the
native, wiping his face. ' 'Tis a family that have made a very large
fortune by the knacker business and tanning, though they be only
sleeping partners in it now, and live like lords. Mr Neigh was
going to pull down the old huts here, and improve the place and
build a mansion – in short, he went so far as to have the grounds
planted, and the roads marked out, and the fish-pond made, and
the place christened Farnfield Park; but he did no more. "I shall
never have a wife," he said, "so why should I have a house to put
her in?" He's a terrible hater of women, I hear, particularly the
lower class.'

'Indeed!'

'Yes; and since then he has let half the land to the Honourable
Mr Mountclere, a brother of Lord Mountclere's. Mr Mountclere
wanted the spot for a kennel, and as the land is too poor and
sandy for cropping, Mr Neigh let him have it. 'Tis his hounds that
you hear howling.' (*HE*, pp. 198–200)

Again this is a translation of the pseudo-active to the real active. The
metaphors of fertility which enhance the Wessex pastoral scene are
replaced by a real dramatization of rural power relations and a real
economic transaction. It is also a specific personal attack. *The Hand of
Ethelberta* was first published as a serial in the *Cornhill*. It was commissioned on the basis of the success of *Far From the Madding Crowd*,

which was in turn commissioned because *Cornhill*'s editor, Leslie Stephen, had been impressed by *Under the Greenwood Tree* (*LTH*, p. 95). The character Neigh is made to resemble Stephen closely; his self-depreciation and his long, burnished beard will have been immediately recognizable within the coterie of literary entrepreneurs. The overtly exploded pastoral is placed, literally, in the house of the man who unwittingly published its concealed explosion in *Far From the Madding Crowd*. Neigh/Stephen's role in *The Hand of Ethelberta*, like Pennyways' in *Far From the Madding Crowd*, is deceptively slight. As the arbiter of literary production at the Doncastles' dinner-table, he is the key figure in the bourgeois production of Ethelberta herself. As Ingham puts it:

> the personal criticism [at the Doncastles'] is reductively sexual whether it comes from men or women. The men are titillated by the self-exposure of publication and the women are shocked by its unwomanliness.[4]

The fiction created by the woman becomes, in effect, the fiction which creates the woman. Because of his centrality in this process, Neigh (whose name is also, phonetically, 'nay'; a refusal of the 'unacceptable') also becomes central to the novel's whole account of its own fictiveness.

Neigh/Stephen is a guard-dog set to prevent the passage of analytical or hostile fictions, or the bowdlerizer Hardy pre-empts in *Far From the Madding Crowd* by doing the job himself and making a fool of Stephen's editorial amendments, designed to make the fiction more 'acceptable' in the area of sexual morality. The character is in this sense a public knacker. By presiding over the act of rejecting and doctoring fictions (by Hardy), he is allowing the continuation of the process of feeding underfed horses (writers; hacks; and it is worth noting that Partridge gives a usage current from c. 1730 of 'hack' as a harlot or bawd, which corroborates Hardy's use of female sexuality as a subversive device) to hounds (critics) which hunt on behalf of the Mountcleres. And by gagging fiction and culture and making them the political tool of the Mountcleres and the Enckworth structure, Neigh is perpetuating every level of exploitation and grotesquerie displayed at Farnfield. Hardy gives an explanation of the power base which enables Neigh to do this: Neigh is Doncastle's nephew, so that his antecedents represent the unassailable cultural power of dons working in association with castles.

Farnfield ought to be a house, but it is not: Neigh's failure to build a house there is attributed to his unwillingness to take a wife, so what goes on in place of the house also goes on in place of a marriage. The image of the horses being starved, killed and fed to the hounds is also an account of the potential fate of a woman (or by the association already established any individual who is not a power-holder) who is forced to accept the power relations she is subject to by aspiring to become the wife of Mr Darcy at Pemberley or Mr Neigh at Farnfield. Hardy's earlier models of the fictional house are also literally demolished at Farnfield. The proposition is no longer that the château the heroine sees *may* turn out to be empty and grotesque; it simply *is*. The château does not translate into an ideal and tranquil version of its former self, as it does in *Desperate Remedies* and *Far From the Madding Crowd*; it simply becomes somewhere else, as Ethelberta makes the personal translation from prospective mistress of Farnfield to real mistress of Enckworth. The bourgeois myths of the heroine becoming mistress of a house like Greshambury Park (the idealized history of England), or a house like Pemberley (the perfectly-proportioned image of her lover) are similarly overturned; Ethelberta marries the elderly and perverse Lord Mountclere and comes to live in his elderly and perverse house. Her control of the estate is practical and in sharp contrast to Bathsheba's passing her farm at Weatherbury into male stewardship. There are no genteel avoidances of money and business here. Christopher Julian is told at the inn at Anglebury that

> 'She's steward, and agent, and everything. She has got a room called "my lady's office", and great ledgers and cash-books you never see the like. In old times there were bailiffs to look after the workfolk, foremen to look after the tradesmen, a building-steward to look after the foreman, a land-steward to look after the building-steward, and a dashing grand agent to look after the land-steward . . . Half of 'em were sent flying; and now there's only the agent, and the viscountess, and a sort of surveyor man, and of the three she does most work . . .' (*HE*, pp. 406–7)

Hardy gives his plainest meanings of the 'governing structure' at Enckworth. The codification is given so clearly here that the description of Enckworth, putting my earlier quotation of the staircase capable of imprisoning an elephant into context, is once again worth quoting at some length.

Enckworth Court, in its main part, had not been standing more than a hundred years. At that date the weakened portions of the original medieval structure were pulled down and cleared away, old jambs being carried off for rick-staddles, and the foliated timbers of the hall roof making themselves useful as fancy chairs in the summer-houses of rising inns. A new block of masonry was built up from the ground of such height and lordliness that the remnant of the old pile left standing became a mere cup-bearer and culinary menial beside it. . . .

The modern portion had been planned with such a total disregard of association, that the very rudeness of the contrast gave an interest to the mass . . . the hooded windows, simple string-courses, and random masonry of the Gothic workman, stood elbow to elbow with the equal-spaced ashlar, architraves and fasciae of the Classic addition, each telling its distinct tale as to stage of thought and domestic habit without any of those artifices of blending or restoration by which the seeker of history in stones will be utterly hoodwinked in time to come . . .

It was a house in which Pugin would have torn his hair. Those massive blocks of re-veined marble lining the hall – emulating in their surface-glitter the Escalier de Marbre at Versailles – were cunning imitations in paint and plaster by workmen brought from afar for the purpose, at a prodigious expense, by the present viscount's father, and recently repaired and re-varnished. The dark green columns and pilasters corresponding were brick at the core. Nay, the external walls, apparently of massive and solid freestone, were only veneered with that material, being, like the pillars, of brick within.

To a stone mask worn by a brick face a story naturally appertained – one which has since done service in other quarters. When the vast addition had just been completed King George visited Enckworth. Its owner pointed out the features of his grand architectural attempt and waited for commendation.

'Brick, brick, brick,' said the king.

The Georgian Lord Mountclere blushed faintly, albeit to his very poll, and said nothing more about his house that day. When the king was gone, he sent frantically for the craftsmen recently dismissed, and soon the green lawns became again the colour of a Nine-Elms cement wharf. Thin freestone slabs were affixed to the whole series of fronts by copper cramps and dowels, each one of substance sufficient to have furnished a poor boy's pocket

with pennies for a month, till not a speck of the original surface
remained, and the edifice shone in all the grandeur of massive
masonry that was not massive at all. But who remembered this
save the builder and his crew? and as long as nobody knew the
truth, the pretence looked just as well . . . (*HE*, pp. 303–5)

Robert Gittings gives a good example of the critical 'rewriting' of this
narrative device in his introduction to the widely-used Macmillan
New Wessex paperback edition of *The Hand of Ethelberta*:

> The truth is that a large part of *Ethelberta* is badly written, and
> often shows Hardy at his worst in style and thought . . . there is
> the padding-out of the story with borrowed factual details. Chief
> among these is the large number of technical terms from architec-
> ture. Even in the novels which are *about* architects – *Desperate
> Remedies* and *A Laodicean* – Hardy does not plunder so wilfully
> his own architectural training. (*HE*, pp. 18–19)

This almost wilfully misses key points in the narrative structuring of
the novel. Ethelberta's three suitors from the bourgeois *bourse*
(balanced against the idealized and ineffectual Julian) form a chain
which takes Ethelberta from Arrowthorne Lodge (or straight-
forward deracination at Anglebury) to Enckworth. Mountclere is
the final consumer, Neigh the arbiter and Ladywell the procurer.
Property ownership and architecture are used to measure this. When
she is floated on the *bourse* of the Doncastles' dinner-party, Ethelberta
owns a very short lease on a house in London. This sets the time
she has available to make a suitable conquest and become mistress
of another house. The first suitor, Ladywell, has no property of
his own, although his family is said to own land near Aldbrickham;
as a dandy, he is the personification of the rigid codes of style by
which the *bourse* members define themselves; as an artist, he is
functionally as well as personally decorative; and, as his painting of
Ethelberta demonstrates, he is purely a fashionable painter, presenting a new commodity to his masters in a polished and acceptable
way. Then Ethelberta is passed on to Neigh, whose property and
function as a cultural entrepreneur have already been dealt with.
    Ultimately this progression brings her to Enckworth and Lord
Mountclere. The concealed Priapus in *Far From the Madding Crowd*
was the 'acceptable' and working class Oak: the revealed Priapus in

The Hand of Ethelberta is the 'unacceptable' and aristocratic Lord Mountclere. The move to Enckworth is precisely connected to Neigh and Farnfield. The horse-flesh at Farnfield is fed to the Hon. Edgar Mountclere's hounds. The way in which Ethelberta and the fiction are fed from arbiter to consumer is clear enough (again the pseudo-active model is inverted; this is the part of the process of male manipulation which should be concealed from the heroine), but she has first to deal with another procurer. In a precise piece of balancing, brother deals with brother in the diplomatic prelude to the marriage. This clarifies the meaning of the marriage contract made at the end of the novel. Where Ethelberta and Lord Mountclere play out the fairytale implausibilities which are the results of Ethelberta's career of social imposture, the two brothers state the socio-economic and moral realities of the situation. Sol Chickerel is a joiner, working for a large firm of London builders, and, like Jude, in a trade which maintains and develops the structure on the most literal level. Edgar Mountclere is, like Ladywell, a dandy. At almost 'the identical time when the viscount was seen to come from the office for marriage-licences in the same place' (*HE*, p. 334), his brother steps from his carriage and picks his way across the builder's yard where Sol works. Both brothers are opposed to the marriage: Sol on the basis of Lord Mountclere's immoral past and Edgar Mountclere ostensibly on the basis of Ethelberta's working-class origins and really on the basis that the marriage threatens his chances of inheritance. Sol speaks first:

'Preposterous! If it should come to pass, she would play her part as his lady as well as any other woman, and better. I wish there was no more reason for fear on my side than there is on yours! Things have come to a sore head when she is not considered lady enough for such as he. But perhaps your meaning is, that if your brother were to have a son, you would lose your heir-presumptive title to the cor'net of Mountclere? Well, 'twould be rather hard for 'ee, now I come to think o' t – upon my life, 'twould.'

'The suggestion is as delicate as the – atmosphere of this vile room. But let your ignorance be your excuse, my man. It is hardly worth while for us to quarrel when we both have the same object in view: do you think so?'

'That's true – that's true. When do you start, sir?' (*HE*, p. 338)

This is very much an ironic refutation of Disraeli's idealist synthesis of class interest. Class antipathy is sacrificed to common interest; and the common interest sustains the antipathy by trying to stop a marriage between master and servant. Lord Mountclere knows about Ethelberta's past before they marry. He learns the truth at about the time of his meeting with her at Corvsgate Castle. We therefore see Ethelberta's vulnerability and agitation most clearly on this occasion, when the appropriately-named Menlove is on the point of revealing everything. The castle is a ruin, and Mountclere sees it as a member of the Imperial Association (a plainly emblematic title), investigating its history through its ruinous state. The building has been stripped for examination by the revelatory passage of time and an account of its history is given by, again appropriately and disruptively, Dr *Yore*. (Other members of the Imperial Association include Lady Jane Joy, Mr Small, a profound writer who never publishes, and three degrees of clergy, from a Very Reverend Dean to a moderately reverend Nonconformist.) If Dr Yore is a don of some sort, which seems likely, the process of his describing the castle becomes a revelatory image of the Doncastles' power.

> The reader buzzed on with the history of the castle, tracing its development from a mound with a few earth-works to its condition in Norman times; he related monkish marvels connected with the spot; its resistance under Matilda to Stephen, its probable shape while a residence of King John, and the sad story of the Damsel of Brittany, sister of his victim Arthur, who was confined here in company with the two daughters of Alexander, king of Scotland. He went on to recount the confinement of Edward II herein, previous to his murder at Berkeley, the gay doings in the reign of Elizabeth, and so downward through time to the final overthrow of the stern old pile. (*HE*, p. 252)

Corvsgate's history is composed mainly of disreputable acts; specifically those concerned with the state imprisoning its potential opponents. The only exception, the resistance to Stephen by Matilda, may not be entirely coincidental: this is after all a subversive fiction about a powerful woman in a journal edited by a man named Stephen. Ethelberta arrives at the castle on a donkey; the Imperial Association, led by Lord Mountclere, spend some time examining the donkey before they look at the castle. Examining the donkey (which is plainly connected with Neigh and his horses) is examining the vulnerability of Ethelberta's real status. This is blatantly rather than reductively sexual: her ass is on public view (Partridge confirms this as a current nineteenth-century alternative to 'arse'). The donkey is directly related to Ethelberta's social climbing. Lord Mountclere says: 'we were engaged in a preliminary study of the poor animal you see there: how it could have got up here we cannot understand' (*HE*, p. 250). The unacknowledged (or at least unstated) sexual element of her ascent is made equally plain:

> The ass looked at Ethelberta as though he would say, 'Why don't you own me, after safely bringing you over those weary hills?' But the pride and emulation which had made her what she was would not permit her, as the most lovely woman there, to take upon her own shoulders the ridicule that had already been cast upon the ass. (*HE*, p. 251)

So Ethelberta's covert history emerges at the same time as a covert history of Imperial England. This is a set-piece which, like the feeding of horses to hounds at Farnfield, can work in two was because the question is left open: who or what is the ruin? Is it Ethelberta's false history of herself? Is her self-narration, and hence the fiction itself, in danger of collapse because of the revelation of its fictiveness? Or is the ruin more obviously Lord Mountclere, here described physically for the first time?

Corvsgate also gives a model for seeing Enckworth as a building which represents a national-imperial history, and which has this history encoded within it. Dr Yore's notes are not necessary a second time. The crucial difference is that Enckworth has been 'built' while Corvsgate has been left in ruins. It is a historicized present rather than a past. Lord Mountclere is decadent, perverse and unexpectedly vigorous. Naturally enough, in this parody of 'natural' 'classic realist' artifices, his house shares these qualities. 'In its main part', the structure has not been standing more than a hundred years; it dates from the time of the first Industrial Revolution and the main wave of enclosures. The new Enckworth develops its image of authority and hegemonic power from 'the original medieval structure', which remains 'the only honest part of the building'; it is the Gothic revival imposing false cultural and political control, as the Stoke-d'Urbervilles do when they misappropriate the d'Urberville name. A Georgian false front (which could not be more obviously or capriciously Georgian: King George saw the structure and complained of its brick facings) has been added; it has a veneer of classical order and stability. The marble and the columns and the plasterwork are misrepresentations of grandeur and power. This is the kind of work Sol and Dan Chickerel do. The most distinctive oddity is the principal staircase. Its artifice and method of support have already been mentioned. The 'twenty or more tons dead weight of stone' are suspended by the theories of geometrical construction which make Sol Chickerel and Edgar Mountclere act together to keep each other apart. But to rise in the bourgeois world, as Ethelberta has chosen to do, this is the staircase you have to climb. When she considers marrying Lord Mountclere for his staircase alone the statement is a remarkably accurate account of what she is really doing.

The Hand of Ethelberta thus becomes, in Brechtian terms, Hardy's most overtly interrogative text. The debates inherent in its treatment of property, marriage and writing cannot easily be refused by a reader. As Widdowson puts it, the novel 'unmistakably draws attention to its own artificiality and to its playfulness about literary forms and expectations'.[5] And in *The Hand of Ethelberta* Hardy also animates and articulates a politically silenced working-class group.

Agricultural labourers had to be rewritten in the bourgeois novel as 'background' characters in a bourgeois parable because of the genuine physical threat they posed to their masters. As Williams says,

> The image of a mob of starving and rebellious labourers haunts the literature of the countryside, from Disraeli to *Felix Holt*, and the impact of this mob action on the consciousness of educated and enlightened observers is a central theme in the country novel before Hardy.[6]

Hardy's individuation of workfolk into slow-witted figures like Jan Coggan, Cainy Ball, Joseph Poorgrass and Laban Tall in *Far From the Madding Crowd* dismantles the threat posed by this mob. But in *The Hand of Ethelberta* he does the opposite, empowering domestic servants in a revolutionary fantasy. Butlers and lady's maids are by definition deferential and do not carry with them any inherent spectre of revolution. In 1861, as Richard Altick shows, there were slightly more than a million domestic servants in the United Kingdom. This represents a work force larger than the textile industry's.[7]

Here Hardy unites them in the equivalent of industrial disruption: the master/servant relation is fictionally challenged, and overthrown, by the surrogate spectre of female sexuality. The idea of a working-class woman, having rewritten her class, using her sexuality to exploit *haute-bourgeois* and aristocratic men and gain executive control of (their) Structure (hence the importance of Ethelberta being her own bailiff at Enckworth) overthrows, at least fictionally, a crucial erotic paradigm. The male–female relation, as I have already argued, in many ways mirrors a capital–labour power relation. Contemporary evidence suggests that this was very often specifically magnified into a pattern of male sexual fantasy about female servants. Lord Mountclere does not abandon Ethelberta when he learns her true history; on the contrary, he accelerates his attempts to marry her. His erotic response increases when he knows that she is really a servant. Stallybrass and White cite two striking examples of this eroticized power relationship: Freud's 'Rat Man' and his infant memory of two nurses, Fräulein Peter and Fräulein Lina and the abscesses on Fräulein Lina's buttocks[8] (another revelation of Ethelberta's ass), and Arthur J. Munby's diaries.[9] Munby's diaries, together with Hannah Cullwick's, written between 1854 and 1873, detail a relationship in which the upper middle class Munby secretly married Cullwick, his maid-of-all-work. Munby's photographs of Cullwick show her in sexually exposed positions covered in dirt. Her diary entries show an anxious deference to his erotic projections of her. Hardy provides a fantasy which, while avoiding the literal presentation of Ethelberta doing dirty and demeaning work (unless, of course, you regard the writing of fiction which reproduces working class experience for a bourgeois readership as 'dirty' and 'demeaning') accepts the existence of this control by sexual fantasy in order to attempt to overthrow it.

The overthrow is intimately linked to the overall project of the self-subverting fiction. As Boumelha puts it:

Ethelberta, like Meredith's Diana, is a writer of sorts . . . It . . . gives a congruence to her creation of her own best, if least plausible, story – the romance of free choice and action. She tells her sister 'But don't you go believing in sayings, Picotee: they are all made by men, for their own advantages. Women who use public proverbs as a guide through events are those who have not ingenuity enough to make private ones as each event occurs'. Faith Julian and the other women who rebuke Ethelberta's lack of womanliness speak the public proverbs that consolidate male advantage, while Ethelberta's story-telling is a unique case of the private saying made into a public spectacle. She makes speech for herself, and in doing so transgresses all the determinations of class and kin. And yet it is evident from the first that her power of free choice cannot forever be evaded. The free subject is a fairy-tale, which takes on a most ironic inflection when her chosen suitor proves more frog than Prince. An elderly aristocrat with a mistress in tow, Lord Mountclere is an almost parodically exaggerated instance of the patriarchal male.[10]

Widdowson argues that 'Hardy's own social and intellectual aspirations seem to be displaced on to his female characters, who are then held in check by the novels' deployment of patriarchal strategies'.[11] In Ethelberta's case this is tellingly accurate. Ethelberta begins, like the Hardy created in the autobiography, as a poet who turns to story-telling.

The woman Ethelberta is produced initially by the *bourse* of the Doncastles' dinner-party. The first agency of this is her poetry. In order to escape from Lady Petherwin's control (an identity based on Ethelberta's status as the widow of a son who has not lived to come into his inheritance), Ethelberta literally writes her own identity. The obvious double meaning of an authorial hand and a hand in marriage in the book's title makes its analytical purpose very clear. Poetry, by convention (as a fictional mode which yields such low financial rewards that it is supposed to transcend the market), expresses Ethelberta's emotional state:

These 'Metres by E' composed a collection of soft and marvellously musical rhymes, of a nature known as the *vers de société*. The lines presented a series of playful defences of the supposed strategy of womankind in fascination, courtship and marriage – the whole teeming with ideas bright as mirrors and just as unsubstantial, yet forming a brilliant argument to justify the ways of girls to men. The pervading characteristic of the mass was the means of forcing into notice, by strangeness of contrast, the single mournful poem that the book contained. It was placed at the very end, and under the title of 'Cancelled Words' formed a whimsical and rather affecting love-lament, somewhat in the tone of many of Sir Thomas Wyatt's poems. This was the piece which had arrested Christopher's attention, and had been pointed out by him to his sister Faith. (*HE*, pp. 47–8)

The title of the single mournful poem implies that it must negate itself; it is an appeal to Julian, sent as an admission that Ethelberta regrets having misidentified herself. But the means of sending the poem is more widespread publication, and it is placed at the end of the collection, so that its presentation has wider implications. It becomes a public statement of the fact that Ethelberta's attempt to appeal to 'natural' identity and romance must lead not to the achievement of any naturalness (unless you believe that freestone facings are natural), but to the assumption of a high degree of artifice. The true end of a search for naturalness is Enckworth, at least in the artificial terms *The Hand of Ethelberta* prescribes for itself; but because at this early stage of the novel it is not yet available, it seems that the search has ended in self-cancellation.

The publication of the 'Metres by E,' 'floats' Ethelberta on a commodity market which is both literary and personal and which is, not coincidentally, presided over by her father's employer:

A few weeks later there was a friendly dinner-party at the house of a gentleman called Doncastle, who lived in a moderately fashionable square of West London. All the friends and relatives present were nice people, who exhibited becoming signs of pleasure and gaiety at being there; but as regards the vigour with which these emotions were expressed, it may be stated that a slight laugh from far down the throat and a slight narrowing of the eye were equivalent as indices of the degree of mirth felt to a Ha-ha-ha! and a shaking of the shoulders among the minor traders of the kingdom; and to a Ho-ho-ho! contorted features, purple face, and stamping foot among the gentlemen in corduroy and fustian who adorn the remoter provinces.

The conversation was chiefly about a volume of musical, tender, and humorous rhapsodies lately issued to the world in the guise of verse, which had been reviewed and talked about everywhere. This topic, beginning as a private dialogue between a young painter named Ladywell and the lady on his right hand, had enlarged its ground by degrees, as a subject will on those rare occasions when it happens to be one about which each person has thought something beforehand, instead of, as in the

natural order of things, one to which the oblivious listener replies
mechanically, with earnest features, but with thoughts far away.
And so the whole table made the matter a thing to inquire or reply
upon at once, and isolated rills of other chat died out like a river
in the sands. (*HE*, p. 75)

Ethelberta has tried to free herself from the Petherwin contract, and
thus, it seemed, the right of the aristocratic family she married into
to write her identity. But by 'publishing' herself she has made a
public share issue of her own emotions and presented herself for
evaluation. The members of the 'friendly' dinner-party discuss her
sex, her age, her experience and her marital status; woman as private
commodity becomes woman as writer; woman as writer thus becomes woman as public commodity. Ethelberta's naive mistake has
been to believe that the 'laws' of contract and identity are a control
system in themselves, rather than the articulations of a governing
structure. The Doncastles' cultured and self-confident world is
built on a market, as well as on the labour of Ethelberta's father.
Ethelberta's real class position is made clear by the fact that she only
learns about the response to her poems because her father has served
the guests and overheard their conversation. Her family are really
just beggars at the cultural feast they have prepared and served.

Then poetry gives way to storytelling. The poems express emotion and (more often) attempt to justify manipulative behaviour,
either by the author herself or by women in general. Why not? What
else should you do? The stories state, very simply, that the fiction
consists of the invention of something plausible and untrue and its
publication for financial gain. The poems are written when Ethelberta
is attached to no property, and is instead carefully deracinated.

Ethelberta begins by staying with Lady Petherwin, first at the inn
in Anglebury, and then at Wyndway House. This places her precisely: she is Lady Petherwin's creature, unable to either own property or marry it; she is as much a transitory guest at Wyndway as she
is at Anglebury. Her first lover, Julian, is equally outside Structure.
He owns no house, and his family's financial ruin has led to his
becoming a professional musician. This means that his relationship
to the structure is purely ornamental; and it means also that his
relationship with Ethelberta is not politicized as her other relationships are, so that it provides an 'ideal' romantic model to which the
other relationships ironically refer. The fact that Julian is a lover
whose knowledge of Ethelberta pre-dates her first marriage is also

important: it means that his misperception of her is based not on her contractual status, but on his conviction that she was a lady in reduced circumstances when she was not. So even the ideal of 'natural' love is subject to the same kind of male misapprehension as Lord Mountclere's. This is the context in which the 'Metres by E'. and their justification of female strategy are published.

In London Ethelberta is still hypothetically a lady; because she still holds the short remaining lease of her town-house, she is technically only under notice to quit the Petherwin contract. And as a widow who has not even reached her majority her status is equally hypothetical and disconcerting. Her story-telling exploits the ambivalence of the position. The poems took her into the market by talking about her manipulative skills; having become aware of her new context, the stories represent an instrumental use of those skills. The narrator of the novel chooses to give only one extract:

> He came forward until he, like myself, was about twenty yards from the edge. I instinctively grasped my useless stiletto. How I longed for the assistance which a little earlier I had so much despised! Reaching the block or boulder upon which I had been sitting, he clasped his arms around from behind; his hands closed upon the empty seat, and he jumped up with an oath. This method of attack told me a new thing with wretched distinctness; he had, as I suppose, discovered my sex; male attire was to serve my turn no longer. The next instant, indeed, made it clear, for he exclaimed, 'You don't escape me, masquerading madam,' or some such words, and came on. My only hope was that in his excitement he might forget to notice where the grass terminated near the edge of the cliff, though this could easily be felt by a careful walker: to make my own feeling more·distinct on this point I hastily bared my feet . . . (*HE*, p. 113)

This is a narrator's account of a blatant dissimulation (including a misrepresentation of gender) carried out by her and now related as if it were true. She is being pursued and she is on the edge of a cliff; she has been driven, in her story's metaphor, to a geographical margin which is also life-threatening. The story Ethelberta holds in reserve is her own, and this extract from one of her other stories prefigures the situation in which it will eventually be told. The stories are composed and rehearsed at Arrowthorne Lodge and presented in London; so a calculated fraud is worked out in the servants' hall and then practised on the masters. In many ways this is also an account of the deception which Hardy has already perpetrated in *Desperate Remedies* and *Far From the Madding Crowd*. And the money earned from the stories is used to finance duplicity: it keeps up Ethelberta's London house, as well as the fiction that she is a lodger there.

Ethelberta's main anarchies of transaction begin when the stories are publicly told to the *bourse*. Its members have misconstructed Ethelberta (which suggests a telling connection with Hardy's note in the autobiography about 'the author of *Far From the Madding Crowd* having been discovered to be a house-decorator(!)' (*LTH*, p. 102)), and she responds by telling them lies about herself. This is, I believe, also the essential response of Hardy's prose fictions to a similar situation. The question of whether Ethelberta's series of 'dares' will be discovered becomes the novel's principal source of suspense. If the overt conclusion of *Far From the Madding Crowd* is correct, and if patriarchy governs, what follows is an exercise in how to manipulate it most effectively; Ethelberta moves from a poet, an object of discussion at a fashionable dinner-table, to a storyteller who will eventually become Lady Mountclere. If Hardy's professional and social aspirations are indeed displaced on to Ethelberta, he offers a clear justification of his financial project here: the aim of successful deception is, quite straightforwardly, to intrigue your way into the Structure at the highest possible level and then exercise as much control as possible. In this sense Ethelberta's acceptance, for practical purposes, of the existing structure and her strategy of corrupting it by making herself a desirable commodity exactly mirror Hardy's novelistic practice.

But like the last of Ethelberta's poems, the novel ultimately becomes self-defeating and cancels itself out. Because the self-conscious disruption is foregrounded, its narrator renders himself virtually powerless. Nothing is held in reserve; the narrative strategies have been revealed in the surface of the text. This is the crucial inadequacy of presenting such a sophisticated interrogative text to a culture unprepared for it (except perhaps by Meredith), and this also suggests a central reason for *The Hand of Ethelberta*'s minimal impact, until recently, on Hardy criticism. There has been no need to 'rewrite' or 'unwrite' the book because its whole project is to unwrite itself. In this sense *The Hand of Ethelberta* is an unexpectedly naive sequel to *Far From the Madding Crowd*. Without the reserved area of power in the author-controlled gap between Wessex and the counter-text, and its potential for concealment, the entire fiction is presented for evaluation on trading terms only, and in this case the 'price' of publishing the fiction is the public surrender of a counter-text. In this sense *The Hand of Ethelberta* represents the first of two crucial watersheds (*A Laodicean* is the second) in the published Hardy's process of learning to 'trade' wholesale subversion effectively.

4

The Return of the Native (1878): Arcadia Overthrown

> On the question of recognition [Eustacia] was somewhat in-
> different. By the acting lads themselves she was not likely to be
> known. With the guests who were assembled she was hardly
> so secure. Yet detection, after all, would be no such dreadful
> thing. The fact only could be detected, her true motive never.
> (*RN*, p. 151)

D. H. Lawrence describes *The Return of the Native* as 'the first tragic
and important novel'.[1] John Paterson rightly argues that it is more
accurately described as an attempt at tragedy:

> the facts of its fiction simply do not justify the application of
> so grand, so grandiose, a machinery. Its men and women are
> seldom equal to the sublime world they are asked to occupy.
> In the Vyes and Yeobrights, Hardy evidently intended a little
> aristocracy fit to bear the solemn burdens of tragedy. But they
> remain a species of stuffy local gentility and as such incapable
> of heroic transformations.[2]

The notion of tragedy has been close to the centre of the critico-
political rewriting of Hardy. For the purposes of this exercise I want
to regard 'tragedy' as a bogus entity which has been part of the
'educational' process of using the culturally created 'Thomas Hardy'
in the project of bourgeois liberal education. *The Return of the Native*
is, very plainly, an ersatz tragedy traded in the Victorian fiction
market as a tragedy. To become involved in a debate about whether
it 'succeeds' or 'fails' in Aristotelian terms is to be directed away
from Hardy's dangerous subversions of mode and market. The 'tragedy' is part of the same authorial exercise in pastiche which invites
the definitions of 'sensational' for *Desperate Remedies*, 'Arcadian' for
Far From the Madding Crowd and 'comic' for *The Hand of Ethelberta*.

Like its predecessors, *The Return of the Native* is a pastiche because it is, in terms of the counter-text, an exercise in destruction, not self-education. The two go hand in hand (as *Jude the Obscure* makes very clear) throughout Hardy's business as a novel-writer, and *The Return of the Native* is no exception.
This novel's genre contains, as before, its dangerous dares. Lawrence takes the 'tragic' line through to its logical conclusion.

What is the real stuff of tragedy in the book? It is the Heath. It is the primitive, primal earth, where the instinctive life heaves up. There, in the deep, rude stirring of the instincts, there was the reality that worked the tragedy. Close to the body of things, there can be heard the stir that makes us and destroys us. The heath heaved with raw instinct. Egdon, whose dark soil was strong and crude and organic as the body of a beast. Out of the body of this crude earth are born Eustacia, Wildeve, Mistress Yeobright, Clym, and all the others. They are one year's accidental crop. What matters if some are drowned or dead, and others preaching or married: what matters, any more than the withering heath, the reddening berries, the seedy furze, and the dead fern of one autumn of Egdon? The Heath persists.[3]

Wessex returns to Hardy's fiction with a vengeance. *The Return of the Native* is set on a topographical margin between civilization and wilderness. Its action is framed by rituals which (transcending literal dates in the novel) define the beginning and end of a pagan winter. Mikhail Bakhtin describes the force of such unofficial carnivals:

As opposed to the official feast, one might say that carnival celebrates temporary liberation from the prevailing truth of the established order; it marks the suspension of all hierarchical rank, privileges, norms and prohibitions. Carnival was the true feast of time, the feast of becoming, change and renewal. It was hostile to all that was immortalized and complete.[4]

The fictional mode of tragedy is the celebration of the immortal and the complete. The 'official feast' (the bourgeois novel premised on notions of money and power; the context which tries to silence the mummers) is overthrown from the start of *The Return of the Native*. The fiction starts at Samhain, set originally on 31 October as the

division of summer and winter. As Hole points out,[5] Bonfire Night
on 5 November is a re-arrangement of this ceremony. It is thus
also a political ceremony which celebrates an (attempted) burning
of the Houses of Parliament also celebrated in *Desperate Remedies*.
Bonfires on Rainbarrow open the novel's dramatic action. Then
Eustacia joins the mummers, pretending to be a man. This adumbrates the later notion that she is a witch, because Samhain/
Hallowe'en is also one of the four sabbats when local covens meet
in general assembly.[6] Eustacia's travesty immediately threatens the
ritual's luck; because a woman has taken part in the ritual, any
fertility in the season which follows this mumming will be blighted.
The counter-text attacks the characterological 'tragedy' of the traded
text from its inception. As Wotton puts it:

> What we are confronted by as we gaze into Egdon's grim and
> solitary old face is the history of the life and labour of the work-
> folk and the better informed class. Egdon signifies the material
> unity of their world at its moment of transition. Egdon awaits
> not change but overthrow.[7]

The Hand of Ethelberta's interrogative openness on behalf of the servant class is followed by a full deployment of the reserved power of
rural detail in *The Return of the Native*. The counter-text's clearest
rules of engagement are presented (once the trader has successfully
sold his ersatz tragedy, this time to Chatto & Windus's *Belgravia* –
what title could imply greater ignorance of Wessex?) after the drama
seems to be over. Hardy uses innocently picturesque rural detail to
do this.

> Venn soon after went away, and in the evening Yeobright
> strolled as far as Fairway's cottage. It was a lovely May sunset,
> and the birch trees which grew on the margin of the vast Egdon
> wilderness had put on their new leaves, delicate as butterflies'
> wings, and diaphanous as amber. Beside Fairway's dwelling was
> an open space recessed from the road, and here were now col-
> lected all the young people from within a radius of a couple of
> miles. The pole lay with one end supported on a trestle, and
> women were engaged with wreathing it from the top downward
> with wild-flowers. The instincts of merry England lingered on
> here with exceptional vitality, and the symbolic customs which

tradition has attached to each season of the year were yet a reality on Egdon. Indeed, the impulses of all such outlandish hamlets are pagan still: in these spots homage to nature, self-adoration, frantic gaieties, fragments of Teutonic rites to divinities whose names are forgotten, seem in some way or other to have survived medieval doctrine. (*RN*, p. 401)

Like Eustacia, the narrator does not object to the detection of the pagan allusions which enrich his bourgeois tragedy in the confidence that the real motive for using them will remain undetected. This dare is particularly clear because the 'homage to nature' is so much at odds with the results of the relationship between character and environment, here represented (apparently) by the preparations for May Day. May Day is the first day of a pagan summer, and these celebrations end the winter which was blighted by Eustacia's mumming. Egdon, it seems, can now look forward to a future without the corrupting influence of Eustacia and Wildeve. But the pattern of the fertility rituals disrupts this at once. Summer is not a new planting season but the season when the crops planted after Samhain are harvested. Eustacia has blighted these crops and any celebration is foolish and premature. The state of the characters in the Aftercourses makes this very clear.

Clym Yeobright (in full Clement: mild, gentle) has turned, grotesquely, into a half-blind, faithless and unregarded preacher who, as Goode points out,[8] prefigures Jude Fawley as an allusively-constructed Christ figure. Thomasin Yeobright and Diggory Venn will marry and leave Egdon. Mrs Yeobright, Eustacia and Damon Wildeve are all dead. Like *Far From the Madding Crowd*, the bourgeois parable concludes with death punishing transgression and a synthesis of property and propriety. After the deaths the reader's focus seems to have been sharpened and the fiction normalized. Egdon, where tragedies happen, has somehow receded. This is done not by moving the narration away from the Heath but by a shift in the balance of metaphor. Within the single paragraph I quote a satiric account of Egdon's taming and subordination is offered.

First Egdon becomes its margin; then its trees become, in anthropomorphic cliché, dryads dressing themselves; then, passing the two key determinants of civilization, a dwelling and a road, the tree becomes a maypole, a dryad now being passively dressed with wildflowers; and so the conquest of nature is completed and ritually celebrated. This is, as I have already suggested, double-edged to say the least. Hardy seems to be offering an account of the narrator's ability to overcome natural forces in the creation of his bourgeois fiction, but his attempt at tragedy has been premised on the notion that natural forces determine character and fate. And the overthrow of gender which blighted the winter is repeated at the start of the summer as tree changes to maypole and dryad changes to phallus, caressed by the women dressing it. On this demonstrably implausible basis, the equally implausible 'instincts of merry England' linger on.

The narrative's function seems to be clear and unproblematic: having subordinated Egdon, the narrator exists in order to tell the reader what the characters think, why they think it and what it causes them to do. The surface of this epilogue is not dissimilar, at first glance, to the pastoral of *Under the Greenwood Tree*. This is not the retrograde step it seems. The change from the main body of the novel on Egdon represents a covering up of what has gone before (the revelatory concealment of Manston's guilt or Ethelberta's ass). The very presence of the change in the narrative is disruptive, and the delicate wit of its execution outside Fairway's cottage draws attention to the attacks which make it necessary. The Aftercourses depend on two essential certainties which have been destroyed: the certainty of community and civilization and the certainty that a fiction may be stably presented and perceived.

In this sense *The Return of the Native* represents a use of the counter-text which differs significantly from what has gone before. The project is still to bring the subversions of *The Poor Man and the Lady* as close to the surface of the traded text as possible. Actually trading a counter-text has failed in *The Hand of Ethelberta* and the experiment of running counter-text and traded text alongside each other in *Far From the Madding Crowd* is not repeated. Here Hardy again uses fictional mode as the vehicle of his counter-text. The relationship between character drama and topographical setting is the source of the overthrow, and the fiction is actually shifted from traded text to counter-text and (transparently and satirically) back again. It should also be pointed out that the May Day celebrations have, like the modernized Samhain of Guy Fawkes night, political connotations which echo the burning and destruction at the start of the pagan winter; as Robert W. Malcolmson points out,[9] May Day was often celebrated on 29 May rather than 1 May because it was reintroduced as a celebration of Charles II's Restoration in 1660. This fits well with its use in *The Return of the Native* as a falsely imposed restoration of order and control. The scene of (unreal) restoration at Fairway's cottage is seen by Clym. His damaged eyesight has at this point stabilized into a permanently inadequate vision. This is part of an overthrow of narrative rules of engagement which takes the form of organic damage and decomposition, of a return to a native state. The end of winter and political restoration is also (to use an appropriately organic and mock-autumnal metaphor) a false end to a fictional decomposition. The eyes see the text and the narrator's 'vision' sees the events of the novel, and so the hero's eyesight is strategically the most important thing the corrupt narrator can damage and, by this de-naturing, manipulate. Clym's ophthalmia is brought about by reading, by his attempt to produce meaningful knowledge from printed material. This is done in the course of his plan to set up a school on Egdon. As Wotton puts it:

> on his return from Paris with his head full of vague, Messianic, Saint-Simonian ideas based on the antagonism between workers and idlers, he fails to see what is as plain as a pikestaff to the workfolk; to dream of educating them in the 'humaner letters' before solving the problem of their poverty was absurd. Clym loves Egdon and he loves its people; it is just that he no longer sees them, but gazes past them, beyond them to that utopian vision of a conflict-free altruistic world of universal consciousness. Clym becomes the focus of conflict between these two worlds.[10]

And it is a focus which, literally, becomes incapable of focus when Clym prepares to put his plans into operation. To offer cultural wealth in place of economic sufficiency is as naive and corrupt as the factory system of bourgeois liberal fiction-writing, production and prescribed reproduction. Both are challenged at the same time by the interrogative narrative conceit of making the blindness a 'real' fact in the dramatic action of the traded text. The counter-text's metaphor thus becomes the traded text's 'reality', inverting the anticipated norm and the power relations which might be expected to supply the reader with a secure framework for reproducing the narrative.

> One morning, after a severer strain than usual, he awoke with a strange sensation in his eyes. The sun was shining directly upon

the window-blind, and at his first glance thitherward a sharp pain obliged him to close his eyelids quickly. At every new attempt to look about him the same morbid sensibility to light was manifested, and excoriating tears ran down his cheeks. He was obliged to tie a bandage over his brow while dressing; and during the day it could not be abandoned. Eustacia was thoroughly alarmed. On finding that the case was no better the next morning they decided to send to Anglebury for a surgeon.

Towards evening he arrived, and pronounced the disease to be acute inflammation caused by Clym's night studies, continued in spite of a cold previously caught, which had weakened his eyes for the time. (*RN*, p. 270)

Endeavouring to take the trouble as philosophically as possible, [Clym] waited on till the third week had arrived, when he went into the open air for the first time since the attack. The surgeon visited him again at this stage, and Clym urged him to express a distinct opinion. The young man learnt with added surprise that the date at which he might expect to resume his labours was as uncertain as ever, his eyes being in that peculiar state which, though affording him sight enough for walking about, would not admit of their being strained upon any definite object without the risk of reproducing ophthalmia in its acute form. (*RN*, p. 271)

Hardy manipulates the refractive index of his narrative in *The Return of the Native* to such an extent that the diamonds Clym trades in Paris become (through reading and naive utopianism) the furze he cuts when he returns to Egdon. The move from diamonds to furze seems, from the point of view of the traded text, completely bizarre. What the two have in common is that they are both 'natural' and both need to be cut in order to realize their cash, or 'instrinsic', value. To change from selling cut diamonds to cut furze is to make the whole notion of any natural object having an intrinsic cash value ridiculous. Catherine Belsey defines the illusionistic narrative of the classic realist text as 'narrative which leads to *closure*, and a *hierarchy of discourses* which establishes the "truth" of the story'. Closure, she argues, is disclosure and 'the dissolution of enigma through the re-establishment of order'.[11] As the subversive re-establishment of order at Fairway's cottage demonstrates, *The Return of the Native* turns this on its head. If vision and narrative stability have been incurably corrupted, both closure and disclosure become incurably problematized. If the refractive clarity of diamond can be changed to the refractive density of furze (and if the notions of cash value which evaluate the difference between the two have been wilfully ignored) by narrative caprice, how can you judge what the author has chosen to show you?

G. H. Lewes gives an account of the assumed contract of shared vision between writer and reader: '*My* world may be my picture of it; *your* world may be your picture of it; but there is something common to both which is more than either'.[12] The 'something common' is (although of course this may not be Lewes's belief when he makes the comment) the mode of production which presents the (fictional) picture, and in this sense Lewes is really celebrating his own entrepreneurial role. The concept of a transcendent vision is made to stand for the authority of the fiction's 'real author'. The novel becomes simultaneously a vehicle and an emblem: without the contract of shared vision, bourgeois fiction risks losing its hegemonic authority. Hardy's artistically pretentious visual descriptions and analyses are, in this context, once again interrogatively and destructively self-conscious. The author plays dangerous dares and threatens to give the game away in terms of the connection between producer power and authorial vision. This is particularly clearly done in *The Return of the Native*.

The first description of Clym (or rather, in the narrator's structuring of reader-perception into one character's *sight* of another, Eustacia's first vision of him) is a striking example of this narrative practice. Here it multiplies an underlying disruption, because Eustacia first sees Clym during the mumming, when she presents herself in a state of sexual travesty. Clym's face is seen 'with marked distinctness against the dark-tanned wood of the upper part' of a settle. 'The spectacle constituted an area of two feet in Rembrandt's intensest manner' (*RN*, pp. 161–2). The narrator's final observation in this passage hypothetically divides his function into philosopher (explaining his text) and artist (presenting it), sets one against the other and problematizes both.

When standing before certain men the philosopher regrets that thinkers are but perishable tissue, the artist that perishable tissue has to think. Thus to deplore, each from his point of view, the mutually destructive interdependence of spirit and flesh would have been instinctive with these in critically observing Yeobright. (*RN*, p. 162)

The creation of 'perishable tissue' and 'point of view' by an author constitute, as much as any two elements can, the narrative power of the project of realistic fiction. Because the power this creates resides not with the author but with the reproductive medium he does not own, the author is attempting here, within the acceptable trading bounds of his medium, his own overthrow. Egdon is also revolutionary and destructive in terms of time and space. Each is related to the other and consequently there are no governing absolutes (which have in any case been symbolically burned down on Bonfire Night). The narrator chooses to introduce this, in the manner of patronizing rural comedy, as the mummers wait for Charley (who will be trangressively replaced by Eustacia) to arrive.

> The next evening the mummers were assembled in the same spot, awaiting the entrance of the Turkish Knight.
> 'Twenty minutes after eight by the Quiet Woman, and Charley not come.'
> 'Ten minutes past by Blooms-End.'
> 'It wants ten minutes to, by Grandfer Cantle's watch.'
> 'And 'tis five minutes past by the captain's clock.'
> On Egdon there was no absolute hour of the day. The time at the moment was a number of varying doctrines professed by the different hamlets, some of them having originally grown up from a common root, and then become divided by secession, some having been alien from the beginning. West Egdon believed in Blooms-End time, East Egdon in the time of the Quiet Woman Inn. Grandfer Cantle's watch had numbered many followers in years gone by, but since he had grown older faiths were shaken. Thus, the mummers having gathered hither from scattered points, each came with his own tenets on early and late; and they waited a little longer as a compromise. (*RN*, p. 154)

When she arrives, Eustacia brings space and time with her. As Wotton observes, 'As she roams over Egdon, she bears with her the twin symbols of Kantian subjective *Anschauung*, space and time, "her grandfather's telescope and her grandmother's hour glass"'.[13] The hour glass is an otherwise pointless flourish, because it is pointed out that she also wears a watch.

So space and time are located in one central protagonist and vision is located in the other. They marry, disastrously. The contract which makes the fiction in a creative sense is represented by the contract which makes it in a cultural-political sense, so that the author-created disasters in Eustacia's marriage to Clym are also author-induced disasters in the making of a bourgeois fiction. As Boumelha points out, '*The Return of the Native* is the first of Hardy's novels to deal with marriage, not simply by employing marriage, more or less ironically, as a plot resolution, but by presenting the relationship itself as a continued, lived process'.[14] But to foreground a process on Egdon is to dismember it. The marriages in *The Return of the Native* are necessarily concerned with property as well as propriety. The structure that maintains the Structure needs to be financed. The Yeobright inheritance represents this. Any notion that cash-power represents intrinsic value is overthrown when the inheritance is gambled away under Rainbarrow. Again I want to quote at some length.

> Down they sat again, and recommenced with single guinea stakes; and the play went on smartly. But Fortune had unmistakably fallen in love with the reddleman to-night. He won steadily, till he was the owner of fourteen more gold pieces. Seventy-nine of the gold pieces were his, Wildeve possessing only twenty-one. The aspect of the two opponents was now singular. Apart from motions, a complete diorama of the fluctuations of the game went on in their eyes. A diminutive candle-flame was mirrored in each pupil . . . Wildeve played on with the recklessness of despair. 'What's that?' he suddenly exclaimed, hearing a rustle; and they both looked up.
>
> They were surrounded by dusky forms between four and five feet high, standing a few paces beyond the rays of the lantern. A moment's inspection revealed that the encircling figures were heath-croppers, their heads being all towards the players, at whom they gazed intently.
>
> 'Hoosh!' said Wildeve; and the whole forty or fifty animals at once turned and galloped away. Play was again resumed.
>
> Ten minutes passed away. Then a large death's head moth advanced from the obscure outer air, wheeled twice round the lantern, flew straight at the candle, and extinguished it by the force of the blow . . . [Wildeve] went hither and thither until he had gathered thirteen glowworms – as many as he could find in a space of four or five minutes – upon a foxglove leaf which he pulled for the purpose . . . shaking the glowworms from the leaf [Wildeve] ranged them with a trembling hand in a circle on

the stone, leaving a space in the middle for the descent of the dice-box, over which the thirteen tiny lamps threw a pale phosphoric shine. The game was again renewed . . .
   The incongruity between the men's deeds and their environment was great. (*RN*, pp. 253–4)

This set-piece has implications which make it impossible to return to the previous narrative mode. Two value systems, one emotional-psychological and the other material-economic, encounter each other on the heath. The agent who causes the encounter in the first place is a simpleton named Christian (the superstitious system of values which has maintained the 'world' in false equilibrium). The inheritance, whether it is an inheritance of characteristics or of wealth, is the passing of treasure from one generation to another. Because the inheritance shown here is in cash, a completely negotiable indicator of value, it is simply a gambling stake. The inheritance is, to a very significant extent, the story; and the conflict between the two value systems thus shows the way the story of *The Return of the Native* is told on the point of its collapse.

The narrator's power to light the scene seems theatrical or even cinematic; here it is a particularly blatant and self-conscious decision to illuminate or obscure dramatic action at the point where cash changes hands. As the first sight of Clym shows, this is part of a sustained narrative technique; Eustacia shivers when flashes of reason dart 'like an electric light upon [Wildeve]' (*RN*, p. 92). The account of the death's head moth blowing out the light, and the continuation of the game by the light of glowworms is not an overloaded or over-indulgent nature description but the accurately scored account of a critical change. A conventional artificial light source (the assumed premise of a story in which the characters go into the heath for a scene, taking their lighting with them like travelling actors) is withdrawn, to be replaced by a bizarre natural one; as if, because of this passage of money and the gambling transaction, the heath is assuming the right to light itself, the characters and the action. It is only after the dice-throwing that the heath really begins to show the force Lawrence identifies.

At this moment of fictional insurrection, the reader's position is defined, described and summarily undercut. The readers take on the role of the heath-cropping ponies: having been allowed to move in close to the action, and having seemed to have such complete control that it is possible to see a diorama in the players' eyes, they are shooed away. Later they have stones thrown at them when they try to come back. The image states the change from a 'safe' fiction, controlled by its story about characters, to a wild and dangerous one (however hypothetical the danger to the reader may be); the reader depends on the heath for narrative sustenance as the ponies depend on it for food.

In the middle of a novel which depends implicitly on a contract of plausibility between writer and reader (and which does not, like *Desperate Remedies* and *The Hand of Ethelberta*, offer an implicit modal apology for its artifice), in which the writer has already abused that contract by unusually sustained and detached landscape description, Hardy presents a gambling sequence which makes no more pretence to plausibility than the description of Farnfield in *The Hand of Ethelberta*. This may have mythic resonance, and it might very well be cited as evidence in support of Paterson's thesis about a clumsy attempt at tragedy, with an unimaginative and pedestrian Fate supporting Diggory Venn. But in the context of these fragmentations and subversions a greater one becomes clear. Where the Yeobright inheritance changes hands, an *idea* of fiction meets the currency which should verify or falsify it. The hypothesis implicitly put forward at the start of *The Return of the Native* is that it is possible to write a 'stable' narrative about people who might be real when their world is governed by material rather than organic determinants; the currency, plainly, is the money which buys the book, pays its author and maintains the Structure. This gives further meaning to the creative taunt of beginning with an extended landscape description. When narrative and money meet, the whole basis of narrative threatens to collapse. The narrator uses the supposedly stable, empirical system of cash value which is supposed to validate his traded text as the means of overthrowing it.

It is partly a critique of the arbitrary nature of money that the narrative of a book which sets itself out as a major tragedy should depend on the throw of a dice; the reconciliation of cash and sexual 'morality' is an arbitrary and fragile business when the means of owning property is apparently a matter of hazard (or 'fate'). And in such a self-referential fiction, the throw of the dice also makes the statement that the rules of writing and reading are firmly broken: the only facts that can be known about this fiction are that the writer has written it and that the reader is reading it. The novel is a secession from structure, in every sense. If money and power are represented, as they are at Greshambury Park, Pemberley and Enckworth Court,

by the ownership of land, the return to a lost organic world on
Egdon is, by ironic conceit, a return of money and power to a native
state; money and power become arbitrary gambling tokens illumi-
nated by the land itself. But the basis of land ownership is heavily gendered in bourgeois
society, and Hardy does not abandon his engagement with this
question here. Egdon is theoretically common land and two men
gamble for the tokens which imply ownership of it. This could
hardly be a more important transaction. Neither Venn nor Wildeve
is a Yeobright, yet both gamble for the Yeobright inheritance
on behalf of a woman. Kinship and marriage define patterns of
ownership in both the traded text and the counter-text of *The
Return of the Native*. As Rosalind Coward argues, contextualizing
Hardy's position on patriarchy in terms of late nineteenth century
debate:

> In so far as social explanations were sought for kinship, the ex-
> planations of the emergence of the paternal, that is, procreative
> family were explanations for the emergence of individual prop-
> erty rights. These arguments about the emergence of individual
> property rights worked on certain conditions. First, indi-
> vidual interests were conflated with the procreative family
> with transmission from father to genetic offspring. Second,
> because of the theory of work as the origin of private property,
> it became possible to 'sex' property, assuming a natural division
> of labour between the sexes. Men created it, therefore property
> was masculine. Finally, there is an assumption of an essential
> male psychology which seeks power through genetic self-
> perpetuation. It is this which in many accounts is the motor for
> the break-up of former collective society into individual units.[15]

This change is enforced on the Egdon workfolk (whose divisions of
labour and recreation are significantly ungendered; Susan Nunsuch
and Olly Dowden are not silenced or disempowered by the presence
of Christian Cantle or Timothy Fairway) by the marital transactions
of the Egdon bourgeoisie: the Vyes (a sea captain and his grand-
daughter), Wildeve (a civil engineer turned publican), Venn (the son
of a dairy farmer who becomes a dairy farmer himself) and the
Yeobrights. Hence the centrality of the passage of the Yeobright
inheritance in the text's self-destruction.

Four assumed stabilities underwrite marriage as the principal subject for the bourgeois novel: money, gender, character and christianity. In *The Return of the Native* money is problematized in the dice-throwing. Gender is problematized in the mumming. Character is problematized by the narrator's subversion of his own means of writing and seeing character on the reader's behalf. Christianity is problematized by the whole notion of the novel's action being set in an atavistic pagan winter. The old religion is used to overthrow the new. Eustacia is the agency of overthrow (or tragedy), and she is specifically linked to the practice of witchcraft. This is also part of mumming: Hole notes, for example, that Northamptonshire 'guisers' were referred to as 'witch-men'.[16]

The christian church is made the site of this struggle for hegemonic control. The idiotic *Christian* Cantle tells Mrs Yeobright about Susan Nunsuch's attempt to use a well-known device of witchcraft to end the witching of her children by Eustacia. (This is not particularly anachronistic: Hole gives examples of a Lincolnshire farmer sacrificing a calf to save his cattle from murrain in 1866 and the burning of a pin-studded effigy outside the American Embassy in London in 1900[17]).

'This morning at church we was all standing up, and the pa'son says "Let us pray." "Well," thinks I, "one may as well kneel as stand"; so down I went; and, more than that, all the rest were as willing to oblige the man as I. We hadn't been hard at it for more than a minute when a most terrible screech sounded through church, as if somebody had just gied up their heart's blood. All the folk jumped up, and then we found that Susan Nunsuch had pricked Miss Vye with a long stocking-needle, as she had threatened to do as soon as ever she could get the young lady to church, where she don't come very often. She've waited for this chance for weeks, so as to draw her blood and put an end to the bewitching of Susan's children that has carried on so long. Sue followed her into church, sat next to her, and as soon as she could find a chance in went the stocking-needle into my lady's arm.' (*RN*, pp. 200–1)

Eustacia brings fire on to the heath when she lights a beacon to attract Wildeve, and fire is used, as it is in the fire at the Three Tranters in *Desperate Remedies*, to destroy images of stability. Eustacia

carries fire with her throughout the novel; metaphorically, for in-
stance, she is the source of the fiery sunset on the heath when Mrs
Yeobright dies after Eustacia has failed to answer the door to her.
Eventually she is extinguished in the only way possible, by water.
Everything goes to heat the cauldron of the weir in which Eustacia
drowns.

The Return of the Native begins with a marriage (between Thomasin
and Wildeve) which has failed to take place because of a technicality.
This apparently superficial reason for the failure of contract is amplified into the failed marriage at the centre of the novel's action, and
effectively explained by it. The real conflict here is between Egdon
and the attempt to colonise it by the patriarchal, private property-
holding project of marriage and the novel.

The four main protagonists of *The Return of the Native* are precisely
balanced: of the two men, Wildeve is an outsider who has come
to Egdon and who becomes anxious to escape, and Clym is a native
who has left, returns, and does not want to leave. Of the two
women, Eustacia is an outsider who has been brought to Egdon and
is anxious to escape, and Thomasin is a native. Both men's occupa-
tions are most easily read as analytical propositions, and are, again,
ludicrous otherwise: Wildeve is a failed engineer who has turned
publican, and Clym is a Parisian diamond salesman. Clym, the 'lad
of whom something was expected', has been forced by the imperatives of career and achievement into the paradigm, indeed the bur-
lesque, of civilization, which is appropriately set in Paris; a man
making his living by selling an entirely useless commodity which
is valuable only because its ownership is regarded as a high symbol
of material 'achievement'.

Wildeve is in many ways Clym's complement. He has come to
Egdon as it were in Clym's place and his marriage to Thomasin
blocks the possibility of a semi-incestuous contract between the
Yeobright cousins. He has been an engineer, and thus involved in
the processes of manufacture and technology which really produce
materialist civilization. Having failed at that, his new business is
running an inn, although he still keeps his engineer's plate on the
door. This occupational transition is as bizarre and disruptive as
Clym's. In fact each transition parallels the other. Wildeve is, in a
way, engineer of intoxication on the heath, of a state which results
in a blurring and breaking down of perception. He provides a
mechanical/material model of the decomposition of consciousness
and sight which is also represented by Clym's ophthalmia.

The marriage Wildeve blocks would represent an apparently 'ideal' contract between Egdon's sensitive conscience (Clym) and its goodness and fertility (Thomasin); because this kind of idealistic relationship between individual and state and land would be untenable in a materialist society, it could only be made without reference to the outside world; and Wildeve is the outside world. On this basis Wildeve is the exploiter and Clym the exploited (a role emphasised by Wildeve's sexual attractiveness and Clym's somewhat asexual ethereality); and Eustacia, with her crude and violent craving for civilization, even Budmouth's, is Wildeve's ideal partner, just as Thomasin is Clym's.

The two miscontracts and the attempts to escape from them lead to the deaths of both exploiters; Egdon seems to exact a revenge on behalf of the good. In this sense the trader's policing of sexuality appears to govern the novel's conclusion. As Stubbs argues,[18] Eustacia is one of Hardy's women characters who are strongly sexualized only at the cost of inherent self-destructiveness, and Wildeve is very much her inferior male counterpart. But it is not possible, except in the satire of the Aftercourses, to argue that the Yeobrights maintain their integrity after the deaths, or that anything positive can be hoped for. Thomasin has left the heath with Venn, like two emigrants leaving England, and Hardy takes the trouble to disrupt his narrator's status with a footnote explaining an original intention to leave her a widow: 'Readers . . . with an austere artistic code can assume the more consistent conclusion to be the true one' (*RN*, p. 413).

Clym thus takes on the narrative of Egdon's future alone. This is a narrative which, like the self-cancelling conclusion of *The Hand of Ethelberta*, can supply only meaningless meaning:

> Yeobright had, in fact, found his vocation in the career of an itinerant open-air preacher and lecturer on morally unimpeachable subjects; and from this day he laboured incessantly in that office, speaking not only in simple language on Rainbarrow and in the hamlets round, but in a more cultivated strain elsewhere – from the steps and porticoes of town-halls, from market-crosses, from conduits, on esplanades and on wharves, from the parapets of bridges, in barns and outhouses, and all other such places in the neighbouring Wessex towns and villages. He left alone creeds and systems of philosophy, finding enough and more than enough to occupy his tongue in the opinions and actions common to all

good men. Some believed him, and some believed not; some said
that his words were commonplace, others complained of his
want of theological doctrine; while others again remarked that
it was well enough for a man to take to preaching who would not
see to do anything else. But everywhere he was kindly received,
for the story of his life had become generally known. (*RN*, p. 423)

Clym's decomposed sight has robbed him of the ability to perceive
and his 'vocation' is to proselytize. What could be more ridiculous
than an evangelist preaching an absence of religion and system?
How can you conceivably determine 'the opinions and actions common to all good men' without 'creeds and systems of philosophy'?
As a fictional character whose 'life has become generally known'
he moves, notionally, from the 'reality' of the fiction to the more
improbable 'reality' of a life beyond it. Only this improbable state
can accommodate the continued co-existence of the heath and the
fictional mode which has effectively overthrown itself in the act
of 'creating' it.

5

A Laodicean (1881): Made of Money (I)

'Cornegidouille! nous n'aurons point tout démoli si nous ne démolissons même les ruines! Or je n'y vois d'autre moyen que d'en équilibrer de beaux édifices bien ordonnés.'

('We shall not have succeeded in demolishing everything unless we demolish the ruins as well. But the only way I can see of doing that is to put up a lot of fine, well-designed buildings.')

(Alfred Jarry, *Ubu Enchaîné*)[1]

What is most obviously missing in *The Return of the Native* is Hardy's previous analytical use of architectural structure. Plainly there are buildings in the novel: the Quiet Woman, Blooms-End, Captain Vye's cottage, Eustacia and Clym's cottage; but they are seen only in terms of their function as dwellings, not in terms of their architectural qualities or the code of meaning that such a presentation would imply. This omission might be seen as a statement that, while Hardy assumes the necessary existence of some form of structure in order to shelter the characters from the weather, or to contain them within a narrative, he does *not* presuppose that socio-economic structure (or for that matter narrative and perceptual structure) has any place on the heath. But this would be to reduce *The Return of the Native*'s counter-text to another self-cancelling overthrow.

The point is that *The Return of the Native* simply does not take on the concept of a great house, or a château, which is so important in the first three texts I examine. Nothing in its tragic mode demands that it should. *A Laodicean*, in contrast, takes on the same questions of decomposition, overthrow and fictional representation and focuses them on the largest and most architecturally meaningful great house Hardy ever presents. This is done without the protection of genre-writing and without the protection of Wessex. These absences have made the novel almost impossible to approach in terms of the 'rewritten' Hardy. *The Return of the Native* has 'travelled well' historically because its tragic mode and its Wessex setting have been regarded as somehow historically transcendent. This is really non-sense; *The Return of the Native* is as much the product of its moment and mode of production as *A Laodicean*. Debates on architecture, religious denomination and photography demand analysis, which has almost invariably been refused, on the terms the author pre-scribes, whereas tragedy in Wessex can be analysed in terms of extrinsic, ideologically-informed notions of 'tragedy' and 'Wessex'. Thus *A Laodicean*, subtitled 'A Story of Today', has 'travelled badly' and been misconstituted as an 'unwelcome' anachronism.

Hardy was seriously ill during the writing of *A Laodicean*, and it seems likely that the novel was only published in its present form because a trading contract had to be fulfilled. This fact has been eagerly seized on because it provides an excuse for explaining *A Laodicean* away as Hardy's worst novel and retaining the individual genius Thomas Hardy without inconvenient revisions (J. I. M. Stewart, for instance, argues that in this text 'inspiration falters and found-ers'[2]). In fact the influence of the illness has been overestimated and misused. William Lyon Phelps noted that Hardy (by then retired from novel writing and defending his reputation) told him in 1900 that

> *A Laodicean* contained more of the facts of his own life than any-thing else he had ever written . . . That was published in 1881; during its composition he was dangerously ill, and did not be-lieve he could recover. He thought it was his last illness, and perhaps that was why he put in so much of himself.[3]

This is curiously misleading. There are obvious connections between Hardy and his character George Somerset because both men are architects; and the narrator of Hardy's autobiography talks at some length about Hardy's interest in the question of whether he should be baptised as an adult at the time when he was apprenticed to the architect John Hicks in Dorchester in the late 1850s (*LTH*, pp. 29–31). But by the time Hardy became ill (and remained so ill, whether through the original illness or bad medical advice, that much of the novel was dictated to Emma Hardy) the first thirteen chapters were already written[4] and the 'predetermined cheerful ending' Hardy refers to in his 1896 Introduction already established. The areas of personal experience were therefore established as subject matter before Hardy realized that he might shortly die; so any idea either that Hardy chose his subject matter through desperation or through the attempt to write a conscious memorial is wrong. This also means that Hardy's decisions about plot and character were already made. The question of dictation is more productive, because since there is no evidence that Hardy dictated on any other occasion, it almost certainly implies a surrender of narrative control. The will to power in the overall structuring of the text is present but the narrative authority which conceals it elsewhere is greatly reduced. This suggests the possibility that Hardy is less well protected here than in any other text because the gap between trader and narrator is in danger of being eroded. *A Laodicean* is a Hardy text which is only partly narrated by Hardy. Like the other Novels of Ingenuity it does not succeed in *covering* its own ingenuity, and in this sense it is extremely revealing.

The traded novel is primarily a story of fascination, love, and satisfaction deferred. In terms of mode it mixes the sentimental with the sensational. Somerset is confronted in his quest for Paula by obstacles which can be attributed either to difficulties of character (like Paula's Laodiceanism) or to problems posed by malign forces (like Dare's plots against him). Each balances and explains the other. The château of Castle de Stancy follows Macherey's Radcliffean model, but with the modification that where in *Desperate Remedies* Springrove and Manston compete merely for stewardship on the grounds of their own eligibility, Somerset and Havill compete to rebuild the château on the grounds of the quality of their plans. The hero is threatened by the structure and its contents; he desires the contents sexually; and he has in his hands the means of modifying the structure and gaining sexual satisfaction. Strategies and contrivances are thus, not surprisingly, central. The Laodiceanism of the title is, like Gabriel Oak's Laodiceanism in *Far From the Madding Crowd*, a deceptive lukewarmth.

John Power, like Napoleon in *The Trumpet-Major*, is an omnipresent absence in *A Laodicean*. His wealth, his purchases, his bequests and his daughter are the prizes for which Somerset competes. The biblical source of Laodiceanism comes from *The Revelation of St John the Divine*:

> And to the angel of the church in Laodicea write;
> These things saith the Amen, the faithful and true witness, the beginning of the creation of God: I know thy works, that thou art neither hot not cold: I would thou wert cold or hot. So because

thou art lukewarm, and neither hot nor cold, I will spew thee out of my mouth. Because thou sayest, I am rich, and have gotten riches, and have need of nothing; and knowest not that thou art the wretched one and miserable and poor and blind and naked: I counsel thee to buy of me gold refined of fire, that thou mayest become rich; and white garments, that thou mayest clothe thyself, and that the shame of thy nakedness be not made manifest; and eyesalve to anoint thine eyes, that thou mayest see. As many as I love, I reprove and chasten: be zealous therefore, and repent.[5]

'Power' is plainly the creator of Laodicea's wealth and equivocation: and as John, his (posthumous) revelations to the church in Laodicea try to call it to order. Like Gabriel Oak, the qualities suggested by this (absent) character's name are highly contradictory; but we are not given a 'real' character, as we are in *Far From the Madding Crowd*, to cover schematically-presented issues of power and revelation. Vision is necessary to revelation and John Power's 'revelation' to this Victorian Laodicea claims to offer the eyesalve which would have cured Clym's ophthalmia in *The Return of the Native*. The efficacy of the eyesalve will depend on the hegemonic control of cash-ownership and the 'truth' of the revelation it offers. As Dare's misleading photographic images show, even a quasi-scientific realism produced by these determinants is open to corruption by the practitioner. In this sense the novel is very centrally about the nature of bourgeois fiction and the cultural power built on the 'truth' of its revelation. *A Laodicean*'s obsession with buildings is thus Hardy's attempt, however incompletely executed, to analyse the nature not only of John Power's power but also of his own.

John Power is self-made economically, just as Hardy is self-made culturally. The absent Power represents the notionally absent Hardy. Imposture and the means of learning how to make the imposture are the inextricably linked issues of the novel: the materials which will make an acceptable story about life in Castle de Stancy will also make a bomb to destroy it. The revelation and learning of *A Laodicean* are principally expressed through George Somerset. At first his interpretative and strategic skills are too eclectic and naive for him to assess the truth of the revelation. In Belsey's terms he cannot comprehend 'closure' because he has been presented with many discourses but no hierarchical context in which to establish the power relations which structure them. This is particularly ironic because his business as an architect is, as the narrator clearly explains, to use a macaronic style to mask the structures which represent those power relations. As a dilettante he is subject at first to the myth that it is possible to observe the Structure without personal involvement in its power relations. Castle de Stancy disabuses him of this very specifically. English Gothic (the architectural style of the House of Commons rebuilt after Manston's and Eustacia's fires) is a productive first clue.

> The spectacle of a summer traveller from London sketching medieval details in these neo-Pagan days, when a lull has come over the study of English Gothic architecture, through a re-awakening to the art-forms of times that more nearly neighbour our own, is accounted for by the fact that George Somerset, son of the Academician of that name, was a man of independent tastes and excursive instincts, who unconsciously, and perhaps unhappily, took greater pleasure in floating in lonely currents of thought than with the general tide of opinion. When quite a lad, in the days of the French-Gothic mania which immediately succeeded to the great English-pointed revival under Britton, Pugin, Rickman, Scott, and other medievalists, he had crept away from the fashion to admire what was good in Palladian and Renaissance. As soon as Jacobean, Queen Anne, and kindred accretions of decayed styles began to be popular, he purchased such old-school works as Revett and Stuart, Chambers, and the like, and worked diligently at the Five Orders; till quite bewildered on the question of style, he concluded that all styles were extinct, and with them all architecture as a living art. Somerset was not old enough at that time to know that, in practice, art had at all times been as full of shifts and compromises as every other mundane thing; that ideal perfection would never be achieved by Greek, Goth or Hebrew Jew, and never would be; and thus he was thrown into a mood of disgust with his profession (*L*, p. 39)

This showing-off of architectural knowledge provides a lightly ironic account of Somerset's development, his youth, and his limitations. His eclecticism seems to have its complement in Paula's boudoir.

> On the tables of the sitting-room were most of the popular papers and periodicals that he knew, not only English, but from Paris, Italy and America. Satirical prints, though they did not unduly preponderate, were not wanting. Besides these were books from

a London circulating library, paper-covered light literature in
French and choice Italian, and the latest monthly reviews; while
between the two windows stood the telegraph apparatus . . . [the
sleeping-room] was a pretty place, and seemed to have been
hastily fitted up. In a corner, overhung by a blue and white
canopy of silk, was a little cot, hardly large enough to impress
the character of a bedroom upon the old place. Upon a counter-
pane lay a parasol and a silk neckerchief. On the other side of
the room was a tall mirror of startling newness, draped like the
bedstead, in blue and white. Thrown at random upon the floor
was a pair of satin slippers that would have fitted Cinderalla. A
dressing-gown lay across a settee; and opposite, upon a small
easy chair in the same blue and white livery, were a Bible, the
Baptist Magazine, Wardlaw on Infant Baptism, Walford's County
Families, and the *Court Journal*. On and over the mantelpiece
were nicknacks of various descriptions, and photographic portraits of the artistic, scientific, and literary celebrities of the day.
(L, pp. 66–7)

As John Power's sole legatee, Paula owns the château. Somerset's
investigation of this structure is, as he penetrates Paula's boudoir,
covertly sexual. The objects he sees (reflected, as Paula will be, in a
'mirror of startling newness') present a complementary set of cultural, economic, religious and sexual signs. These, by convention,
determine Paula. The outer room presents a balanced, cosmopolitan,
fashionable modernity. The inner room offers an account of its com-
ponents. Satin slippers and a dressing-gown define femininity; the
book on country families and the *Court Journal* define social standing; the book on baptism and the bible define religious denomination and establish Paula, according to the contemporary categories
Hands describes,[6] as a 'New Light', searching for an eclectic religious
philosophy. All these are self-conscious assumptions which struggle
to impress themselves on the castle which contains them: the 'photographic portraits' of contemporary celebrities are representations of
the Powers' cultural modernity, sitting uneasily above the represen-
tational history of the de Stancy history and the family portraits
by Holbein, Jansen, Vandyck, Lely, Kneller and Reynolds.

    Castle de Stancy has been paid for by the money John Power
made from building railways. In the traded text this offers meanings
concerned with modernity and the conquest of landscape by capital.

The counter-text adds sexual meaning. After Somerset has been given a room in the castle to facilitate his investigation and his plans for rebuilding (and hence an invitation by the power structure to rewrite Paula's female identity), he goes to see the tunnel John Power built. Unexpectedly Paula, chaperoned by Charlotte de Stancy, joins him. Building the tunnel was the act of penetration which produced Paula and the château. The sexualized description of the vaginal tunnel and Somerset's virginal discovery of it are barely concealed in the traded text. (Like all the quotations before page 133, this comes before Hardy's illness and the start of dictation.)

Somerset did not forget what he had planned, and when lunch was over he walked away through the trees. The tunnel was more difficult of discovery than he had anticipated, and it was only after considerable winding among green lanes, whose deep ruts were like Cañons of Colorado in miniature, that he reached the slope in the distant upland where the tunnel began . . .

'It is most natural,' said Paula instantly. 'In the morning two people discuss a feature in the landscape, and in the afternoon each has a desire to see it from what the other has said of it. Therefore they accidentally meet.' . . .

Somerset looked down on the mouth of the tunnel. The popular commonplace that science, steam and travel must always be unromantic and hideous, was not proven at this spot. On either side of the deep cutting, green with long grass, grew drooping young trees of ash, beech, and other flexible varieties, their foliage almost concealing the actual railway which ran along the bottom, its thin steel rails gleaming like silver threads in the depths. The vertical front of the tunnel, faced with brick that had once been red, was now weather-stained, lichened, and mossed over in harmonious rusty-browns, pearly greys, and neutral greens, at the very base appearing a little blue-black spot like a mouse-hole – the tunnel's mouth . . .

Down Somerset plunged through the long grass, bushes, late summer flowers, moths, and caterpillars, vexed with himself that he had come there, since Paula was so inscrutable, and humming the notes of some song he did not know. The tunnel that had seemed so small from the surface was a vast archway when he reached its mouth, which emitted, as a contrast to the sultry heat on the slopes of the cutting, a cool breeze, that had travelled a mile underground from the other end. Far away in the darkness of this silent subterranean corridor he could see that other end as a mere speck of light. (*L*, pp. 120–1)

Then Somerset's presence is replaced by a train (presumably ejaculating steam as it goes), mechanically penetrating the tunnel on his behalf; and the 'mere speck of light' at the far end of the tunnel parallels Dare's and Captain de Stancy's voyeuristic, concealed view of Paula in her gymnasium.

This sexual conquest of landscape and its implications of conquest by a Trojan, patrilinear hegemony have been naturalized by time: lichen and moss give the tunnel, which cannot possibly have been in existence for more than forty or fifty years, a speciously organic appearance. This is linked sexually with Castle de Stancy: in terms of Somerset's sexual fascination with Paula, the tunnel arch builds a castle around a vagina. Somerset finds exactly this when he finds Paula in her castle, and at the end of the novel he will build his own new house around Paula to perform the same function. This combination of mock history and sexual containment are at the heart of Paula's Laodicean conflict, because she cannot at first see beyond the imposition of age and power as she tries to make a pseudo-active choice between autonomy (paid for by men's money) and a place in the patrilinear hierarchy (meaning that she would use the money to buy up the de Stancys as well as their castle, becoming Lady de Stancy in the process). The false historicism of the tunnel's mouth has its equivalent in the 'real' history of the castle. One again this is a structure built by men to contain women which is temporarily under female government; by this means power is asking for cultural definition. In the ironic terms which define *A Laodicean*, it is necessary for a woman to ask a man to compete to build a new version of her old structure, in order to contain her; and it is similarly 'natural' that the new version of the old structure should ultimately be accompanied by another new version of an old structure, a marriage contract.

In the context of this proposed rebuilding the Victorian vogue of 'unlimited appreciativeness' and its consequent colonization of all available styles make direct expression or fresh expression impossible. After the collapse of authorial vision in *The Return of the Native*, the only available fictional and architectural structures are those based on macaronic parody.

A Laodicean's first image is of Somerset sketching an unspecified English village church at sunset. The sun is setting on Anglican hegemony and, since night follows sunset, natural light is about to disappear. In terms of his intention and his practice in observing the church, Somerset is automatically analogous with the reader of a new fiction: he is perceiving an object and taking its measure with all the skill at his disposal. From this perception he will form his judgement and definition and will add what he learns to what he considers the store of his knowledge. Hardy offers Somerset two ways of perceiving, just as he offers the reader two ways of perceiving. He can either reflect on the sunset, and its 'meditative melancholy' and 'contemplative pleasure,' or he can continue with the brief with which he has approached the church, or the text, and make a technically accurate analysis of the object under examination. Hardy is unambiguous about the choice that needs to be made: the obvious decision would be to indulge in the romantic escapism of looking at the sunset, but

> The sketcher, as if he had been brought to this reflection many hundreds of times before by the same spectacle, showed that he did not wish to pursue it just now, by turning away his face after a few moments, to resume his architectural studies. (*L*, p. 37)

It would be a generally 'acceptable' idea for the object being perceived, the sun setting on an English village church, to be seen as an unproblematic form of pleasing diversion. But in this case it is to be analysed. Hardy presents what seems to be a story of love and satisfaction deferred, but instead of presenting the escapist plot, and its concomitant assumption that its 'realistic' background exists only to give it a plausible base (as the church and Somerset would exist only to provide such a base for reflections about the sunset), he does the opposite. The plot he presents is fragile and interrogative and it consistently directs attention towards its underlying structure, the plausible base which ought to be its background.

It is thus crucial that Somerset (originally destined for the church) is an architect and that the first image is an English village church. Somerset's function has something in common with Jude's. Where Jude must literally maintain the structure, as a stonemason, Somerset interprets the structure, intellectualizes it according to what he has learned, and then plans and supervises its development and reconstruction. This, you might say, is the brief Hardy tries to give to the reader of *A Laodicean*. The opening sequence of architectural structures establishes this; and the fact that the reader has been closely identified with Somerset suggests, and the meaning of the architectural structures determines, that this level of perception may be offered as a serious alternative to reading the more obvious story of love and intrigue.

The village church, at the appropriately named village of Sleeping-Green, effectively represents myths of stability, unity, and organic continuity. If it were true that John Power's industrial state also developed organically there would be no need to look further. The traded text depends on the shared acceptance of this principle. But all the architectural structures in *A Laodicean* are essentially ideological structures, and further examination produces the revelation implied by the title. Why else should the reader's position be equated with an architect's? This is an apparently classic realist text destroyed from within by the presence of 'classic realist' buildings. Hence the lichened tunnel, satirizing (quite apart from its sexual subversion) any notion of 'fixed unchangeability' by investing a recent technological rape of the land with the signifiers of nature and age.

The stabilities of the village church are almost immediately overthrown by a building which specifically describes the power relations which created it. Having gone beyond the idea that the Anglican village church might somehow have occurred naturally Hardy develops his examination of structure and religion by presenting John Power's new red brick Baptist chapel in the middle of a field. A credible Dorset model for this is the isolated Baptist chapel Kerr describes, built at Fifehead Magdalen in 1863 and 'almost hidden by great beech and chestnut trees'.[7] The general tendency, as Kerr also points out, was for Nonconformist chapels to be built by working-class communities in centres of light industry like Stoke Abbott, Burton Bradstock and Charmouth where there were sufficiently strong groups of spinners, weavers or rope-makers to raise a congregation and the money to build. In Sleeping-Green the Nonconformist work ethic is artificially reproduced by capital rather than labour.

The Baptist chapel stands as a transition between the village church and Castle de Stancy. Somerset is led to the chapel by 'New Sabbath,' a hymn tune he remembers from his Anglican boyhood. The Anglican tradition, which has been 'betrayed' by the Tractarian Revival,

has ironically moved to this new and very unnatural-looking building, which is part of the same process of technological conquest
as John Power's railways and telegraph wires, mapping and meas-
uring the country on their own terms. An extraordinarily sustained
cluster of ironies and paradoxes occurs in the description of the
chapel, the Baptist service, and the baptism which does not take
place. It is as if Hardy mutates and subverts literal meaning so
furiously in this short section of *Laodicean* in order to turn his fiction
from the given object of the opening into an object in which no
statement can easily be taken at face value, thus re-establishing the
overthrow of *The Return of the Native*.

The Baptist chapel is a christian church without any protecting
Anglican mythos. It has been built in the middle of a field without
local invitation. The man who has placed it there is called Power;
and the only information we are at first given about John Power
and the chapel is its inscription:

Erected 187–
AT THE SOLE EXPENSE OF
JOHN POWER, Esq, M.P.'
(*L*, p. 43)

'John' universalizes him, and makes the connection with St John the
Divine; 'Power' gives the reason for his having been able to build the
chapel; 'expense' describes both his means of holding power and of
paying for the chapel to be built (and 'sole expense' suggests, ironically, that it may have been done at the expense of his soul); and
'M.P.' confirms that he represents this interest in parliament. Like
Sergeant Troy's stone placed on top of Fanny Robin in *Far From the
Madding Crowd*, this erection of a male monument to power in what
must previously have been a fertile field also represents the act of
impregnation described by the railway tunnel; and the fact that
we next see Power's daughter would tend to support the point. In
offering a chosen, designed, impersonal revelation of himself,
St John the Divine is about to offer what is, in Hardy's terms, a true
revelation. But the seed falls, in biblical terms, on stony ground. The
chapel building is new and ugly, and it exists in order to propagate
a form of dogma and a sense of community which are quite alien
to the area it is built in. This is made clear by the difficulty
Mr Woodwell (again, a type-name; a man naively attempting to do
good; the angel of the church in Laodicea) has in maintaining his

The Hidden Hardy

congregation; and Mr Woodwell is himself one of the ironies of this section of the novel, as a good man carrying out this probably pointless and certainly unwelcome function. The more closely you examine the larger meanings and implications of the Baptist chapel, particularly as information is added in order to explain Paula and her part in the service, the more subversive ironies proliferate.

Paula's refusal to immerse herself is due to her Laodiceanism; being lukewarm she is half way between hot and cold. Her baptismal garments cover the shame of her nakedness, as St John the Divine suggests. Her wealth, her position and her problematic construction of her own identity are all the result of her inheritance. She is, as Captain de Stancy puts it, 'Miss Steam-Power'. She has therefore been produced, exactly, by the interaction of hot and cold. (Mr Woodwell even has a 'steaming face' when he denounces her.) All the forces she represents are forces produced in England by the steam-powered second Industrial Revolution. John Power died of the interaction that made him: the Laodicean mixture of hot and cold creates steam power, and he died from a chill caught after a hot bath, so that obeying his own allusive exhortation to be hot or cold killed him. In refusing baptism, Paula is refusing immersion in a tank of cold water that can very easily be read as the unheated boiler of a steam engine. It will take the fire of the burning castle to heat it, boil the water, produce the steam and ultimately the gold (the ring which traditionally binds the marriage contract) refined by fire.

The third building Somerset sees is Castle de Stancy, which contains the English Gothicism which has been rendered 'organic' and docile in the village church (and will be made sexual and subversive in the railway tunnel). The castle is presented as a third level of analysis. The old church has been stripped back to a new baptist chapel. The chapel has been presented by the Powers, who now own the castle; and the castle therefore represents the powers which have built the structure in the field as a means of securing their position in the castle. When Somerset and the second architect, Havill, first meet at dinner in the castle, Havill mistakenly argues that the castle's origins are Saxon. (Havill is a deacon of the baptist chapel; evidently eyesalve has done nothing for his historical vision.) Somerset demonstrates that they are Norman. This debate is made to carry considerable weight.

If the castle is Saxon (as opposed to Norman: the Saxon conquest has not been celebrated as a historical event) it represents an uninterrupted succession in which changes in hegemonic control have been a matter of assimilation into a 'natural' power structure. If it is Norman it represents a power structure built to enforce conquest and the notion that changes in hegemonic control are produced by invasion and struggle. Again the great house becomes a schematized history of England: the castle was severely damaged in the Civil War, for instance, and never fully rebuilt afterwards. This unrepaired erosion of the *ancien régime's* defences has made it possible for the bourgeois Powers to take the place of the aristocratic de Stancys. The way John Power became owner of the castle, arriving to dinner as guest and leaving as owner, repeats *The Return of the Native's* use of hazard to disrupt money. This directs attention away from the literal means of purchase to the metaphorical explanation contained in the two architects' competing histories. Paula is capable of being fooled by Havill on this important point. She does not know the true history and implications of the power she has inherited; Somerset must earn the right to teach her. Paula is specifically made a consumer of books and magazines in the description of her boudoir, and like the inscribed feminine reader she waits to be given the 'correct' patriarchal hierarchy of meaning which constitutes a 'true' history of the structure she inhabits. In this sense the competitive attempt at interpretative invasion (Somerset against Havill) runs alongside the competitive attempt at amorous invasion (Somerset against Captain de Stancy).

The unresolved issues in Paula's Laodiceanism and the question of where new money will exercise its economic power culturally are represented by her pseudo-active choice of lovers. The christianity which will endorse a marriage contract with one or other lover is also, as Mr Woodwell's fight for a congregation shows, a site of competition and struggle. Valentine Cunningham argues that

> Paula Power's dilemma about whether to become a Baptist like her father, and opt for the railway and telegraph age, or to choose tradition, an ancient name in marriage, and Anglicanism, to go with her castle, is real enough, and Hardy leaves it unresolved.[8]

This is revealing. Cunningham's ideas that the dilemma is real and that the author can resolve it in a meaningful sense are based on the assumption that *A Laodicean* is the uncorrupted 'classic realist' text

Hardy 'trades'. In fact the pseudo-active choice Paula makes, whether it is between lovers or architects, is obscured by the conflicting artifices of vision (Somerset's architectural sketching, analysing structure, and Dare's photographic process, corrupting technologically precise pictures of its surface) which compete for the perceptual space left by the collapse of Clym Yeobright's vision. In this circumstance resolution would be possible only in the satiric terms of *The Return of the Native*'s Aftercourses. Hardy's anti-resolution follows this model:

> 'We will build a new house from the ground, eclectic in style. We will remove the ashes, charred wood, and so on from the ruin, and plant more ivy. The winter rains will soon wash the unsightly smoke from the walls, and Stancy Castle will be beautiful in its decay. You, Paula, will be yourself again, and recover, if you have not already, from the warp given to your mind (according to Woodwell) by the medievalism of that place.'
>
> 'And be a perfect representative of "the modern spirit"?' she inquired; 'representing neither the senses and understanding, nor the heart and imagination; but what a finished writer calls "the imaginative reason"?'
>
> 'Yes; for since it is rather in your line you may as well keep straight on.'
>
> 'Very well, I'll keep straight on; and we'll build a new house beside the ruin, and show the modern spirit for evermore. . . . But, George, I wish – ' And Paula repressed a sigh.
>
> 'Well?'
>
> 'I wish my castle wasn't burnt; and I wish you were a de Stancy!' (*L*, pp. 436–7)

Somerset is originally aware of the architectural difference between a Saxon and a Norman Castle de Stancy but he is not fully aware of its implications. The original plan for the rebuilding of the castle, made by Somerset, stolen by Dare, submitted by Havill and accepted by Paula, is striking but in this sense naive:

> Dare uncovered the drawings, and young Somerset's brainwork of the last six weeks lay under their eyes. To Dare, who was too cursory to trouble himself by entering into such details, it had very little meaning; but the design shone into Havill's head like a light into a dark place. It was original; and it was fascinating. Its originality lay partly in the circumstance that Somerset had not

attempted to adapt an old building to the wants of the new civilization. He had placed his new erection beside it as a slightly attached structure, harmonizing with the old; heightening and beautifying, rather than subduing it. His work formed a palace, with a ruinous castle beside it as a curiosity. (*L*, p. 164)

It simply does not occur to Paula that her ideals of Hellenism, which would allusively imply another masculinist Trojan invasion, and her plans to build another Saltaire or New Lanark in a place which has no means of production and which would therefore offer its occupants no chance of earning a living, represent an implausible fantasy. Equally it does not occur to Somerset that he must take account of considerations which are not aesthetic. The literal plot and the de Stancy family disabuse him. As the original Norman invaders, the de Stancys are presented as a great family in a late stage of decay. The family, or the dynasty, has devolved into the functions which originally created its power, and its members and their various threats to Somerset 'explain' the contents of the English Gothic château.

Sir William de Stancy, originally a baroque rake, takes on the cryptic colouring of an elderly bourgeois, with a modern villa and considered opinions about life and money. Charlotte de Stancy ends (in a reflection of the novel's first image) in an Anglican nunnery, taking refuge in structure and dogma. Captain de Stancy, a soldier, and thus ostensibly a figure of conquest and power, has impaired his constitution in India (where he has been enforcing an invasion), and spends his time fretfully at Toneborough barracks. His most potent attempts at seduction come under assumed identities, in the amateur play, and when he dresses up in his ancestor's armour, stands by the portrait of an ancestor who looks like him, and recites a poem he has learned by heart. Captain de Stancy is sympathetic but unenterprising: the sexual element of his pursuit of Paula is manipulated by his illegitimate son.

Dare is the principal agent of the architectural and marital plots against Somerset, This makes him the third bastard, following Manston and Troy, at the manipulative centre of Hardy's first five full-scale novels. He is a contractual outlaw and he is ageless, featureless and Mephistophelian. His name, Willy Dare, describes the sexual transgression which produced him, and in this sense reproduces the narrative sexual subversions which Hardy uses to illicitly disrupt his traded texts. Dare is a photographer, as well as

Somerset's draughtsman. His business is to take superficial and incontrovertibly accurate pictures, using a new and popular scientific technique. But his idiosyncratic method makes it possible to manipulate a negative image in order to corrupt the positive image which has been presented to the reader, and this is used to discredit Somerset. This form of manipulation closely parallels Hardy's simultaneous corruption and non-corruption of the 'classic realist' and photographically 'credible' novel. And Dare's corrupt use of the telegraph to invent, and corroborate, non-existent gambling debts for Somerset has a similar function.

The marriage between Paula and Somerset at the end of the novel is evidently its 'predetermined cheerful ending,' but it would not be correct to say that *A Laodicean* only concludes on this level. The question of how the steam engine may best be contained is also resolved, although the resolution is heavily qualified. A marriage between Paula and Captain de Stancy would have been a contract, and, since Paula represents both power and authority in a larger sense, a base for the future building of England, founded on Dare's manipulation and fraud and Paula's naive obsession with tradition. It would have produced a state governed by a superstructure of romantic reaction but actually controlled by the amoral exercise of power. The contract between Paula and Somerset is a contract, and a base for the future, between Paula's new money and power and Somerset's educated liberal idealism; but here the novel's analysis avoids the crucial question of whether such a future is really possible, because it depends on the fictionally accelerated entropic process of the de Stancys evaporating and their castle burning down.

The novel is thus essentially a competition between histories. John Power (and Abner Power and his more blatantly explosive history), the de Stancys and Dare are a history of power relations, and this has been set against Somerset's *reading* of the effects of those power relations on the structure they have built. The past, like any narrative, cannot be expected to tell the truth about itself. The conclusion is heavily ironic rather than optimistic. Jarry's implausible ideal can be accomplished only when the evidence of power relations has been obliterated (by fire; another desperate remedy), a Victorian bourgeois liberal reading substituted and a more generally 'acceptable' history written in the fabric of the new house. Now that Somerset has won Paula and patrilinear authority has been re-established, a new power structure can be built using the same materials.

6

The Mayor of Casterbridge (1886): Made of Money (II)

'I haven't more than fifteen shillings in the world, and yet I am a good experienced hand in my line. I'd challenge England to beat me in the fodder business; and if I were a free man again I'd be worth a thousand pound before I'd done o't. But a fellow never knows these little things till all chance of acting upon 'em is past.' (*MC*, p. 10)

'Very well,' said Henchard quickly, 'please yourself. But I tell you, young man, if this holds good for the bulk, as it has for the sample, you have saved my credit, stranger though you be. What shall I pay you for this knowledge?' (*MC*, p. 49)

'Then the wheat – that sometimes used to taste so strong o' mice when made into bread that people could fairly tell the breed – Farfrae has a plan for purifying, so that nobody would dream the smallest four-legged beast had walked over it once. Oh yes, everybody is full of him, and the care Mr Henchard has to keep him, to be sure!' concluded this gentleman.
'No, he won't do it for long, good-now,' said the other.
'No!' said Henchard to himself behind the tree. 'Or if he do, he'll be honeycombed clean out of all the character and standing that he's built up these eighteen year!' (*MC*, p. 107)

When Susan Henchard and her daughter arrive in Casterbridge Michael Henchard is at the height of his power and influence in the town, celebrating his mayoral authority at the banquet at the King's Arms. The narrative thus contains two opposed extremes, both contained in the novel's principal character. At Weydon-Priors he got drunk and sold his wife and daughter to a sailor; at Casterbridge he is the most prominent figure in the town. There is no clear narrative continuity offered to explain the two versions of the subtitled 'Man of Character'; and consequently narrative stability gives way almost

115

from the first to the 'staging' devices of *The Return of the Native*. Hardy's dangerous dare here is contained in the subtitle, and notions of stable character are replaced by the 'elemental' capitalist instabilities of cash and credit. Character and narrative are sacrificed to these non-humanistic imperatives. The bourgeois liberal fictional trick is displaced at its roots (which are, literally, the fertile roots of Henchard's trade, his 'character' and his 'credit'). As Goode shows,

> All Henchard's decisive acts are theatrical and the story is constructed around them – the auction, the oath, the banquet, the meeting with Susan in the arena, the embrace of Farfrae, the visit to the soothsayer, the greeting for the royal personage, the reading out of Lucetta's letters, his meeting with her in the arena, the fight with Farfrae, the last exit. The self-begotten, arranged significant and egocentric gesture is the dominant unifying force of the narrative. Susan and Elizabeth-Jane enter Casterbridge as though it were a theatre . . . There is even a band to welcome them and their first glimpse of Henchard is in tableau, performing a role.
>
> This theatricality does not enter and transform the novel: it is the very condition of its existence. We have no indication of the details of Henchard's rise from journeyman to Mayor and are surely not intended to think that being teetotal is a guarantee of such success.[1]

We see Henchard at Casterbridge through Susan and Elizabeth-Jane's arrival. We follow the two women into the town in order to see, as they see, that an alchemical change has taken place in Henchard. Like them we are given no psychological data to help analyse the change. And like them we do not see the change but are asked to construct it from the two analogues of alchemical change Hardy offers: the changing of wife into cash at Weydon-Priors fair and Farfrae's changing of grown wheat to wholesome.

These two transactions are absolutely connected and they order the making of the whole fiction. Farfrae is the instigator of Henchard's downfall, and thus of almost all the novel's dramatic action. Henchard is the drama: Farfrae is the staging machinery. This function is nearly as blatant as Dare's in *A Laodicean*. Farfrae *causes* so much of the novel because he contains the allegorical proposition it devotes itself to falsifying, that it is possible to make grown wheat wholesome, to reverse malign (organic?) processes which have already taken place. The sample has been changed by Farfrae's alchemical process, so that the remaining question is whether the same process will hold good for the bulk. The novel's full title is *The Life and Death of the Mayor of Casterbridge*. Henchard is mayor for less than a third of its length, and what we really see is the process by which Henchard loses his power and Farfrae gains it. The point is that the mayor is *seen* to be created by the trading practices which enforce the power of money, and Casterbridge, over the field. In terms of the traded text Henchard's ascent to power, which we do not see, is assumed to be an earlier version of Farfrae's: Henchard is the 'rule o' thumb sort of man' and Farfrae his technological successor. Henchard's emotional need for Farfrae naturalizes, even physicalizes, one stage of a historical, material process trying to retain its power against a successor. The proposition that this is 'A Story of a Man of Character' actually proposes the question of whether the individual is stronger than the material process which makes him, and whether character can overcome the cash which in every sense creates him. 'Character', 'credit' and 'standing' become virtually coterminous. Plainly this strikes at the heart of all notions of liberal 'individualism'.

'You must be, what – five foot nine, I reckon? I am six foot one and a half out of my shoes. But what of that? In my business, 'tis true that strength and bustle build up a firm. But judgement and knowledge are what keep it established. Unluckily, I am bad at science. Farfrae; bad at figures – a rule o'thumb sort of man. You are just the reverse – I can see that, I have been looking for such as you these last two year, and yet you are not for me. Well, before I go, let me ask this: Though you are not the young man I thought you were, what's the difference? Can't you stay with me just the same? Have you really made up your mind about this American notion? I won't mince matters. I feel you would be invaluable to me – that needn't be said – and if you will bide and be my manager I will make it worth your while.' (*MC*, pp. 49–50)

But the 'rule o'thumb' is far more than this, Henchard's judgement is based on guesswork and superstition. These are the qualities which have built his 'character', 'credit' and 'standing' in Casterbridge. In terms of the historical moment of the novel's production, as opposed to its earlier setting, this represents an appeal to fatalism which was part of the workfolk's response to the 1880s agricultural depression: Kerr cites the example of *Raphael's Book of Fate*, a best-seller guaranteed to 'tell the fate of anyone'.[2] This becomes the vehicle of the authorial will to power. Henchard's failed gamble on harvests and prices when he tries to overpower Farfrae and retain control without his new ally resembles a real transaction Kerr also refers to. A plausible part-model for Henchard is Shadrach Dunn of Gillingham (1799–1867), a self-made seed merchant and pioneer of artificial grasses reputed to have made £10,000 from grain deals in 1848, having bought cheap after the good summer of 1846 and held his stocks until the 1848 harvest was washed out by summer rains.[3] Henchard's failure to capitalize in the same way seems to be attributable to his superstition, and Farfrae's consequent success to the lack of it.

This brings into play a whole alternative structure based on the essentially volatile discourses (in terms of the 'rational' constructs of 'science' and 'history') of magic and witchcraft. In the traded text these devices are used to colour and validate a Wessex setting and a 'Wessex' protagonist, the superstitious countryman faced with a centralizing cash economy and its threatening scientific devices. In the counter-text Henchard is 'made of money' at Casterbridge after he has been magically created at Weydon-Priors. Hardy's use of the Wild Man figure is again central in this process. Like the mock Wild Man brought out of the woods in a pageant to greet Elizabeth I at Kenilworth in 1575,[4] Henchard comes out of the wilderness and approaches the margin of civilization at a fair. The fair becomes the Victorian communal equivalent of the individualized, mythologized medieval Wild Man in terms of its dangerous marginality. It is both inside and outside socio-economic structure. As Stallybrass and White put it:

> the fair, like the marketplace, is neither pure nor outside. The fair is at the crossroads, situated at the intersection of economic and cultural forces, goods and travellers, commodities and commerce. It is a gravely over-simplifying abstraction therefore to conceptualize the fair purely as the sight of communal celebration.[5]

Hardy's fair at Weydon-Priors is also at an intersection of historical perspective. Malcolmson quotes an 1875 petition against the two annual fairs at Sawbridgeworth which encapsulates the Victorian bourgeois attempt to suppress the threatening 'low' culture of the fair:

> But whilst these Fairs are of the smallest possible conceivable worth in a commercial point of view, indefensibly and indisputably they are the prolific seed plots and occasions of the most hideous forms of moral and social evil – drunkenness – whoredom – robbery – idleness and neglect of work . . .[6]

This is a remarkably transhistorical gesture. Ebbatson points to Hardy's use elsewhere, notably in 'On the Western Circuit', of the fair's machinery of misrule to express the erotic and sexual activity which the bourgeois onlookers cannot.[7] In *The Mayor of Casterbridge* the device is turned on the bourgeois reader in terms of a more elemental and heretical fertility. The Sawbridgeworth petitioners' 'seed plots' (presumably) unwittingly link the fair to its more general and older source as a subversive celebration of fertility, in which the Wild Man was an essential figure. Bernheimer refers to the early christian writings of St Peter Chrysologus (d. 450) and Caesarius, Bishop of Arles (d. 542), denouncing pagan and partchristian carnivals and their Wild Men, culminating in their (unsuccessful) suppression by decree at the Second Trullan Council in 692.[8] The attempt to remove the individuated figure of the Wild Man becomes the attempt to remove 'moral and social evil' in 1875.

Hardy starts with a reading of the historical moment of *The Mayor of Casterbridge*'s production: the Wild Man, once indispensable, joins the fair as it is about to close. Bernheimer gives this account of the Wild Man's foreknowledge of the land's fertility, which is also the basis of Henchard's 'rule o'thumb':

> as a demon he shares nature's secrets and is thus in a position to give advice about the weather, the harvest prospects, medical herbs, and even about processes in the dairy business. Accordingly he tells the peasants when to sow and to gather the rye, and thus is responsible for the ensuing abundance.[9]

He goes on to say that making the Wild Man drunk reveals his secrets. The secret we are told at Weydon-Priors when Henchard gets drunk is the Wild Man's potential to exploit a cash economy: 'if I were a free man again I'd be worth a thousand pound before I'd

done o't.' Then at Casterbridge Henchard protects his secret that he
sold his wife and child, the human expressions of the same fertility),
and the magical predictive skill which built his character and his
credit, by abstaining from alcohol.

But the drink at Weydon-Priors has been mixed in a witch's
cauldron. This is presented with a minimum of ambiguity.

> At the upper end [of the tent] stood a stove, containing a charcoal
> fire, over which hung a large three-legged crock, sufficiently
> polished round the rim to show that it was made of bell-metal.
> A haggish creature of about fifty presided, in a white apron,
> which, as it threw an air of respectability over her as far as it
> extended, was made so wide as to reach nearly round her waist.
> She slowly stirred the contents of the pot. The dull scrape of
> her spoon was audible throughout the tent as she thus kept
> from burning the mixture of corn in the grain, flour, milk, raisins,
> currants, and what not, that composed the antiquated slop in
> which she dealt. . . .
> But there was more in that tent than met the cursory glance;
> and the man, with the instinct of a perverse character, scented it
> quickly. After a mincing attack on his bowl he watched the hag's
> proceedings from a corner of his eye, and saw the game she
> played. He winked to her, and passed up his basin in reply to her
> nod; when she took a bottle from under the table, slily measured
> out a quantity of its contents, and tipped the same into the man's
> furmity. The liquor poured in was rum. The man as slily sent back
> money in payment. (*MC*, pp. 8–9)

Casterbridge is made up of (apparently) stable structures and a
stable market (and a stable Man of Character); Weydon-Priors is the
portable structure of a portable market. Although the assumed exchange of the fair is a trade in livestock and workfolk, like the trade
at Casterbridge and Greenhill fairs in *Far From the Madding Crowd*,
the exchange we actually see is the purchase of rum-laced furmity
for cash. This magical transaction creates Henchard's Casterbridge
in the counter-text, because the act of making the Wild Man drunk
and engaging him with the cash economy on the margin of the
wilderness (repeated in a Casterbridge where 'Country and town
met at a mathematical line' [*MC*, p. 29]) reveals the means by which
his 'character' and 'credit' will be established. The most notable
constituents in the furmity, 'to those not accustomed to it', are 'grains

of wheat, swollen as large as lemon-pips, which floated on its surface' (*MC*, p. 9). These grains, and the smuggled rum which is part
of the heretical 'low' law and culture of Mixen Lane (a street name
which reprises Mrs Goodenough's act of mixing the contents of her
cauldron; and naturally enough, she comes to Mixen Lane when she
comes to Casterbridge) are the main constituent elements of this
version of Casterbridge. Furmity is possibly the only drink in which
seeds are literally planted and which therefore plants seeds in the
drinker.

In this way corn and rum are mixed inside Henchard. The effect
is immediate. Having used cash to buy rum he gets drunk and in this
uninhibited state he sells his wife and frees himself. The buyer who
emerges, not entering the tent until the auction is under way and
Henchard is already drunk, is a sailor. Rum is traditionally a sailors'
drink, and it has (presumably) been smuggled to Weydon-Priors
from the sea. This connection is repeated when Susan and Elizabeth-
Jane arrive in Casterbridge. Henchard, having abstained from
alcohol ever since the wife-selling, has risen to eminence by corn-
trading. The narrator observes that 'Time the magician had wrought
much here' (*MC*, p. 35). When the two women come to the King's
Arms and see the banquet, which celebrates the success of an economy built on the corn trade, the diners at Henchard's table are
preparing to drink rum. The narrator makes this a parody of the
christian ritual overthrown (by witchcraft and the breaking of
christian marriage) at Weydon-Priors:

> Three drinks seemed to be sacred to the company – port, sherry,
> and rum; outside which old-established trinity few or no palates
> ranged.
> A row of ancient rummers with ground figures on their sides,
> and each primed with a spoon, was now placed down the table,
> and these were promptly filled with grog at such high tempera-
> tures as to raise serious considerations for the articles exposed to
> its vapours. (*MC*, pp. 35–6)

And when Henchard and Susan finally meet again they do so at an
inn called the Three Mariners. Farfrae arrives at Casterbridge at the
same time as the two women, and these arrivals signal the breaking
of the spell cast in the tent. Henchard's 'rule o'thumb' judgement
begins to fail and he is forced to visit Conjuror Fall in order to guess
at the weather and harvest prospects.

This 'magical' disruption of 'realism' is equally a disruption of class and gender structures. In terms of the sexing of property it immediately overturns the notions of male planting of male seed (which inform Casterbridge's entirely male government) at the centre of Victorian evolutionary theories of patriarchy and the beginnings of property: the Henchard created at Weydon-Priors has been mixed in a female witch's cauldron, in which seeds are stirred (and scraped, or potentially aborted) as if they were in a womb. By selling his wife and daughter Henchard becomes a self-dispossessed patriarch, so that Hardy's usual pattern of a fatherless woman is replaced by a wifeless and daughterless man without the human fertility to perpetuate his power structures. His business is to control, buy and sell other people's seed, but he has given up control of his own.

Henchard's chief magistracy at Casterbridge has been achieved, in effect, by a repudiation of paternity which he tries to make good as his 'high' law collapses when it is challenged by the 'low' law of the furmity-woman and Mixen Lane. In regaining his wife and (non-biological) daughter, these power structures collapse. And Henchard's anti-realistic conception, or transformation, at Weydon-Priors produces a class antagonism which adumbrates the basis of his trading success in Casterbridge. As Wotton puts it:

> Henchard negates the festive and celebratory nature of the fair by his egotism. What the people perceive as a joke permissible under the rules of topsy-turvy, the licence of the temporary release from the world of work, Henchard means seriously and in that act which refuses the spirit of the festival he places himself in a position of antagonism to the workfolk, an antagonism which grows with time.[10]

The placing of money, the notes and coins which Newson (a surrogate new son who takes over the patrilinear inheritance Henchard is surrendering) counts out as payment for Susan, in Henchard's magical transformation is an additional and very fundamental subversion of a fiction which makes a claim to 'realism'. As John Vernon argues, potent comparisons can be made between the nineteenth-century novel's claim to represent reality and paper money's claim to represent 'things of (presumably) enduring value: gold and silver'.[11] In this sense the novel's opening at Weydon-Priors uses the dice-throwing on the heath in *The Return of the Native* as its point of departure. Both fallacies are in the hands of a witch in *The Mayor of Casterbridge*.

Hardy makes this connection clear when Henchard visits Conjuror Fall. A conjuror is traditionally a male witch, often regarded as a white witch and a repository of communal wisdom. Conjuror Minterne and Conjuror Trendle are mentioned on this basis at Talbothays dairy in *Tess of the d'Urbervilles*. An additional meaning is that a conjuror may be a priest of the old religion,[12] and the sources of both Minterne and Trendle suggest this more diabolic function. John Minterne was reputed to have made a pact with the devil which enabled him to jump on horseback from Batcombe Down over the church at Batcombe. A pinnacle of the church could not be made to stand and it was said that the hoof of Minterne's horse removed it. Minterne was buried against a church wall because he 'vowed to be buried neither in nor out of church'.[13] Waring connects this with the medieval legend of the church-building devil, in which an architect makes a pact with the devil to assist him in building a church and cheats the devil of his reward, at which the devil kicks an irreparable hole in the church as he departs. This suggests striking connections with Hardy's novelistic practice as an antinomian architect. The Trendle comes from the mummers' play: in the Dorchester play the devil says

> Here comes I, Beelzebub –
> And over my shoulders I carry a club
> And in my hand a frying-pan
> And I think myself a jolly old man.[14]

The Trendle is the club, also brandished by the Cerne Abbas giant.

The narrator's account of Henchard's visit to Conjuror Fall is heavily laden with counter-meanings:

> In a lonely hamlet a few miles from the town – so lonely that what are called lonely villages were teeming by comparison – there lived a man of curious repute as a forecaster or weather-prophet. The way to his house was crooked and miry – even difficult in the present unpropitious season. One evening when it was raining so heavily that ivy and laurel resounded like distant musketry, and an out-door man could be excused for shrouding himself to his ears and eyes, such a shrouded figure on foot might have been perceived travelling in the direction of the hazel copse

which dripped over the prophet's cot. The turnpike-road became a lane, the lane a cart-track; the cart-track a bridle-path, the bridle-path a footway, the footway overgrown. The solitary walker slipped here and there, and stumbled over the natural springes formed by the brambles, till at length he reached the house, which, with its garden was surrounded with a high dense hedge. The cottage, comparatively a large one, had been built out of mud by the occupier's own hands, and thatched also by himself. Here he had always lived, and here it was assumed he would die.

He existed on unseen supplies; for it was an anomalous thing that while there was hardly a soul in the neighbourhood but affected to laugh at this man's assertions, uttering the formula 'There's nothing in 'em,' with full assurance on the surface of their faces, very few of them were unbelievers in their secret hearts. Whenever they consulted him they did it 'for a fancy.' When they paid him they said, 'Just a trifle for Christmas,' or 'Candlemas,' as the case might be.

He would have preferred more honesty in his clients, and less sham ridicule; but fundamental belief consoled him for superficial irony. As stated, he was enabled to live: people supported him with their backs turned. He was sometimes astonished that men could profess so little and believe so much at his house when at church they professed so much and believed so little. (*MC*, pp. 185–6)

The setting of Conjuror Fall's house has striking similarities with a widely reported incident in 1863, in which a wiseman from Sible Hedingham called Dummy, who lived alone in a self-built mud hut on the outskirts of the village, was ducked, and later died, because he was thought to have cursed the landlady of an inn which refused him accommodation.[15] Again we are taken to the margin of the wilderness through a series of obscuring devices. The turnpike-road turning to overgrown footpath is either an invitation to the reader, or a dangerous dare, which moves from the main turnpike-road of the traded text to the concealed creative strategies which make the counter-text. Hardy specifically characterizes an authorial position in Conjuror Fall: the authorial project of producing *The Mayor of Casterbridge* is, very fundamentally, to conjure a fall. In asking how the harvest will grow from the seed Henchard is asking for foreknowledge of his own story, of the seed planted at Weydon-Priors. In this sense the tempest and disaster Conjuror Fall forecasts also accurately foretells Henchard's own future. And Conjuror Fall has, inevitably, predicted Henchard's arrival at his house and set a place for him at his table. Once more cash is exchanged before secrets are revealed, just as cash is exchanged before the reader can reproduce the fiction.

> 'Then take this,' said Henchard. "Tis a crown piece. Now, what is the harvest fortnight to be? When can I know?'
> 'I've worked it out already, and you can know it at once.' (The fact was that five farmers had already been there on the same errand from different parts of the country.) 'By the sun, moon and stars, by the clouds, the winds, the trees and grass, the candle flame and swallows, the smell of the herbs; likewise by the cats' eyes, the ravens, the leeches, the spiders, and the dung-mixen, the last fortnight in August will be – rain and tempest.'
> 'You are not certain, of course.'
> 'As one can be in a world where all's unsure. 'Twill be more like living in Revelations this autumn than in England. Shall I sketch it out for 'ee in a scheme?' (*MC*, p. 187)

There is no need to sketch out any scheme, because the reader already has it in the pages which follow. The harvest and its sequels, foretold by the invocation of pagan, pantheistic signs, will create another anti-christian Revelation of St John Power the Divine. When the rains come, after Henchard has acted against Conjuror Fall's advice and already lost heavily, and it becomes clear that the prediction will come true, the 'Man of Character''s overwhelming egotism in the traded text is juxtaposed with a sense of his counter-textual creation. This threatens narrative dislocation on a major scale.

> From that day and hour it was clear that there was not to be so successful an ingathering after all. If Henchard had only waited long enough he might at least have avoided loss though he had not made a profit. But the momentum of his character knew no patience. At this turn of the scale he remained silent. The movements of his mind seemed to tend to the thought that some power was working against him.
> 'I wonder,' he asked himself with eerie misgiving; 'I wonder if it can be that somebody has been roasting a waxen image of me, or stirring an unholy brew to confound me! I don't believe in such power; and yet – what if they should ha' been doing it!' Even he

could not admit that the perpetrator, if any, might be Farfrae. (*MC*, p. 190)

And so as the spell breaks, a self-knowledge which also threatens to break the traded text begins to emerge. Because this threat is located in a self-creative and self-destructive central protagonist, it is possible to bury the counter-text and the author's concealed will to power in a way which appears to strengthen the traded text; Henchard's overwhelming (and at this point almost paranoid) egotism seems to account for his instinct that he may have been cursed. The introduction of these discourses of magic represents a very important progression from *A Laodicean*, where a surprisingly similar project, in terms of its critique, weakens its traded text because its counter-textual discourses dealing with the technology of perception must necessarily be displayed on the surface of the text without the same potential for integration. *A Laodicean* attempts the integration and fails. The most important change between these two novels is the shift from a counter-text concerned, like *The Hand of Ethelberta* and *The Return of the Native*, with the *destruction* of fictional representation and perception, to a counter-text concerned with a genuine alternative mode of *creation*. In this sense the production of *The Mayor of Casterbridge* is Hardy's first truly revolutionary act, which puts his earlier subversions into context as localized attacks and overthrowings in the campaign of gradual erosion which has made this revolution possible.

Lucas argues that in *The Mayor of Casterbridge* 'the bare fact matters, because [Hardy] isn't writing fable or allegory. On the contrary, actuality is all important'.[16] The point is that because Hardy's heretical creative discourses in this novel create a writing based on *fundamentally* anti-realistic fable and allegory, he is free for the first time to deal with socio-economic actuality. Although Henchard comes from nowhere, his encounter with the outside edge of structure at Weydon-Priors has a firm material basis. Henchard and his family become a paradigm of the landless workfolk his business at Casterbridge sets him against. When Henchard and Susan come to civilization from the field they need work and somewhere to live. Weydon-Priors can offer neither: five houses were cleared away last year and three this. They only go to the fair after learning this information.

All that remains of the fair is 'the clatter and scurry of getting away the money o' children and fools' (*MC*, p. 7). When Susan and

Elizabeth-Jane arrive at Casterbridge, the image is repeated and institutionalized; they come to the town just as the shops are closing and the curfew is being sounded. As in *A Laodicean*, the end of day signals the start of an analytical *walpurgisnacht*. In Casterbridge Susan and Elizabeth-Jane go to a hotel, civilization's image of comfort and welcome, where at Weydon-Priors the Henchards go to a tent. Again the repetition is clear: the choice of the Three Mariners rather than the King's Arms echoes the choice of the shabby furmity tent rather than the opulent-looking beer tent.

At the moment when natural light is lost Casterbridge is brought gradually into focus, as a preparation for its stage lighting. Because the counter-text is now creative rather than destructive, Casterbridge is made revelatory after sunset where Egdon Heath was made obscure. The narrator begins by supporting Elizabeth-Jane's comment about the town's antiquity ('naturalizing' it historically in the 'traded' text) and its visual sense of geometric artifice as an imposition placed in the field, like the Baptist chapel in *A Laodicean*:

> Its squareness was, indeed, the characteristic which most struck the eye in this antiquated borough, the borough of Casterbridge – at that time, recent though it was, untouched by the faintest sprinkle of modernism. It was compact as a box of dominoes. It had no suburbs – in the ordinary sense. Country and town met at a mathematical line.
>
> To birds of the more soaring kind Casterbridge must have appeared on this fine evening as a mosaic-work of subdued red, browns, greys and crystals, held together by a rectangular frame of deep green. To the level eye of humanity it stood as an indistinct mass behind a dense stockade of limes and chestnuts, set in the midst of miles of rotund down and concave field. The mass became gradually dissected by the vision into towers, gables, chimneys, and casements, the highest glazings shining bleared and bloodshot with the coppery fire they caught from the belt of sun-lit cloud in the west. (*MC*, p. 29)

The 'level eye of humanity' capable of mathematical definition and dissection is a significant change from Clym's ophthalmia and Dare's corrupt photography. Because Henchard's Casterbridge has been made in Mrs Goodenough's cauldron, or in Conjuror Fall's mud hut, there is no need to obscure it. First we see a general shape and the emphasized margin of the mathematical line; then we see the town from the height of a bird, perceiving only abstract colour and image; then human vision focuses more closely, seeing specific architectural features as Susan and Elizabeth-Jane come up one of the avenues which run out from the town into the surrounding cornland; then we see people; then we hear voices; then we hear Henchard's name. The stage is set. Now that the arrival at Weydon-Priors has been repeated in an arrival at the more permanent structure the tents adumbrate, the results of the Wild Man's witching can be revealed.

The lamplights now glimmered through the engirdling trees, conveying a sense of great smugness and comfort inside, and rendering at the same time then unlighted country without strangely solitary and vacant in aspect, considering its nearness to life. The difference between burgh and champaign was increased, too, by sounds which now reached them above others – the notes of a brass band. The travellers returned into the high street, where there were timber-houses with overhanging stories whose small paned lattices were screened by dimity curtains on a drawing-string and under whose barge-boards old cobwebs waved in the breeze. There were houses of brick-nagging which derived their chief support from those adjoining. There were slate roofs patched with tiles, and tile roofs patched with slate, with occasionally a roof of thatch.

The agricultural and pastoral character of the people on whom the town depended for its existence was shown by the class of objects displayed in the shop windows. Scythes, reap-hooks, sheep-shears, bill-hooks, spades, mattocks, and hoes, at the iron-mongers: bee-hives, butter-firkins, churns, milking-stools and pails, hay-rakes, field-flagons, and seed-lips, at the cooper's; cart-ropes and plough-harness at the saddler's; carts, wheel-barrows, and mill-gear at the wheelwright's and machinist's; horse-embrocations at the chemist's; at the glover's and leather-cutter's hedging-gloves, thatcher's knee-caps, ploughmen's leggings, villagers' pattens and clogs. (*MC*, pp. 30–1)

The 'celebration' of Susan and Elizabeth-Jane's arrival by fairy lights and a brass band marks the point where Henchard and Casterbridge cease to be fused by the breaking of the witch's spell. For Casterbridge and its economic future it is a genuine celebration, because Farfrae arrives the same night; the tainted bread which threatens civilization's power over the field can be made good. For

Henchard it is ironic, because it marks the start of alienation from the trading process which has made him. The images of trade and selling are contradictory. The narrator suggests that they show 'the agricultural and pastoral nature of the people', invoking the anthropological Myth of Wessex; but their very profusion re-emphasizes the self-conscious artifice of Casterbridge and its trade. In the counter-text these are really stage settings for the analytical drama which follows. Once the curfew has been rung and the shops closed, the reader and the two women are inside the revelatory theatre. A physically revelatory image follows:

> In an open space before the church walked a woman with her gown-sleeves rolled up so high that the edge of her under-linen was visible, and her skirt tucked up through her pocket-hole. She carried a loaf under her arm, from which she was pulling pieces of bread and handing them to some other women who walked with her, which pieces they nibbled critically. The sight reminded Mrs Henchard-Newson and her daughter that they had an appetite; and they enquired of the woman for the nearest baker's.
> 'Ye may as well look for manna-food as good bread in Casterbridge just now,' she said. (*MC*, pp. 31–2)

The increasingly focused, evolving close-up shot of Casterbridge has produced an increasingly rigorous analysis of its function. The relationship between human and agricultural fertility is crucial at Weydon-Priors and it is equally crucial when the two are brought together again. We see the woman walking with her under-linen visible, bringing us close to a source of human fertility (in the non-patriarchal history of Mrs Goodenough's cauldron; and the woman goes on to explain that she has been wife and mother) and this suggests that we are very close to a primary explanation, since the narrator has been stripping layers of misrepresentation and false explanation from Casterbridge just as he has been stripping her clothes. The revealed under-linen has no other conceivable purpose. The woman is carrying bread, and distributing it, and so she exactly describes Casterbridge's business. The town is able to trade, to build itself and to continue trading because it takes corn from the country and turns it into bread. The bread is bad; the man to blame is the man at the centre of the transaction, the corn-factor; the corn-factor is Henchard; and Henchard is the mayor of Casterbridge.

Henchard's business is the very fundamental capitalist transaction which places a cash value (and *makes* and *alters* that value) on the primary process of growing food to eat. The business of trading in corn, of paying a cash price to the grower (Henchard's main creditor at his bankruptcy is a Mr *Grower*) and selling on to the miller and the baker is the paradigm business which can be made to stand for all the further levels and degrees of business which could not otherwise be carried on. Henchard's corn-factoring becomes the primary transaction which enforces the laws of cash on the field, and his monopoly is emphasized: Susan and Elizabeth-Jane learn that 'he's the man that our millers and bakers all deal wi'' (*MC*, p. 32). It is the transaction which makes possible the changing of the workfolk's labour into cash; and so this is the alternative alchemy analysed at Casterbridge. This was the state of alienation Henchard was in when he came to Weydon-Priors, and so his position at Casterbridge follows necessarily from the nature of his transformation at Weydon-Priors.

After his fall has been conjured, his fellow bourgeois' on the town council set Henchard up in a seed-merchant's shop. This is a set-up in both senses (and an ironic precursor of the twentieth century notion of 'seedbed' capital). The un-wild Wild Man has grown and husbanded money instead of crops, and a bad harvest of the latter has also been a bad harvest of the former. Without his credit, character and standing he has no trade. In his little shop, Henchard is using Casterbridge's capital rather than his own to sell the seeds which created him at Weydon-Priors, and in this way the town's power over him is established. He is forced to sell the seeds of new fertility and history when the seeds of his own history have germinated, flourished and overgrown, like the 'growed' wheat. The public display of this cash-alienation comes in the royal personage's visit. The Wild Man is drunk, and the secret he reveals now is the extent of his alienation from the bourgeois hegemony he personified when Susan and Elizabeth-Jane first came to Casterbridge. This was the 'real' secret of his position when he came to Weydon-Priors looking for work and shelter.

When Henchard meets the witch again the only remaining product of the spell is his magistracy. The 'high' law he upholds once protected his economic interests and now it reinforces his alienation. The cauldron and Casterbridge both contain the same dialectic, in which evolutionary patterns of 'natural' law and history are replaced by a conflict between 'high' and 'low', between the materially powerful and materially powerless. The skimmington ride is the clearest example of the attempt to negotiate law and government on this basis. Hole attributes the skimmington's prevalence in the nineteenth century to 'the primitive notion that incest, adultery or immorality blighted the crops',[17] represented in *The Mayor of Casterbridge* by loaves 'as flat as toads, and like suet pudden inside' (*MC*, p. 32). She also gives the instance of participants in a skimmington in Hedon in 1889 making the claim that it had become 'legal' because the victim's effigy had been carried three nights in succession, as if the anti-rational and 'superstitious' discourses of *The Mayor of Casterbridge*'s counter-text can gain hegemonic control of the traded text by insistent covert practice. This is plainly a notional victory when a bourgeois fiction must be traded for the counter-text to exist at all, but it nonetheless indicates a radical shift in the power relations which structure the fiction's competing discourses.

The counter-text comes close to the surface allegorically in the Roman remains at Casterbridge. Bernheimer shows that, as for instance in *Gorboduc*, Wild Men were often identified in England as pre-Anglo-Saxon Britons (and in this sense Henchard supersedes the earlier Aeneas figures, founding England from Rome).[18] In this sense, with the conflict between magical and material histories at issue, the Roman amphitheatre, where Henchard has two critical meetings, becomes a dangerous middle ground between past and present. And the Roman remains are also very much an authorial 'dare': the townspeople of Casterbridge, like the reader of the traded text, regularly dig up Roman antiquities without any sense of their interest or value.

The one building in Casterbridge which does not have a direct relation to corn-trading is Lucetta's house, the unambiguously-named High-Place Hall.

The Hall, with its grey *façade* and parapet, was the only residence of its sort so near the centre of the town. It had, in the first place, the characteristics of a country mansion – birds'-nests in the chimneys, damp nooks where fungi grew, and irregularities of surface direct from nature's trowel . . . The house was entirely of stone, and formed an example of dignity without great size. It was not altogether aristocratic, still less consequential, yet the old-fashioned stranger instinctively said, "Blood built it, and Wealth enjoys it," however vague his opinions of those accessories might be.

Yet as regards the enjoying it, the stranger would have been wrong, for until this very evening, when the new lady had arrived, the house had been empty for a year or two, while before that interval its occupancy had been irregular. The reason of its unpopularity was soon made manifest. Some of its rooms overlooked the market-place; and such a prospect from such a house was not considered desirable or seemly by its would-be occupiers . . . Elizabeth trotted through the open door in the dusk, but becoming alarmed at her own temerity, she went quickly out again by another which stood open in the lofty wall of the back court. To her surprise she found herself in one of the little-used alleys of the town. Looking round at the door which had given her egress, by the light of the solitary lamp fixed in the alley, she saw that it was arched and old – older even than the house itself. The door was studded, and the keystone of the arch was a mask. Originally the mask had exhibited a comic leer, as could still be discerned; but generations of Casterbridge boys had thrown stones at the mask, aiming at its open mouth; and the blows thereon had chipped off the lips and jaws as if they had been eaten away by disease. The appearance was so ghastly by the weakly lamp glimmer that she could not bear to look at it – the first unpleasant feature of her visit. (*MC*, pp. 140–2)

Under Lucetta's tenancy High-Place Hall, which overlooks the corn market, becomes the source of a female overview of a male trade in the seeds of fertility. The house looks two ways, forward to the market, the source of 'blood' and 'wealth''s continuing power and back, through the leering arch, to an alternative history of squalid intrigue. In this sense it is also the analogue of Hardy's cultural power when his fictions enter bourgeois society from the front door and the non-bourgeois sources of the fictions. The leering mask, in the context of the house's pretensions to 'naturalize' power, represents the erosion this duplicity has achieved.

The mask was originally the representation of a human face, just as the novel is originally concerned to represent human behaviour. It is always described as a mask, never as a face; it is plainly a pretence. It is in any case part of a house, not a human body, and its meaning must therefore really refer to the structure, not the conceit that the structure is pretending to be a person. Over the years the face has been eroded, almost to the point of becoming featureless, by thoughtless attack. The mask is the keystone of the arch over the back door of High-Place Hall. In the literal surface of the text, the mask's meanings refer to the world behind, or below, the house, to 'low life' and intrigue: but the placing of the mask means that it can equally be read as referring to the world inside, and in front of, the house. If the arch can be used to go in one direction, it can also be used to go in the other; the intrigue and erosion might equally be said to refer to the market, and the exchanges between Lucetta, Henchard and Farfrae which encompass Henchard's downfall in the traded text.

Farfrae's conquest over the trade in fertility is enforced by his conquest over Henchard's women, first a putative wife and then a putative daughter. And the fertility ritual of the Wild Man's fair is also repeated ironically as part of this process: Henchard's dancing, his attempt to bring the fair to town, is virtually ignored in favour of Farfrae's.

When Henchard and Susan re-court and re-marry, a period of impossible equipoise is introduced. Henchard and Farfrae operate in tandem and it seems that grown wheat can be made good. But the equipoise is based on the belief that Elizabeth-Jane is the daughter Henchard sold. If the new contract with Susan was permanent or productive (if, in other words, Elizabeth-Jane was Henchard's daughter rather than Newsons's, and there was a biological link between Weydon-Priors and Casterbridge), it would be possible for an individual to break his contract with state and society, to have the benefits of operating without the hindrances of the contract, and then to re-contract on his own terms; or, more directly, to have had the use of the capital obtained from the exchange of fertility for cash without penalty. This is not possible. Susan is moribund when she arrives in Casterbridge and Elizabeth-Jane is Newson's daughter. In terms of Mrs Goodenough's mixture she is the daughter of rum, not corn. She is Henchard's by incantatory narrative, not 'natural' blood.

Henchard's second attempt at marriage in Casterbridge is to Lucetta, and since her 'honour' has already been compromised by Henchard this is another attempt to make grown wheat wholesome. This contract would establish a connection which looks forward rather than backward (hence the ambivalent dual aspects of High-Place Hall) because it represents an alliance between new trade and old wealth. Henchard's trade is already superseded when he tries to marry Lucetta, and she marries Farfrae, who has become the newer personification of the corn trade. (Their marriage is witnessed by the ubiquitous Mr Grower.) Farfrae's new horse-drill, literally an image of agricultural efficiency and allegorically an image of sexual proficiency, epitomizes this. Lucetta's pseudo-active choice is, more blatantly than elsewhere, simply between the attraction of past and future stages of capitalism: the two suitors' 'characters' rise and fall as their 'credit' rises and falls. Human fertility is for sale and she falls, like Susan at Weydon-Priors, to the highest bidder.

Lucetta is duly impregnated by the man with the horse-drill, but she dies while she is carrying Farfrae's child, leaving the alliance between trade and wealth unachieved and without issue. Henchard is indirectly responsible for the death, and for this seed failing to grow, because the return of his love-letters leads to the skimmington. Then Henchard sees his own effigy, as if it were his dead body, floating in the river; and this image moves the marriage plot to its concluding stage. The marriage between Farfrae and Elizabeth-Jane has nothing to do with Henchard. He is neither Elizabeth-Jane's father nor the progenitor of Farfrae's business, which has grown up quite independently as a result of his failure. The patriarchal structure has overthrown the Wild Man's transgression, and Henchard's last gift to Casterbridge is a caged bird, which ought to live on seed, starving to death for the lack of it.

All that remains is Henchard's will, the egotistical force which created his business and his 'character' in the traded text. He is not left with no contract, no issue and no business. He is in early middle age and of robust constitution, and there is no practical reason why he should die so quickly. Even a temperance novelist could not expect such a precipitate death from drink, and the narrator offers no evidence that drink kills him. But the vow of abstinence has the counter-textual meanings established at Weydon-Priors and now rum has succeeded corn. Henchard is a drinking man and a field-labourer once more, not a teetotaller buying and selling fields and field-labourers and their produce. His life only existed in terms of his analytical journey from Weydon-Priors to Casterbridge; so now he returns to Weydon-Priors before returning to his obscure origins to die. Once his character and credit are gone he literally ceases to exist. His will represents the necessity of this self-negation: his consciousness, or his willpower, extends only to obliterating the evidence of his own life.

'Michael Henchard's Will.

'That Elizabeth-Jane Farfrae be not told of my death, or made to grieve on account of me.
'& that I be not bury'd in consecrated ground.
'& that no sexton be asked to toll the bell.
'& that nobody is wished to see my dead body.
'& that no murners walk behind me at my funeral.
'& that no flours be planted on my grave.
'& that no man remember me.
'To this I put my name.

'Michael Henchard.'

(*MC*, p. 333)

7

The Woodlanders (1887): The Beginning of the End

As the tree waved South waved his head, making it his fugleman with abject obedience. 'Ah, when it was quite a small tree,' he said, 'and I was a little boy, I thought one day of chopping it off with my hook to make a clothes-line prop with. But I put off doing it, and then I again thought I would; but I forgot it and didn't. And at last it got too big, and now 'tis my enemy, and will be the death of me. Little did I think, when I let that sapling stay, that a time would come when it would torment me, and dash me into my grave.' (*W*, p. 97)

The Woodlanders does not at first sit easily between *The Mayor of Casterbridge* and *Tess of the d'Urbervilles*. They seem at first sight to be accomplished 'tragedies', which deal, or appear to deal, with the life and death of a single protagonist in a public world. *The Woodlanders* exploits the magical realist techniques of *The Mayor of Casterbridge* without its generic protection. In fact it is a rather more sophisticated engagement of the competing discourses of magic and realism, written under the protection of a more obscurely rural Wessex. The protection is now entirely notional and the narrator plays extremely dangerous dares with the reader's credulity in the face of an environmental travelogue or a bourgeois parable. The wilderness contains the 'magic' and the trade which has cut a gap in its margins contains the 'realism'. The novel seeks to use the magic to explode the realism. Hardy's comments in the autobiography when he was correcting proofs for the 1912 edition are cryptic but revelatory:

On taking up *The Woodlanders* and reading it after many years I think I like it, *as a story*, the best of all. Perhaps that is due to the locality and scenery of the action, a part I am very fond of. (*LTH*, p. 358)

This leaves a suggestive gap. The qualities of the 'story' can, in the classic realist project, have little to do with 'the locality and scenery of the action'. Hardy's italics emphasize the separation. The story is the artifice placed in its 'natural' surroundings, which are only presented through the agency of the artifice.

The 'story' is this: a barber arrives at a tiny village in the woods and buys a plain young woman's hair in order to sell it to the rich woman who owns the village. The young woman's father is dying and believes that a tree is trying to kill him. The community's trade is in trees and their by-products: apples, bark, spars. The elderly man in charge of this trade has educated his daughter to be a lady. It was his intention to marry her to a younger, smaller trader, also the beloved of the plain young woman, to whom he owes an inherited debt of honour. The smaller trader's home and half of his livelihood depend on his holding leases which will terminate when the man who believes he is being killed by a tree dies. The larger trader decides that the smaller trader is not of sufficiently high caste for his daughter and the daughter is almost at once courted by a doctor whose caste meets with the father's approval. The doctor is called to the man who believes he is being killed by a tree and orders that the tree be felled; the smaller trader fells the tree and the sick man dies. The doctor marries the daughter and the smaller trader loses his home.

Then the doctor falls in love with the woman who owns the village and sleeps with her, and it becomes apparent to the larger trader and his daughter that marriage to the smaller trader would have been preferable. The couple separate. Attempts are made to obtain a divorce but they fail. The doctor returns and attempts a rapprochement; his wife flees. She arrives by mistake at a hut where the smaller trader is living. He is ill but conceals his illness and insists on sleeping in an inadequate shelter because of his regard for her honour. His illness accelerates: the doctor is called but the smaller trader dies. The doctor's estranged wife gives the plain young woman the impression that she has been sleeping with the smaller trader. The woman who owns the village is shot and killed by another lover. The doctor makes further attempts at rapprochement but his estranged wife has made a pact with the plain young woman to devote herself to the smaller trader's memory. A rapprochement finally occurs and the plain young woman is left to mourn the smaller trader alone.

The story is made of trade, trees, class and marriage. Separated from its 'locality and scenery' it has, as Michael Millgate points out, much in common with the sensational elaboration of *Desperate Remedies*.[1] The novel's main dramatic vehicle is the question of who the larger trader's daughter is to marry, and, having married the wrong man, whether she can unmarry and remarry. Melbury's entrepreneurial business in trees parallels his trading of his daughter. In the traded text (and it is no coincidence that self-made traders are at the centre of these two fictions in which magical discourses overthrow the traded text; nor will it be any coincidence that Jack Durbeyfield is a haggler in *Tess of the d'Urbervilles*) Melbury's attempt to marry his daughter to Fitzpiers, which repeats and develops Fancy Day's father's attempt to trade her upwards socially in *Under the Greenwood Tree*, fails, although the marriage cannot be dissolved, because of the omnipresence of the woods and the workfolk. In terms of the Myth of Wessex both Grace herself and Melbury's business seem to indicate organic essentialism; it is as 'natural' for a man to father a daughter as it is for him to create a successful business. In fact both are artificial productions. There is nothing 'natural' in the Grace who has been produced at her boarding school. Melbury makes it clear that he has tried to use the 'freemasonry of education' (a revealing formulation coming from a self-educated author, linking culturally-produced artifice with the cabalistic reservation of power and thus also describing Hardy's fiction-making) to overcome what he regards as his own inadequacies of class. In the evolutionary process of one generation outgrowing the weaknesses of the last cash is used to buy cultural status:

> 'I heard you wondering why I've kept my daughter so long at boarding-school,' said Mr Melbury, looking up from the letter which he was reading anew by the fire, and turning to them with the suddenness that was a trait in him. 'Hey?' he asked with affected shrewdness. 'But you did, you know. Well now, though it is my own business more than anybody else's, I'll tell ye. When I was a boy, another boy – the pa'son's son – along with a lot of others, asked me 'Who dragged Whom round the walls of What?' and I said, 'Sam Barret, who dragged his wife in a wheeled chair round the tower when she went to be churched.' They laughed at me so much that I went home and couldn't sleep for shame;

and I cried that night till my pillow was wet; till I thought to myself – 'They may laugh at me for my ignorance, but that was my father's fault, and none o' my making, and I must bear it. But they shall never laugh at my children, if I have any; I'll starve first.' Thank God I've been able to keep her at school at a figure of near a hundred a year; and her scholarship is such that she has stayed on as governess for a time. Let 'em laugh now if they can: Mrs Charmond herself is not better informed than my girl Grace.' (*W*, pp. 32–3)

But Grace is incompletely manufactured and thus placed in an untenable middle ground. Her two lovers, Giles Winterborne and Edred Fitzpiers, are both linked with other women, Giles with Marty South and Fitzpiers with Felice Charmond. As Lucas shows, each of the novel's sexual fascinations is also a transgressive class aspiration: 'Marty loves Giles who aspires to Grace who aspires to Fitzpiers who aspires to Mrs Charmond'.[2] The newly bourgeois Grace is pulverized between the feminine models of Marty's 'naturalness' (Grace's biological source in the Hintock woods) and Mrs Charmond's 'artifice' (the new behaviour Grace has been taught at boarding school), which is, since she used to be an actress, literally theatrical. The relation between these two women also describes Melbury's trade: he sells, for a premium, the products of Mrs Charmond's woods using Marty's wage-labour. At the start of the novel, before Grace has been introduced, this transaction is presented without Melbury's agency when Percomb, the somewhat fraudulent 'Perruquier to the aristocracy', buys Marty's hair and sells it (presumably at a healthy profit) to Mrs Charmond. This passage of feminine display represents Melbury's sale of Marty's wage-labour and so Percomb's function adumbrates Melbury's. The actions of these two entrepreneurs thus create the text, which is equally an entrepreneurial act. The dangerous dare here is the gambling of a whole text: the author risks his entire fiction on the premise that its consumers will not recognize a central disruption of its groundrules. Grace's interrogative femininity, which is really her father's entrepreneurial device, fills Percomb's trading gap between Marty and Mrs Charmond. In this sense she fuses and problematizes femininity and trade, the two overriding discourses which create Hardy's cultural enterprise of fiction-writing.

In the traded text the sexually promiscuous Mrs Charmond is 'bad' and the unsexed Marty is 'good'. The relationship between 'bad' capital and 'good' labour also informs the counter-text, but the workfolk, fused with the woods by the labour which simultaneously alienates them from their environment (a situation personified by a singularly alien owner who does not even want what she owns), create a magically malevolent alternative. Giles's group of cottages, where the Souths also live, will go to Mrs Charmond on John South's death. This will take away Marty's home and half of Giles's income. Giles is a copyholder. The end of copyholding represents a crucial change in agricultural power relations. Three-life copyholds in Dorset were generally granted before 1750 by a manorial court, before enclosure became widespread.[3] Copyholding thus represents, at least for Hardy's fictional purpose here, a co-operative, communal use of land.

The period covered by the lease of Giles's cottages is a period characterized by competition: as Kerr puts it, 'by the 1750s common fields [and woodlands] throughout Dorset were collecting grounds for the well-to-do'.[4] After the enclosures it made little economic sense for landowners to charge a fine, or heriot, for re-lifing when immediate cash was available from successful petty-bourgeois' like Melbury. Workfolk who were autonomous, at least in terms of their restrictive bond to the manor, were freed to compete economically for the land they worked and lived on. In practice, as Hardy points out in 'The Dorsetshire Labourer', the effect of this de-stabilizing was the economic and often geographical mobilization of the farmer who stood between lord and worker (*DL*, p. 263). In this sense, though in no other, Melbury's position in *The Woodlanders* exploits the gap left by the thieving bailiff in *Far From the Madding Crowd*. In *The Woodlanders* Hardy almost seems to use this historical struggle to represent the 1880s' battle between writers and producers of fiction, already referred to and focused particularly around the increasingly successful attack on the three-decker (although whether authors' protests would have had any significant effect in a market which was not already collapsing is questionable; and again this collapse seems very much to be represented in the collapsing 'traded' text of *The Woodlanders*).

Plainly the new Darwinian freedom to compete is divisive (or rather, creative) in terms of class. In *The Woodlanders* it provokes the vengeful response of Tim Tangs's man-trap, originally set to catch poaching workfolk but now set to catch a philandering bourgeois. This becomes the analogue of the counter-text's authorial revenge on the traded text's bourgeois parable. The narrator's description is overloaded with extremes of mechanical savagery:

> Were the inventors of automatic machines to be ranged according to the excellence of their devices for producing sound artistic torture, the creator of the man-trap would occupy a respectable, if not a very high, place.
>
> It should rather, however, be said, the inventor of the particular form of man-trap of which this found in the keeper's outhouse was a specimen. For there were other shapes and other sizes, instruments which, if placed in a row beside one of the type disinterred by Tim, would have worn the subordinate aspect of bears, wild boars, or wolves in a travelling menagerie as compared with the leading lion or tiger. In short, though many varieties had been in use during those centuries which we are accustomed to look back upon as the true and only period of Merry England – in the rural districts more especially – and onward down to the third decade of the nineteenth century, this model had borne the palm, and had been more usually followed when the orchards and estates required new ones.
>
> There had been the toothless variety used by the softer-hearted landlords – quite contemptible in their clemency. The jaws of these resembled the jaws of an old woman to whom time has left nothing but gums. There were also the intermediate or half-toothed sorts, probably devised by the middle-natured squires, or those under the influence of their wives: two inches of mercy, two inches of cruelty, two inches of mere nip, two inches of probe, and so on, through the whole extent of the jaws. There were also, as a class apart, the bruisers, which did not lacerate the flesh, but only crushed the bone.
>
> The sight of one of these gins, when set, produced a vivid impression that it was endowed with life. It exhibited the combined aspects of a shark, a crocodile, and a scorpion, (*W*, p. 362)

This violent image (which is also remarkably vaginal; the sequence of 'two inches', totalling eight and ending with 'two inches of probe, and so on' suggests an ironic account of sexual penetration by a man; and this gives an additional sexual dimension to the encroaching undergrowth of the Hintock woods) almost at the end of the text reflects another almost at its beginning. Marty's spar-cutting when

Percomb comes to buy her hair seems to be a way of making a living, but it is a great deal more. In terms of the patriarchal, phallocentric power relations which govern her life it is an attack on the phallic spar. Making a living means that she cuts spars for Melbury and his patriarchal structuring of both Hintock and femininity. It is as if the novel responds to Mill's comparison of human nature to a tree 'which requires to grow and develop itself on all sides, according to the tendency of the inward forces which make it a living thing'[5] on behalf of a violated and exploited human nature which has not been allowed to grow and develop naturally because it is mutilated and stunted to serve the demands of trade and the growth and development of wealth.

John South's life-tree is the key to the meanings which lie beyond this. Historically tree-worship was a persistent subversion of christianity: the Canons of Edgar (963) and the Laws of Canute (1018) both tried to outlaw the practice.[6] Herne the Hunter's oak, on which he was hanged, in Windsor Great Park was regarded as a life-tree; so was Byron's tree at Newstead Park.[7] John South's tree is linked to the falling-in of lives which determines Giles's tenure of the cottages, because his is the last life in the life-holding. Consequently his daughter becomes a dryad in the counter-text. Giles is the Wild Man of the mummers' play. Traditionally he is shown carrying a tree; 'It was [Giles's] custom during the planting season to carry a specimen apple-tree to market with him as an advertisement of what he dealt in' (*W*, p. 36). His move to the woods confirms this. As Bernheimer shows:

> It fell to a somewhat later generation [than Geoffrey of Monmouth's] to introduce the motive of love madness, which from then on was to become the fashionable motive for becoming a wild man. In courtly society, which exalted the lady far above her worshipper and taught him the merits that lie in suffering for love's sake, such motivation was no more than an exaggeration of a knight's normally agitated emotional state. It was, therefore, a flattery for the great lady whose favour was sought, if grief over her inattention or fickleness carried a man to the point of melancholy or irrational violence. The greater the warrior thus brought to grief, the greater the implied prestige of the lady who had caused his fall. Indeed, some of the most renowned knights of romance, Yvain, Lancelot and Tristan, fell victim to this strange occupational disease of knight-errantry.[8]

Giles fits exactly the model of the chivalrous Wild Man retreating into the woods. And he also (being winter-borne) fits exactly the winter mumming's traditional situation of a Wild Man dying in the woods and being brought back to life by a doctor;[9] the only difference being that Fitzpiers, ultimately a false doctor, fails to cure him. Mary Jacobus identifies a further Wild Man association in Giles's connection with Balder, the Teutonic sun-god and source of natural regeneration.[10] The Wild Man's traditional companions as he emerges from the woods to the margins of civilization are wood nymphs, dryads and hamadryads. In the *Aeneid*, Hardy's most important allusive source, the groves which bore primitive man are also the dwellings of woodland divinities (*Aeneid*, 8, 314). In this context, as Giles's 'natural' companion, Marty is a dryad, and this supplies counter-meaning in her initial introduction.

In the room from which this cheerful blaze proceeded [Percomb] beheld a girl seated on a willow chair, and busily working by the light of the fire, which was ample and of wood. With a bill-hook in one hand a leather glove much too large for her on the other, she was making spars, such as are used by thatchers, with great rapidity. She wore a leather apron for this purpose, which was also much too large for her figure. On her left hand lay a bundle of the straight, smooth hazel objects called spar-gads – the raw material of her manufacture; on her right a heap of chips and ends – the refuse – with which the fire was maintained; in front a pile of the finished articles. To produce them she took up each gad, looked critically at it from end to end, cut it to length, split it into four, and sharpened each of the quarters with dextrous blows, which brought it to a triangular point precisely resembling that of a bayonet.

Beside her, in case she might require more light, a brass candle-stick stood on a little round table curiously formed of an old coffin-stool, with a deal top nailed on, the white surface of the latter contrasting oddly with the black carved oak of the sub-structure. The social position of the house in the past was almost as definitively shown by the presence of this article as that of an esquire or nobleman by his old helmets or shields. It had been customary for every well-to-do villager, whose tenure was by copy of court-roll, or in any way more permanent than that of the mere cotter, to keep a pair of these stools for the use of his own dead; but changes had led to the discontinuance of the custom, and the stools were frequently made use of in the manner described. (W, p. 12)

We see this through Percomb. Marty's hair is immediately, and for no other conceivable reason, connected with the woods: it is 'a rare and beautiful approximation to *chestnut*' (W, p. 13) [my italics]. Mrs Charmond's hair is exactly the same colour. The hair which represents the woods' foliage is sold by a wood nymph, because of her poverty (which has come about because John South is no longer able to work), and it passes to the estate's new owner. The specious naturalness of Mrs Charmond's hairpiece, and the sexually exploitative use she makes of it, stand for an equally specious and destructive cash ownership. Effectively she buys the chance to impersonate a dryad. The loss of foliage can be either a seasonal function or a sign that a tree is dying. The tension between these two possible meanings runs through the whole novel, just as the tension between Henchard's finite life and material Casterbridge's renewable life runs through *The Mayor of Casterbridge*. Melbury's (and Percomb's) trade is as renewable as the cash economy which produces it; John South and his life-tree are not.

When Percomb arrives Marty is making spar-gads for Melbury. The act suggests the making of a weapon ('a triangular point . . . resembling that of a bayonet') rather than an innocent piece of thatching material. If she is a dryad mutilating trees she is committing a systematic act of self-mutilation and suicide because she needs the money; and if she is making a bayonet she is mutilating and destroying herself in order to make an offensive weapon. If this weapon is to be used in the creation and maintenance of a cottage it becomes part of the same circular pattern as the tree which has overlooked her father's life. (John South could, after all, have moved away from the tree if his cottage had not been held on the basis of a life-interest.) The visitor, who has watched Marty through the window before deciding to knock and enter, becomes analogous with the reader. Both have come to Hintock, leaving the high road and entering the woods, in order to buy a beautifying and enriching 'natural' product.

Marty is sitting on a willow chair; wood is burning on the fire; the coffin-stools are made of oak and topped with deal. The surface is light, new wood, with a practical function: it is a table being used to hold a candlestick which holds a candle which gives light to enable the spar-cutting to continue. But it also illuminates, and what it shows is its own sub-structure, again wooden, underpinning and at the same time undermining. If Marty is a dryad killing herself by killing her tree, the coffin-stools denote the suicide; if she is making an offensive weapon at the same time they also suggest a death, or deaths. Giles and Marty's affinity is expressed in terms of their shared knowledge of a concealed language peculiar to the woods. This characterizes the area of reserved power which creates the 'finer mysteries' of the counter-text and conceals it from 'the ordinary population'.

The casual glimpses which the ordinary population bestowed upon that wondrous world of sap and leaves called the Hintock woods had been with these two, Giles and Marty, a clear gaze. They had been possessed of its finer mysteries as of commonplace knowledge; had been able to read its hieroglyphs as ordinary writing; to them the sights and sounds of night, winter, wind, storm, amid those dense boughs, which had to Grace a touch of the uncanny, and even of the supernatural, were simple occurrences whose origin, continuance and laws they foreknew. They had planted together, and together they had felled; together they had, with the run of years, mentally collected those remoter signs and symbols which seen in a few were of runic obscurity, but all together made an alphabet. From the light lashing of the twigs upon their faces when brushing through them in the dark either could pronounce upon the species of tree whence they stretched; from the quality of the wind's murmur through a bough either could in like manner name its sort afar off. They knew by a glance at a trunk if its heart were sound, or tainted with incipient decay; and by the state of its upper twigs the stratum that had been reached by its roots. The artifices of the seasons were seen by them from the conjuror's own point of view, and not from that of the spectator.

'He ought to have married *you*, Marty, and nobody else in the world!' said Grace with conviction, after thinking in the above strain.

Marty shook her head. 'In all our outdoor days and years together, ma'am,' she replied, 'the one thing he never spoke of to me was love; nor I to him.'

'Yet you and he could speak in a tongue that nobody else knew – not even my father, though he came nearest knowing –

the tongue of the trees and fruits and flowers themselves.'
(*W*, pp. 340–1)

This relationship is anachronistic in *The Woodlanders* because it is not concerned with sexual passion, marriage or (attempted) divorce. In the traded text it seems to be the ideal and 'natural' base which contrasts with the manufactured complexities of the Giles-Grace-Fitzpiers-Mrs Charmond quadrangle. In fact it is the opposite. Gillian Beer offers this account of the generally multivalent experience of reading Hardy's fiction:

> In reading Hardy's work we often find a triple level of plot generated: the anxiously scheming and predictive plot of the characters' making; the optative plot of the commentary, which often takes the form 'why did nobody' or 'had somebody . . .', and the absolute plot of blind interaction and 'Nature's Laws'.[11]

The Woodlanders shows the strength of this 'absolute plot' (and its far from 'blind' interaction) with particular clarity. What is seen 'from the conjuror's own point of view, not the spectator's', threatens the contract of novel-writing, and all the stabilities that implies, as surely as the adulterous ruptures of marriage. The fiction's prismatic quality is produced not simply by its multiplicity of sights and oversights (Percomb at the window, Fitzpiers with his binoculars) but by the presence of a fully-established counter-text which depends on an antithetical structure of signification made out of 'remoter signs and symbols which seen in few were of runic obscurity'. The shifts in narrative points of view represent this imperfectly-visible alternative. In *The Mayor of Casterbridge* a man came to civilization from the margin of the wilderness; in *The Woodlanders*, set in a clearing in the woods which is civilized only in the most rudimentary sense, the wilderness is fighting back, articulating the erosion of the outbuildings at Knapwater House in *Desperate Remedies*. Melbury himself, as the man at the centre of the financial exploitation of the wilderness, gives evidence of this:

> That stiffness about the arm, hip, and knee-joint, which was apparent when he walked, was the net product of the divers strains and over-exertions that had been required of him in handling trees and timber when a young man, for he was of the sort called self-made, and had worked hard. He knew the origin of every one

of these cramps; that in his left shoulder had come of carrying a
pollard, unassisted, from Tutcombe Bottom home; that in one leg
was caused by the crash of an elm against it when they were
felling; that in the other was from lifting a bole. (*W*, p. 34)

In this way a material transaction, the history of Melbury's life as a
trader working in the woods, is interrogatively 'naturalized' in the
physical disabilities it has created. Fitzpiers's examination of John
South's brain tissue (and his attempt to buy Grammer Oliver's head)
is an equally self-conscious 'pathological' examination of the same
process.

When Fitzpiers enters the fiction, standing above Hintock and
surveying through his binoculars, he offers a retrospective commentary on the processes which have brought the reader to the point
of his first appearance; and from this point the mechanical plot of
marriages and intrigues begins to accelerate. Fitzpiers's remarkably
dilettante medical studies provide the link between trees being cut
and felled and the counter-text's analysis of the process. As a dia-
gnostician he works with a clinical anatomy of the subject before
him. He is in this sense the opposite of the animistic Melbury, looking down where Melbury looks up.

Like a clichéd lone reader he sits alone in his room late at night
with the light burning, rationalizing what he can see through his
binoculars in terms of an eclectic sequence of explanatory formulae.
In many ways this parallels Somerset's position as a solitary sketcher
at the start of *A Laodicean*, and the perception which results is similarly inadequate and revealing. Fitzpiers's courtship of Grace, for
example, only begins because he mistakes her for Mrs Charmond.
The two meet for the first time when Grace visits Fitzpiers in order
to reclaim Grammer's head. He is trying to examine the brain of
the oldest woman in the community. This naturalizing of material
process into biological 'fact' is a patently emblematic project, and
Grace's arrival marks an important transition. The analytical aim of
Fitzpiers's project does not necessarily change; it is simply that the
pursuit of Grammer's head is replaced by the pursuit of Grace's
hand. The attempt to buy the head, taken in conjunction with the
sale of Marty's hair, makes the point that every part of the workfolk
as well as the woods may be bought and sold on at profit according
to its utility. Even dead flesh has a price. This returns to the image
of Neigh's horse-knacker business in *The Hand of Ethelberta*. As Jacobus
puts it,

As John South's brain tissue is dissected under Fitzpiers'
microscope, so Nature has lost its soul to modern science. A
malfunctioning world of necessity and circumstance replaces one
of organic relationship, just as Grace and Fitzpiers are reunited at
the end of the novel by the malfunctioning of Tim Tangs' man-
trap.[12]

Having repudiated his claim on Grammer's brain, Fitzpiers shows
Grace the section of brain he is now examining, which is John South's.
No serious explanation of Fitzpiers's purpose in examining brains is
offered. The meaning of this image therefore has to be found in its
dramatic function. Fitzpiers thus begins his real engagement with
Hintock by courting Grace and examining John South's brain tissue.
South died after his life-tree was felled on Fitzpiers's advice; and this
is a transgressive act, since it was done without Mrs Charmond's
permission. This was a criminal offence, technically a theft. Kerr
notes that in 1816 William Sartin of Corscombe was sentenced to
six months' hard labour for felling a maiden ash tree.[13] The 'high'
law which protects the tree's owner also paradoxically protects the
'low' pagan culture of vestigial tree-worship. Fusion between man
and tree has been clearly established in South's case and the shift
in Fitzpiers's investigation comes after Grace leaves; 'Instead of re-
suming his investigation of South's brain Fitzpiers reclined and
ruminated on the interview' (*W*, p. 138). This change in perspective
is immediately confirmed in the seasonal life of the Hintock timber
trade. A page later we learn that the barking season has just
begun, and that Marty is one of the most expert barkers. The process of stripping the trees, like the process of stripping the brains,
has begun.

Grace's pseudo-active choice of husband is really no more than a
move from one paternally-arranged marriage to another. She has
culturally outgrown Giles, despite the literal debt of history Melbury
owes to Giles's father, and Fitzpiers presents himself as a suitably
aristocratic replacement. The balance between the two men is schematic and ironic, because Giles is given the chivalrous qualities
which, in a 'natural' social structure, should belong to Fitzpiers's
class.

Henchard is first seen at Casterbridge at the centre of a celebration
of fertility under a civilized roof in the King's Arms, and we first see
Giles as he is preparing his party for the Melburys at his cottage.
Since both celebrations are conducted by Wild Men, they assume

that pagan ritual and its popular roots can co-exist with the larger structure represented by these architectural structures. This also represents a superficial fusion of traded text and counter-text. Each state of impossible equipoise is broken by the imperatives of Melbury's trade in trees and Hardy's trade in fictions. Like Henchard, Giles is disgorged by the structure and sent back to the wilderness when his capacity for work and his health fail. He is driven to this stage by the parallel machinery of Hardy's traded text and Melbury and Mrs Charmond's economy. As an independent trader (which puts him in the position of the self-employed venetian blind-maker exploited by the large contractors in Robert Tressell's *The Ragged-Trousered Philanthropists*: self-employment is ultimately only an amplification of Marty's piecework spar-cutting) he lacks the workfolk's last remnants of feudal protection, which at least kept John South in his own home until he died.

Giles dies from a pre-existing organic disease, and in the counter-text this reiterates the metaphor of Fitzpiers's pathology of Hintock. It is the general disease which also killed John South, produced by an enforced naturalization of Hintock's power relations on the organic tissue of workfolk and small traders. In this sense a single death justifies the novel's collective title.

> While speaking thus to herself [Grace] had lit the lantern, and hastening out without further thought took the direction whence the mutterings had proceeded. The course was marked by a little path, which ended at a distance of about forty yards in a small erection of hurdles, not much larger than a shock of corn, such as were frequent in the woods and copses when the cutting season was going on. It was too slight even to be called a hovel, and was not high enough to stand upright in; appearing, in short, to be erected for the temporary shelter of fuel. The side towards Grace was open, and turning the light upon the interior she beheld what her prescient fear had pictured in snatches all the way thither.
>
> Upon the hay within her lover lay in his clothes, just as she had seen him during the whole of her stay here except that his hat was off, and his hair matted and wild.
>
> Both his clothes and the hay were saturated with rain. His arms were flung over his head; his face was flushed to an unnatural crimson. His eyes had a burning brightness, and though they met her own, she perceived that he did not recognize her. (*W*, p. 322)

Giles moves from house to hovel to shelter; specifically a wood-cutter's fuel shelter. This states the wood god's function in a cash economy: he has been fuel and is burning away, like the fire Percomb saw at the Souths' cottage at the start of the novel. From civilized man, he has returned to a native state of grunting animal.

The moral code of behaviour prescribed by the christian marriage contract accelerates Giles's death; he refuses to share his hut with Grace because she is still married to Fitzpiers. A divorce would have meant that, from Melbury's point of view, it was possible to make grown wheat wholesome. In *The Mayor of Casterbridge* a divorce is enacted under the heretical law of Weydon-Priors fair. In *The Woodlanders* the notion of legal divorce is introduced for the first time, and it is suggested that the trap which kept Cytherea imprisoned in the château in *Desperate Remedies* might be sprung. This has profound implications. Hardy's 1895 Preface begins:

> In the present novel, as in one or two others of this series which involve the question of matrimonial divergence, the immortal puzzle – given the man and woman, how to find a basis for their sexual relation – is left where it stood; and it is tacitly assumed for the purposes of the story that no doubt of the depravity of the erratic heart who feels some second person to be better suited to his or her tastes than the one with whom he has contracted to live, enters the head of reader or writer for a moment. From the point of view of marriage as a distinct covenant or undertaking, decided on by two people fully cognizant of all its possible issues, and competent to carry them through, this assumption is, of course, logical. Yet no thinking person supposes that, on the broader ground of how to afford the greatest happiness to the units of human society during their brief transit through this sorry world, there is no more to be said on this covenant; and it is certainly not supposed by the writer of these pages. (*W*, p. 5)

This offers a contradictory justification which comes very close to making the division between traded text and counter-text overt. For 'the purposes of the story' a shared morality is assumed between writer and reader, but this is problematized by being stated at all. And 'enters the head of reader or writer for a moment' is sufficiently sarcastic to suggest that what is really shared between thinking people is a desire to rewrite the covenant. The division between 'the story' and 'the writer of these pages' makes clear the writer's own awareness of his separation from the production of his fiction. The rules of production prescribe that contract cannot be openly broken within a published text. The tactical alternative Hardy chooses is the manufacture of a traded text which does everything but break the rules. The threat posed by the encroaching wilderness of the counter-text is met by a traded text which is in retreat in that, although Grace's divorce from Fitzpiers is unobtainable, it produces the wholesale disruption of a conclusion which is blatantly unfair and unbalanced.

In the hierarchy of discourses which orders the conclusion of *The Woodlanders*, the authority of Melbury's trading control (which has taken clear precedence over Mrs Charmond's ownership after her departure and subsequent death) is overwhelmed by the power of the marriage contract. His autonomy is ultimately as unprotected as Giles's. The trip to London with Beaucock to try and obtain Grace's divorce from Fitzpiers is as implausible as Beaucock's legal credentials. Melbury's trade (carried out, like all his actions, in a spirit of credulous self-improvement) has been built on the separation of woods and workfolk. This destroys the woodland divinities and leaves him with the false gods of Fitzpiers's aristocratic antecedents and his 'rational' science. These fail him and he tries to return his manufactured daughter, paid for by the wealth generated by the separation, to the already moribund woodland god. His money cannot accomplish this. In dealing with the forces which can unmake the marriage contract he sees only part-revealed runic signs and hieroglyphs.

Melbury's treasured investments are promissory notes (deposits of paper money at the bank, Port-Bredy harbour bonds) issued and validated by the 'high' law which will not now repay on demand when Melbury tries to reclaim his miscontracted daughter. His capital has done the work required of it by destroying the heresies of Hintock and the 'high' law protects the structure, not the individual investor who has chosen to maintain and develop it. This is just the position of the entrepreneurial fiction-writer 'investing' workfolk and small traders in the larger business of novel-production, and this is the failure to repay which is met by a self-sabotaging text.

The Mayor of Casterbridge is, if you like, the first revolutionary act; *The Woodlanders* is a second, the miniature *Götterdämmerung* of a

152   *The Hidden Hardy*

miniature civilization. The conjuror has retained control of his text and further weakened its producers and their larger ideological devices. The fictional and physical structures which proved indestructible in *A Laodicean* are now sufficiently eroded for an attempt at full-scale *Götterdämmerung* in *Tess of the d'Urbervilles*.

8

Tess of the d'Urbervilles (1891): *Götterdämmerung*

It was less a reform than a transfiguration. The former curves of sensuousness were now modulated to lines of devotional passion. The lip-shapes that had meant seductiveness were now made to express supplication; the glow on the cheek that yesterday could be translated as riotousness was evangelized to-day into the splendour of pious rhetoric; animalism had become fanaticism; Paganism Paulinism; the bold rolling eye that had flashed upon her form in the old time with such mastery now beamed with the rude energy of a theolatry that was almost ferocious. Those black angularities which his face had used to put on when his wishes were thwarted now did duty in picturing the incorrigible backslider who would insist upon turning again to his wallowing in the mire. (*TD*, pp. 383–4)

The same question is put again: is it possible for grown wheat to be made wholesome? In *Tess of the d'Urbervilles* it applies to Alec d'Urberville and Angel Clare as well as Tess Durbeyfield. Each failed reformation depends on a different ideological system: Alec's on christian revelation, Angel's on a secular revelation of intellectual 'truth', Tess's on a reversal of biological essentialism. Each man's system of reform through revelation seeks to control the biological facts of the woman's life, her sexuality and her fertility. Hanging over all three is the larger question of whether the fictional mode of the novel can re-form after a failure which, in the course of this text, parallels Alec's rape, Angel's naive inadequacy and Tess's 'fall'. As Boumelha puts it,

> the novel's narrative method in a sense enacts the relativism of its structuring argument. But there is more to the discontinuities than this, they also mark Hardy's increasing interrogation of his own modes of narration. The disjunctions in narrative voice, the

contradictions of logic, the abrupt shifts of point of view . . . disintegrate the stability of character as a cohering force, they threaten the dominance of the dispassionate and omniscient narrator, and so push to its limit the androgynous narrative mode that seeks to represent and explain the woman from within and without.[1]

This is in the context of Hardy's position, by 1891, as arguably the most celebrated living English novelist. The threats to the omniscient narrator are made by a writer who has traded himself into a position of considerable cultural power during the period of the Triumph of Fiction, so that any disruption which actually damages the surface of the traded text must be seen as an act of extremely public self-destruction. In the context of the earlier counter-texts, the magical realism of *The Mayor of Casterbridge* and the vengeful wilderness of *The Woodlanders*, the interrogation here is not just an attack on the narrator's omniscience but a revelation of the alternative structures which have been essentially (if barely) concealed until now. The system of building a fiction with antithetical traded text and counter-text places Hardy in a uniquely strong position to disempower his traded text without weakening the novel's dramatic force, and indeed to use this surrender of omniscience to enforce more, not less, on the consumer-reproducer. In *Tess of the d'Urbervilles* this is a highly coherent and integrated manipulative exercise. The traded text enforces its own destruction on the reader through the unavoidable experience of Tess's life and death, and on a more minor but more overtly confrontational level through the challenges it offers to the moral code which defined a fiction acceptable for production, particularly by serial publishers. Jacobus describes the response from Tillotson's to proofs for the part of the novel culminating in Sorrow's death, Hardy's withdrawal of the manuscript in the face of the major changes demanded, and the subsequent rejection by Edward Arnold, editor of *Murray's Magazine*, on the grounds that he would not publish 'stories where the plot involves frequent and detailed reference to immoral situations'.[2]

The will to power represented internally by the counter-text's attacks on the traded text is not superseded, but rather now magnified, by a well-publicized attempt to trade a fiction which is openly transgressive. This entrepreneurial aggression is accompanied by a counter-text of similar scale and ferocity, which very plainly dominates the eroded dramatic/realistic narrative. The act of rape in the wilderness of the Chase, which is at the centre of the traded text's debate about purity, makes overt the fact that subordination to power relations is not a matter of choice but an unsought submission to brute force, and within the text the part-concealed, anti-realistic strategies hold a similar control. The narrator enforces his counter-fiction on the reader as Alec enforces his power over Tess.

Again the medieval notion of wildness is used to locate this; here the Wild Man changes sex. Bernheimer identifies the widespread Northern European legend of a Wild Woman chased and persecuted by a 'hunting and riding demon who chases through the country-side alone or in rowdy company and ends, when he has found his victim, by tearing her apart'.³ Plainly Alec is the 'hunting and riding demon', and Car Darch and the other women at Trantridge are the Maenads who provide his rowdy company. The Maenads are also, as Williams points out, an example of the dissolute and youthful gangs of rootless agricultural workers Marx describes in Lincoln-shire.⁴ This typifies the novel's fusion of real event and mythos. Waring notes that Maiden Castle is thought to have been built by a Wild Woman,⁵ and in terms of a counter-text which deals with the sacrifice of the land this immediately adds moment to the titles of the novel's first two Phases, 'The Maiden' and 'Maiden No More'.

We first see Tess at the Marlott club-walking, a female fertility ritual which has, anachronistically, survived intact into the nine-teenth century. This comes immediately after the revelation that she is a d'Urberville. The novel's title is *Tess of the d'Urbervilles* and this makes it clear that whether the d'Urbervilles are the Stokes of Trantridge or the d'Urbervilles of Kingsbere, labour (and the Durbeyfields) must necessarily belong to capital. Ultimately the trading equation which creates the traded text is the 'truth' of its subtitle. The magical transformation of Durbeyfield to d'Urberville is itself the analogue of the bourgeois novel's position of 'traded' power, really the response of a naive consumer ('Sir John') to a credible fiction produced by a parson, who by virtue of his trade has hegemonic control of knowledge in Marlott. Jack Durbeyfield is carrying an empty egg-basket when he hears the news. The eggs grow to chickens when Tess moves to the Stoke-d'Urbervilles' and takes charge of the fowls there. This replicates the Durbeyfields' relation to the d'Urbervilles in the image of a cottage built for humans now occupied by hens, overlooked by a blind woman whose inability to mediate Alec's power over Tess resembles the decrepit and blind godhead in the poem 'Nature's Questioning'

(*SP*, pp. 288–9). Then after the rape an egg is germinated in Tess herself; the birth of Sorrow follows. The eggs thus become (as *Jude the Obscure* demonstrates in more ironic detail) a protean unit of fertility, the seed which has been planted and already sold when the action of the novel begins. Tess is the only girl at the club-walking with a red fillet in her hair:

> A young member of the band turned her head at the exclamation. She was a fine and handsome girl – not handsomer than some others, possibly – but her mobile peony mouth and large innocent eyes added eloquence to colour and shape. She wore a red ribbon in her hair, and was the only one of the white company who could boast of such a pronounced adornment. As she looked round Durbeyfield was seen moving along the road in a chaise belonging to The Pure Drop, driven by a frizzle-headed brawny damsel with her gown-sleeves rolled above her elbows. This was the cheerful servant of that establishment, who, in her part of factotum, turned groom and ostler at times. Durbeyfield, leaning back, and with his eyes closed luxuriously, was waving his hand above his head, and singing in a slow recitative –
> 'I've-got-a-gr't-family-vault-at-Kingsbere – and knighted fore-fathers-in-lead-coffins-there!' (*TD*, p. 51)

The red makes her the scapegoat of Holman Hunt's picture. The scapegoat is white with red wool wound around its horns. According to Talmudic usage (the Talmud arguably begins the mutation of paganism into Paulinism) the scapegoat is sent out into the wilderness on the Day of Atonement as a propitiation for the community's sins to die amongst the bones of its ancestors (the 'forefathers-in-lead-coffins' at Kingsbere). The clearest image of a scapegoat dying among the bones of its ancestors, and therefore of the sacrifice of Tess's life being accepted, is the point where Angel carries her from the room which contains the effigies of the dead d'Urberville ladies and enacts a mock burial. Because Angel is the first person to see Tess at the club-walking he is the first person to see her transfiguration from village girl to scapegoat; and so, ironically, he is the person who most disastrously misperceives her and therefore miscontracts with her. If the christian forces Angel represents still informed the world the sacrifice might be acceptable and Tess might be allowed to die without further humiliation; but the burial only takes place in a dream, in a larger sense in the dream of christian power over the land and the workfolk.

Casting Tess as scapegoat is effectively a sin-eating. As John Aubrey shows, using the model of sin-eating in seventeenth-century Herefordshire, normally the poorest person in a community is paid to eat the sins of someone who has just died[6] (this practice is still current; a sin-eating was recorded at Wainfawr in North Wales in the late 1960s; it is also used in Mary Webb's *Precious Bane*). Jack Durbeyfield's mock grandeur when he hears about his fictional elevation is undercut by the egregious status his daughter has implicitly accepted by wearing the red fillet. The scapegoat's sacrifice is accepted by the gods only if red turns to white. This does not happen. On the contrary the scapegoat becomes a blood sacrifice. Tanner describes the novel's obsessive sequence of red and white images[7]; the horse's blood, splashed over Tess when he is killed by another cart; the bright red newness of 'The Slopes'; the red brick of Wintoncester gaol; the 'red coal' of Alec's cigar; the red reaping machine; the 'vermilion words' left all over the countryside by the painter of religious texts; Tess's arm bleeding from the stubble in the harvest field; the shot pheasants' 'plumage dappled with blood'; the 'blood-stained paper' Tess sees when she walks to see Angel's parents; Alec's blood when Tess slashes him across the face with her gauntlet; the 'scarlet blot' of Alec's blood coming through the white ceiling after Tess has killed him; the 'crimson damask hangings' of the last bed Tess sleeps in before her arrest at Stonehenge.

Partly this redness reflects a systematic allusion to sun mythology which is very much related to Friedrich Max Müller's work, published in the 1870s.[8] Max Müller's central proposition is that primitive man's impulse to myth, legend and religion is located in a response to the rising and setting of the sun. Tess is fused with the land she lives and works on and the sun brings her fertility to life. This fusion has been produced, impossibly, by generations of labour which have alienated the Durbeyfields from the land they once owned (at least according to Parson Tringham's fiction). In this sense Tess becomes Gaia, the land of the Greek creation myth. The world is created by the marriage of the earth (Gaia) and the sun. When the Aeschylan 'President of the Immortals' finishes his sport with Tess he is Cronos destroying Gaia. In this sense creation, of land, life and fiction, has ended when Tess dies. Angel and Tess get engaged at sunset: and this ill-starred relationship is man's inadequate attempt to intervene in the process of *Götterdämmerung*.

Angel, Tess's christian guardian angel (complete with harp), initially seen walking between two christian priests, has seen the start of *Götterdämmerung* at the Marlott club-walking but failed to realise what was going on. In fact he is an impossible contradiction in terms, a post-christian guardian angel. And you might also argue that his first perceptions of Tess and of the farm at Talbothays represent the position of the 'purchaser' of the 'traded' text naively consuming Wessex; so Angel's interpretative inadequacy and Tess's class and gender experience are enforced on the reader at the same time as dual tests, or proofs, of the subtitle's notions of 'purity' and 'faithful' representation.

The presence of Anglican priests at the start of the blood-letting is also engaged with the literal economic reality of the text. It is worth remembering that tithes were levied in Dorset until 1868.[9] Having bled the land for centuries, the priests now seem to stand by and watch the result; for now the land seems to bleed spontaneously. Tess's non-christian allusive context in the counter-text expresses their absolute irrelevance. Christian dogma and its church's failing hegemony can do nothing for working-class lives except damage them by disinformation. Even in the traded text the do-gooding Clare parents are met with contemptuous narrative satire. How are Emminster Vicarage and the sons' university education paid for if not by the same process of allegorized rape which gets Tess pregnant?

Gaia's complementary divinity is Maia, a Wild Woman usually pictured with huge, hanging breasts (like the cows at Talbothays).[10] This links the 'high' Greek and 'low' English cultures of the counter-text, creating a fusion where in the 'traded' text there is division: Tess's position there is an impossible cultural and linguistic suspension between 'high' and 'low'. Her partial education produces a partially manufactured 'cultural automaton' who by reason of the incomplete process has the revelatory quality of the clock with exposed machinery in *Far From the Madding Crowd*. This use of an incomplete transformation marks a significant development from Hardy's earlier presentation of working-class characters. When Ebbatson talks about linguistic division in *The Return of the Native* he is dealing with a fiction in which workfolk and bourgeois speak different languages:

In the conflictual relationship between regional dialect and standard English, the novel unconsciously mirrors and re-works issues of class-division and a history of appropriation and centralisation.[11]

There is nothing unconscious about the way these issues and this history are related to Tess: her two languages characterize her in terms of both sides of a long historical fight between class and class, appropriation and autonomy, capital and labour, d'Urberville and Durbeyfield (and the change from 'field' to 'ville' is, of course, the transformation of rural to urban which Tess undergoes when she becomes 'Mrs d'Urberville' of Sandbourne). Hence her spontaneous bleeding as the fight necessarily continues and hence the emergence of the scapegoat, sent out to die in the wilderness not by one side or the other but, now that Tess is a d'Urberville, by both.

(Mrs Durbeyfield habitually spoke the dialect; her daughter, who had passed the Sixth Standard in the National School under a London-trained mistress, spoke two languages; the dialect at home, more or less; ordinary English abroad and to persons of quality.) (*TD*, p. 58)

It is significant (though hardly surprising) that the narrator chooses to define the 'English' which privileges the story he tells and its consumers' bourgeois constructions of language and class as 'ordinary'. As Wotton puts it, 'Hardy's writing was produced out of, and is now a hundred years later used to reproduce, a linguistic division in education';[12] which is one very significant reason for the continued cultural power of Hardy of Wessex and the bourgeois liberal 'literature' produced by his trading process. The difference between Tess's conflictual languages and the treatment of the same issue eight years earlier in 'The Dorsetshire Labourer', the zenith of Hardy's business in misrepresenting the workfolk since it has no 'plot' or 'character' to subvert, illustrates the traded text's giving ground on this crucial point.

Having attended the National School [children] would mix the printed tongue as taught therein with the unwritten, dying, Wessex English that they had learnt of their parents, the result of this transitional state of their being a composite language without rule or harmony. (*DL*, p. 254)

In 'The Dorsetshire Labourer' Hardy deploys transparent linguistic strategies which avoid going beyond observation to analysis. As the anthropologist of Wessex he retains a privileged knowledge (from a bourgeois point of view) of 'the unwritten, dying, Wessex English', of the picturesque materials of his novels. This potentially subversive integer is the only way of identifying the 'composite language"'s lack of 'rule or harmony' as against the (apparently) ruled and harmonious language of the bourgeois consumer of the essay, and so the consumer is simply told that it exists, not what it *is* or what it does. (If this does not seem to be a political act, remember that the essay is written by a leading advocate of the Dorset dialect poet William Barnes.) Nothing is done to erode the trader's cultural power over his subject or his ability to mesmerize his market by unrevealed means. Certainly no conflict is implied in the apparently organic and 'natural' process of transition, even if it seems to be regretted.

In *Tess of the d'Urbervilles* Angel 'sees' and 'hears' what the consumer of 'The Dorsetshire Labourer' 'sees' and 'hears'. In the 'traded' text this is presented as inadequate and deleterious. What he sees as 'composite' is the conflictual process which creates the 'modernism' which is the source of his fascination with Tess. He also seeks to naturalize the processes which have created Tess, thus mirroring the bourgeois liberal consumer's project of reading her and the larger project of 'naturalizing' fictions of Character and Environment on artificial constructions of identity, class and power relations. As Goode puts it,

> [Angel] is precisely drawn to Tess by her 'ache of modernism', but then he has to make of her a 'daughter of the soil' constructed in terms of a nature that has already been doubly denied both by blighted planet and by mental harvest.[13]

This is exactly the Myth of Wessex Hardy has traded for twenty years: fetishization of a landscape created by its work practices in the context of a fictional project which reinforces the division and exploitation behind those practices, which blight the planet and produce the workfolk's mental harvest. The creative force behind the runic signs and hieroglyphs Angel cannot read is the predictive narrative power which is appealed to when the conjurors are mentioned at Talbothays dairy. This is contained in the narrator's description of the fortune-telling book Joan Durbeyfield consults before Tess is sent to claim kin with the Stoke-d'Urbervilles.

'And take the *Compleat Fortune-Teller* to the outhouse,' Joan continued, rapidly wiping her hands, and donning the garments.
   The *Compleat Fortune-Teller* was an old thick volume, which lay on a table at her elbow, so worn by pocketing that the margins had reached the edge of the type . . .
   Tess, being left alone with the younger children, went first to the outhouse with the fortune-telling book, and stuffed it into the thatch. A curious fetichistic fear of this grimy volume on the part of her mother prevented her ever allowing it to stay in the house all night, and hither it was brought back whenever it had been consulted. Between the mother, with her fast-perishing lumber of superstitions, folk-lore, dialect, and orally transmitted ballads, and the daughter, with her trained National teachings and Standard knowledge under an infinitely Revised Code, there was a gap of two hundred years as ordinarily understood. When they were together the Jacobean and Victorian ages were juxtaposed.
   Returning along the garden path Tess mused on what the mother could have wished to ascertain from the book on this particular day. She guessed the recent ancestral discovery to bear upon it, but did not divine that it solely concerned herself. (*TD*, pp. 60–1)

The 'gap of two hundred years' only erases the 'lumber of superstitions' (lumber being a product, to make a connection with *The Woodlanders*, of Hintock's magically corrupted timber trade) in terms of a history which accepts the hegemony of a Victorian age built on Angel's intellectual authority and Alec's economic authority. Otherwise it does no such thing. In the narrator's dangerous dare it is a book of magical prediction which is being used to (fore)tell Tess's story to credulous consumers, and this form of conjuring is Hardy's governing fictional practice here. The book is kept in the thatch and not allowed in the house; it is an unacknowledged but *known* insertion in the novel's architectural structure. When Angel learns the 'truth' about Tess he describes the change he perceives in her as if he were the victim of a conjuring trick:

'O Tess, forgiveness does not apply to the case. You were one person; now you are another. My God – how can forgiveness meet such a grotesque – prestidigitation as that!'

He paused, contemplating this definition; then suddenly broke into horrible laughter – as unnatural and ghastly as a laugh in hell. (*TD*, p. 298)

If the notion of forgiveness is christian (or post-christian), it simply cannot deal with this kind of narrative heresy. Again this is a matter of power relations. In a patriarchy a man can be forgiven what a woman cannot, as Angel's failure to forgive Tess what she has already forgiven him shows. Because men make the rules, Angel and the reader have the cultural power to create a Wessex which is ideological and fictive. The conjurors' and workfolk's Wessex, created by labour and small trade, is material and magical, built from powerlessness instead of power.

This is particularly clear at Talbothays, where Angel and Tess become romantically involved and the conflict between notions of Wessex becomes overtly politicized when a marriage contract is brought into play. This happens when the traded text is at its most picturesque. Tess's club-walking at Marlott seems (to Angel and the consumer of the traded text) to be part of a rural idyll; so does the blooming organic fertility and female sexuality at Talbothays dairy. In the material terms which are clearly articulated in the text the opposite is true. At Marlott we see Tess when Jack Durbeyfield has been condemned to death by the doctor at Shaston because of the circle of fat around his heart (the blood-pump which keeps the red and white imagery circulating). This means that a beleaguered working-class family will shortly lose its breadwinner. The dairy at Talbothays is just as fragile. As Kerr shows,[14] the dairyman's was the weakest entrepreneurial position in mid and late nineteenth-century farming in Wessex. At Whitchurch Canonicorum in 1851 all the men who entered 'dairyman' on their census return had it altered to 'agricultural labourer'. Leases were usually only annual and because of the need to show a profit within a single season turnover in cows was also high. This is the insecurity which creates the display of Dairyman Crick's broadcloth and his pew in church, as if those animistic tokens could secure his financial status. Before she comes to Talbothays Tess is in milk after Sorrow's birth and she becomes a dairymaid (according to the conjuror's narrative, which Angel and the reader do not see) because she, like the cows, is artificially kept in milk by the economic demands made on the small-scale entrepreneur. This is the extent of Gaia/Maia's value to the economic machine which really defines her.

Abused female fertility offers a third explanation for the blood in the allegorical imagery of the counter-text. Tess's bleeding arm (and there is blood-letting also at Flintcomb-Ash, where turnips are grown for cattle feed as part of a programme designed to make poor land fertile again, and where the somewhat phallic agricultural engine Tess is forced to ride on, just as she is forced sexually by Alec, enforces the irresistible mechanism of the process) represents the bleeding which comes from a female fertility which does not end in the birth of a future: menstrual period, abortion, miscarriage. All these are effectively placed at the mercy of a patriarchal economy able to enforce its power by rape.

The Vale of Blackmoor, Tess's starting-point in the text, is the Vale of the Little Dairies; Talbothays is in the Vale of the Great Dairies. The (deeply conflictual) combination of human poverty and agricultural richness in the Vale of Blackmoor has already been noted. Talbothays is an amplification of the same situation. The history enforced on the Vale of Blackmoor is dramatized on a larger scale.

> The district is of historic, no less than of topographical interest. The Vale was known in former times as the Forest of the White Hart, from a curious legend of Henry III's reign, in which the killing by a certain Thomas de la Lynd of a beautiful white hart which the king had run down and spared, was made the occasion of a heavy fine. In those days, and till comparatively recent times, the country was densely wooded. Even now, traces of its earlier condition are to be found in the old oak copses and irregular belts of timber that yet survive upon its slopes, and the hollow-trunked trees that shade so many of its pastures. (*TD*, p. 49)

This seems at first a rather obvious adumbration of Tess's story, and this is its function in the traded text. The land of Blackmoor Vale is described, then Tess is alchemically fused with it by the hearsay legend which rehearses her story. But the description of the legend also reprises *The Woodlanders'* conjured counter-text, 'traces of' an 'earlier condition' which override the history written by kings: 'irregular belts of timber' and 'hollow-trunked trees' emptied by Giles's death still survive to tell the tale. The anachronistic survival of the club-walking (like the mummers' play) has the same function.

Tess is killed, according to the law which finds her guilty of murder, at Wintoncester gaol. This is an epilogue to the blood sacrifice which has been made to the sun at Stonehenge.

> She ceased, and he fell into thought. In the far north-east sky he could see between the pillars a level streak of light. The uniform concavity of black cloud was lifting bodily like the lid of a pot, letting in at the earth's edge the coming day, against which the towering monoliths and trilithons began to be bleakly defined.
> 'Did they sacrifice to God here?' asked she.
> 'No,' said he.
> 'Who to?'
> 'I believe to the sun. That lofty stone set away by itself is in the direction of the sun, which will presently rise behind it.'
>
> (*TD*, p. 485)

The sun rises and Tess is arrested. Christianity and post-christian modernism, personified by the guardian Angel sent to oversee Tess's life at the point where she is chosen as scapegoat, has failed to rescue her, conceivably because the angel can no longer believe in god. Since the orphan of Paulinism has failed her (and since, not coincidentally, she has killed an ex-Pauline preacher), she is abandoned to the cruder forces of paganism and sun-worship. In the traded text the sun is presented as a benign god overseeing the harvest at Marlott, a mythic-allegorical part of Wessex's 'timeless' beauty:

> It was a hazy sunrise in August. The denser nocturnal vapours, attacked by the warm beams, were dividing and shrinking into isolated fleeces within hollows and coverts, where they waited till they should be dried away to nothing.
> The sun, on account of the mist, had a curious sentient, personal look, demanding the masculine pronoun for its adequate expression. His present aspect, coupled with the lack of all human forms in the scene, explained the old-time heliolatries in a moment. One could feel that a saner religion had never prevailed under the sky. The luminary was a golden-haired, mild-eyed, God-like creature, gazing down in the vigour and intentness of youth upon an earth that was brimming with interest for him.
> His light, a little later, broke through chinks of cottage shutters, throwing stripes like red-hot pokers upon cupboards, chests of

drawers, and other furniture within; and awakening harvesters who were not already astir.

> But of all the ruddy things that morning the brightest were two broad arms of painted wood, which rose from the margin of a yellow cornfield hard by Marlott village. They, with two other below, formed the revolving Maltese cross of the reaping-machine, which had been brought to the field on the previous evening to be ready for operations this day. The paint with which they were smeared, intensified in hue by the sunlight, imparted to them a look of having been dipped in liquid fire. (*TD*, p. 136)

But there are two harvests here, one of the season's crop and the other of Tess's crop, the baby we see her feeding. Alec's fertilization of Tess parallels the sun's fertilization of Gaia; so in this sense Alec becomes also a solar surrogate.

The sun (Alec) fertilizes the land (Tess/Gaia) and he thus 'makes' the text which is worked out on its subject, Tess the woman. This is the predictive, magical text of the fortune-telling book. So the creation of the novel is presented interrogatively as an elemental creation of the world. The unequivocal power relation between Alec and Tess is also the relation, now being dismantled, between Hardy the 'trader' and the workfolk he fictionalizes. The limitations and patent artifices of Alec's characterization are very much a part of this dismantling of the traded text. He begins as a fictional cliché with an assumed sexual *droit de seigneur* and the characteristics of a wicked squire in a melodrama:

> He had an almost swarthy complexion, with full lips, badly moulded, though red and smooth, above which was a well-groomed moustache with curled points, though his age could not be more than three- or four- and twenty. Despite the touches of barbarism in his contours, there was a singular force in the gentleman's face, and in his bold rolling eye.
>
> 'Well, my Beauty, what can I do for you?' said he, coming forward. (*TD*, p. 79)

When Alec returns, transformed (or re-formed) into a preacher, the narrator says:

> The lineaments, as such, seemed to complain. They had been diverted from their hereditary connotation to signify intentions for which nature did not intend them. Strange that their very

elevation was a misapplication, that to raise seemed to falsify. (*TD*, p. 384)

The intentions of 'nature' are the narrative conjuring trick which created an Alec out of the 'natural' functions of land-owning and male sexual power over women, the functions which establish the 'natural' structure of the novel and the consumer's reproduction of Wessex. Alec's limited characteristics serve the structure of the counter-text, as a creative deity translated into a demon by the material structure which creates his power over Tess. This is the basis on which the 'androgynous narrative mode' is pushed to its limits.

In this context the politics of light and illumination become central, and this develops the similar exercise in *The Return of the Native*. Bullen argues that

> In *Tess of the d'Urbervilles* the meaning which Hardy attributes to objective phenomena lies neither in the sense of light nor within the things themselves, but almost entirely in the way in which they are illuminated.[15]

In fact the meaning comes from the alternative narrative structure of the counter-text, which provides both the source of light and the meanings contained 'within the things themselves'. The technique, as Bullen goes on to show, is a development of Ruskin's suggestion that Turner's treatment of sunlight uses a Greek attitude to solar phenomena; but again this is a superficial method of revealing information which is now very imperfectly concealed by the traded text. The shift in point of view in the harvest field is a case in point, as Alec oversees the harvest of the seed he has caused to germinate in Tess/Gaia. In *The Return of the Native* Clym's hyper-sensitivity to light destroys his perception, but the light is supplied and withheld by a narrator who does not articulate his practice in the dramatic action of the text. Here Alec is light and Angel is obscurity, so that both destroyer and destroyed are characterized; Angel's flawed perception cannot see Tess's purity because he cannot see beyond the destructive act of Alec's violation. The red and white images represent the coeval action of dramatic narrative and sun on Tess and it is significant, as Bullen also points out, that so many journeys are made by night in the novel. These are in effect the earth's unconscious attempt to escape the sun's action on her, but the counter-text's allegorical imperatives make this impossible. The horse's death when Tess is driving beehives to market, for instance, happens in darkness. But the light which would have prevented the accident is the sun-god she has been sacrificed to; and darkness cannot protect her from rape and impregnation.

In the harvest field Tess's function as scapegoat has turned her own community to wilderness. At first she is nameless, an unindividuated worker defined only by her labour and invested, in the Wessex travelogue, with 'the charm which is acquired by woman when she becomes part and parcel of outdoor nature' (*TD*, p. 137). Then she is named: she is 'the same, but not the same; at the present stage of her existence living as a stranger and an alien here, though it was no strange land that she was in' (*TD*, p. 139). At the same time the sun-intensified red reaping-machine defines the work practices and power relations which alienate any worker from her harvest field. Instead of red turning to white it has become 'liquid fire'.

The cycle now starts again. The seeds of the next section of allegorical narrative are found, appropriately, in the harvest field. Tess's baby dies and cannot be buried in consecrated ground. Her fertility seems to be reconstructed at Talbothays, where it is really exploited by another manifestation of the reaping-machine. Patriarchy is benign under Dairyman Crick, but the contradiction between a friendly and communal means of production and the capitalistic selling-on of milk into large urban centres coincides with the increasing threat that the Durbeyfields left at Marlott will lose their home either through collapse of the building itself or Jack's death, and be reduced to landless workfolk. The Rally is simply another abuse of the scapegoat. Patriarchy (which is ultimately governed by Alec and the sun) cannot be made benign; Crick has to milk the most difficult cows himself because only a man can draw the last drop. There is no significant difference between the power relations at Talbothays and Flintcomb-Ash, and both farms are part of the same cycle of fertilization, lactation and selling-on. Flintcomb-Ash and Farmer Groby simply show the processes which Angel and the reader cannot see at Talbothays.

The *apparent* difference between the two farms is in available and withheld female sexuality, represented by verdant pasture on one hand and starve-acre rendsinas on the other. In *Jude the Obscure* Sue withholds herself sexually as an (impossible) attempt to retain an autonomy which is intellectually based: this follows Gaia's equally impossible attempt to withhold herself from the sun by the defeminization Tess tries to practice at Flintcomb-Ash. On a literal level this makes the point that you cannot ungender yourself when your gender is an ideology practised on you a power relation which renders you powerless. But the impossibility and hopelessness are not unavoidable. They are precisely as unavoidable as the scapegoat's victimization, built on the 'essentialisms' of nature, capital and gender, which the reader is forced to experience and respond to with appropriate outrage. This kind of nature, like 'traded' Wessex, is surely presented here in order to invite the kind of 'real' overthrow which has previously only been represented by Hardy's internally competing fictions.

In fact female sexuality becomes potentially subversive and powerful at Talbothays until it is brought under contractual-ideological ownership by Angel. The dangerous dares of sexually allegorized landscape in *Far From the Madding Crowd*'s swordplay and *A Laodicean*'s tunnel entrance come to the surface in the fusion of the dairymaids and their working environment. Sexual arousal *without* the actual presence of a man is more threatening than mere sexual response because (in spite of 'cruel Nature's law', a law in the process of being refuted) it implies Gaia's potential for dangerous gender autonomy and collectivity:

> The air of the sleeping-chamber seemed to palpitate with the hopeless passion of the girls. They writhed feverishly under the oppressiveness of an emotion thrust on them by cruel Nature's law – an emotion which they had neither expected nor desired. The incident of the day had fanned the flame that was burning the inside of their hearts out, and the torture was almost more than they could endure. The differences which distinguished them as individuals were abstracted by this passion, and each was but part of one organism called sex . . .
> They tossed and turned on their little beds, and the cheese-wring dripped monotonously downstairs. (*TD*, pp. 204–5)

Plainly the dripping cheese-wring undercuts the polite fictional convention of locating sexual desire in the heart (pushed to its limits in any case by the narrator's placing of the 'flame' inside rather than outside the heart). This is the attack on the proprieties of the traded text a producer has invested in. The landscape of Talbothays, also dripping rather than merely 'acceptably' moist with fertility, has much the same function in the counter-text's attack on the proprieties of Wessex. Angel's incorrect ideological construction of both woman and land neither contains this successfully (from the point of view of the patriarchal structures he unknowingly represents) nor provides the protection he believes he can offer.

The d'Urbervilles are temporal stewards of the land; the Clares are the spiritual stewards who have maintained the creed which maintained their power, and so created the powerlessness of the Durbeyfields. (Remember that a christian priest tells Jack Durbeyfield that he is a d'Urberville and so begins the dramatic action.) They have also maintained the marriage contract which, although Angel tries to revise it by attempting to marry in a registry office, has maintained the structuring of sexual relations and male ownership of female fertility which suppressed Gaia and the Wild Woman, and which for the working class Durbeyfields became the only ideology they could give their daughter. The Clare parents are 'good' in terms of the moral code *Tess of the d'Urbervilles* sets out to savage, and they are presented almost as satirical cartoons:

> 'But – where's your wife, dear Angel?' cried his mother. 'How you surprise us!'
> 'She is at her mother's – temporarily. I have come home rather in a hurry because I've decided to go to Brazil.'
> 'Brazil! Why they are all Roman Catholics there surely!'
> 'Are they? I hadn't thought of that.' (*TD*, pp. 333–4)

This belongs to the same disruptive-interrogative mode of characterization as the comic Durbeyfields and the one-dimensional Alec. The Clares' spiritual engagement with the gods and the land and the people is offered up for destruction on the same basis as Jack Durbeyfield's aristocratic pretensions. *Götterdämmerung* is in progress; the land will sacrifice itself to the sky and the gods will be dead; all Pauline christianity has produced in these circumstances is a creed with a notion of individual spiritual renewal so pernicious that it will allow Alec, who has raped the country, to become its evangelist. When Alec appears to Tess as an evangelist for a second time he is carrying the marriage contract which would give a christian blessing to his (undeclared) first violation, unless of course you accept the implausible christian reformation. Mr Clare's seeds, life in Angel and faith in Alec, are both used to help bleed the scapegoat to death.

The christening and burial of Sorrow make the same point emblematically. Having been nameless for so long the baby is given a 'name suggested by a phrase in the book of Genesis' (*TD*, p. 145). Genesis is the judaeo-christian creation myth which has usurped Gaia's Greek creation myth (and her pre-Hellenic matriarchy) and the Wild Woman's ritual power over her own fertility. If Tess is Gaia she has borne a world, as she is now bearing its sins as scapegoat, and seen it sicken and grow moribund. Now she christens her baby herself according to the only ritual available to her, since the ritual tradition she might have learned from her mother has been stolen by the National School. The christian church denies the baby a burial because its spiritual vision is so obscured by a moral code that it finds a non-marital creation of the world unacceptable. What seems at first to be misplaced narrative irony imperfectly masks a point where Tess/Gaia's divinity cannot avoid coming to the surface if the counter-text is to be maintained without compromise:

> She did not look like Sissy to them now, but as a being large, towering, and awful – a divine personage with whom they had nothing in common.
>
> Poor Sorrow's campaign against sin, against the world, and the devil was doomed to be of limited brilliancy – luckily perhaps for himself, considering his beginnings. In the blue of the morning that fragile soldier and servant breathed his last, and when the other children awoke they cried bitterly, and begged Sissy to have another pretty baby. (*TD*, p. 146)

Angel's eclectic ideological modernism presents literally, without the allegory of buildings, George Somerset's inability to escape from a pre-existing structure. The snobbery which makes him impressed that Tess is 'really' a d'Urberville also makes clear his continuing attachment to the class structure which makes Mrs Crick seat him apart from the workfolk to eat. His attempt to divert the Clare legacy of spirituality from university scholarship and christian ministry to the Gaia-worship he tries to learn at Talbothays is another impossible gesture of autonomy, correct in terms of the counter-text's creative myth; he recognizes what he could not see at the Marlott club-walking, but recognition comes too late. The moral system which is still a christian inheritance sends him away from Tess and almost ludicrously to Brazil, where he expects to find the El Dorado of Gaia and Talbothays without any blemish of the corrupting ideological history and the material violation which are his own real inheritance. Angel (and here his reader-identification is very clear) is the only character who is given all the information necessary to see Tess as Gaia and scapegoat: but his narrative of Tess collapses into an incomprehensible product of 'grotesque prestidigitation' when he learns about the past and the crucial violation he has not been shown. In Brazil Angel meets a mystical and disruptive god-surrogate, appropriately in what turns out to be an infertile and fever-ridden earthly paradise, created only as a speculative capitalistic project. He dies and Angel buries him, thus reprising the mock burial of Tess:

> The cursory remarks of the large-minded stranger, of whom he knew nothing beyond a commonplace name, were sublimed by his death, and influenced Clare more than all the reasoned ethics of the philosophers. His own parochialism made him ashamed by its contrast. His inconsistencies rushed upon him in a flood. He had persistently elevated Hellenic Paganism at the expense of Christianity; yet in that civilization an illegal surrender was not certain disesteem. Surely then he might have regarded that abhorrence of the un-intact state, which he had inherited with the creed of mysticism, as at least open to criticism when the result was due to treachery. A remorse struck into him. (*TD*, p. 422)

An ironically-conceived Christ, the 'large-minded stranger''s commonplace remarks are sublimed by his death, and supplant a tradition of philosophical reason. This quite implausibly (in terms of the traded text) frees Angel from his inconsistencies and liberates the Hellenic paganism of Tess's counter-textual conception from the obscuring mysticism of his christian inheritance. Unfortunately this death of god prefigures Tess's death, which is ultimately due to Angel's failure to get back to England from El Dorado in time to save her from the sun.

Immediately after this revelation Tess is summoned back to Marlott from Flintcomb-Ash, where she went to work only because she had to pay for repairs to her family's cottage, because her mother is ill and expected to die. When she arrives her mother is sleeping. Her father has the idea of maintaining himself and his nobility by public subscription. Alec, the real beneficiary of an enforced subscription (the farming rents and profits the workfolk and small traders create) arrives, disguised as an agricultural labourer and thus reversing

Durbeyfield and d'Urberville. He offers to help support the family. Joan Durbeyfield recovers and Jack suddenly dies. The circle of fat around his heart is now complete. The life-hold on the cottage now terminates and the family becomes landless and rootless. The Durbeyfields refuse Alec's offer of the hen-house, an obvious enough statement of their position, which would create the rural fictional idyll aspired to by the kind of text Hardy's corrupted Wessex explodes. Williams quotes this credo from William Howitt's *The Hall and the Hamlet* (1848): 'The hall may, and must, do much to elevate the hamlet, and the hamlet, in a more enlightened and prosperous condition, can add much to the interest of living at the hall'.[16] In this case the hall, having raped and impoverished the hamlet, proposes to transport it to a position where it can be more easily used and abused. This is the real result of Alec's reformation. Instead of going to Trantridge the whole family takes up Tess's destiny as scapegoat. When Joan is unable to find lodgings in Kingsbere, where she has gone because of the d'Urberville connections, she tries to claim a freehold interest in the d'Urberville family vault and suggests that the family live there until they find somewhere better. Alec arrives again, Marian and Izz write to Angel at Emminster Vicarage to warn him: and the novel moves to its final stage, Fulfilment.

Angel learns that Tess is at Sandbourne, goes there, and finds that she is living there as Mrs d'Urberville. On his way he has visited Marlott and paid for the tombstone commemorating 'John Durbeyfield, rightly d'Urberville', thus in a sense paying a tiny part of the price of the christian alchemy which created Tess's red fillet and her journey in the wilderness. Sandbourne is a fashionable resort, a bourgeois institutionalization of the fair which, as Stally-brass and White note,[17] retained some semblance of its old identity in the nineteenth century by moving further and further away from towns and cities, eventually arriving at the seaside. This is where the Wild Woman is now kept and displayed, like the Wild People displayed in freak shows and carnivals until the mid-twentieth century.[18] At first Angel regards 'Mrs d'Urberville' as a positive sign; Tess must be using her 'ancestral' name. In fact she is using it because she has yielded to a pressure which has been unavoidable since her first arrival at 'The Slopes'. She only uses her ancestral name as Tess Durbeyfield covering her violated honour. The haggler/trading novelist who sent his daughter to claim kin with the d'Urbervilles has got his price for the eggs in his basket.

When Tess kills Alec Gaia kills the sun god and she will be killed herself in consequence. Her guardian Angel, whose return brought about the murder, takes her to the place of her formal sacrifice at Stonehenge, where he is again met by a disruptive conjured image, this time of Stonehenge surrounded by policemen. As Bullen shows,[19] this is the conclusion of a sequence of druidical symbols which have followed Tess through the text, most strikingly in the image of (white) mistletoe on the trees on the Chase at the time of the rape and above the bed at Wellbridge. Later she contemplates suicide under mistletoe. This has an additional resonance in the sacrificial killing of Alec; in Germanic myth Loki kills the sun god Balder with a spear of mistletoe.

This *Götterdämmerung* has not ended the world but, since Gaia is dead, the earth is no longer under even the vestigial protection of the non-christian divinities of the earlier counter-texts, all of whom ultimately find their source in Gaia/Maia. But the material-ideological forces which produced Tess as their scapegoat retain their power; their representatives sentence Tess to death and hang her at Wintoncester gaol, so they are unquestionably guilty of Gaia's killing. The real overthrow demanded by this outrage can therefore now only be made in material-ideological terms, by an attack on the material-ideological 'Structure' itself.

9

Jude the Obscure (1895): High Farce

Jude the Obscure is in many ways a self-consciously complete inversion of Victorian novelistic practice. Nineteenth-century English fiction seems often to adapt the *Bildungsroman* into an ameliorative parable, dealing often with a young, male bourgeois protagonist thrust by circumstance into an alien working-class or petty bourgeois world. There he becomes *déclassé* (it seems) and by strength of character finds his way through a quasi-Gothic 'château' of previously unmapped class and cultural experience to a lost inheritance of authority and money. He achieves this by learning 'real' human values from his working-class and petty bourgeois companions, seeing at the same time the callous values of his 'own' class of origin when he experiences its behaviour from a working-class point of view. A gentleman is made a gentleman once more by what he learns from 'nature''s gentlemen (and ladies), and so the bourgeois code seems to be revised. *Nicholas Nickleby* is perhaps the purest example of this. Hegemony is maintained by the organization of working-class experience into bourgeois narrative and language and a bourgeois aesthetic through a means of production and reproduction with this tendency at its heart, and is always mediated by the 'character' and qualities predicated on the hero.

The revolutionary sequence of novels which begins with *The Mayor of Casterbridge* and ends with *Jude the Obscure* comes at a point where the novel's hegemonic means of production and reproduction is in the process of major mutation, if not collapse. This crisis is not confined to the manufacture and trading of fiction. Hardy's process of overthrowing a bourgeois propagandist commodity from the mid-1880s parallels similar threats to order in industrial and social relations: Bloody Sunday, the Sack of the West End, successful strikes by unskilled and semi-skilled dockers and gas-workers in 1889. The contrast between these events and the Lib-Labism and control of industrial relations by the conciliatory Junta leaders which preceded them is very much the contrast between the narrative strategies of *Jude the Obscure* and *Far From the Madding Crowd*. A crucial change in Hardy's characters' trading also reflects this. Until now all of Hardy's male protagonists have traded either in the product of fertility (grain, trees) or in management and planning (bailiffs, farmers, architects). The entrepreneurial ambivalence of these jobs, all in some sense on the margin between powerless and powerful, is very much the force behind the traded text/counter-text equivocation. *Tess of the d'Urbervilles* shatters the equivocation by presenting a protagonist who simultaneously trades labour and fertility, both from a position of powerlessness and without strategy. Jude simply has nothing to trade but his wage-labour.

But this development is far more than a matter of what the characters do for a living, although that remains absolutely central. Lewes sets three governing principles for an 'acceptable' author's contribution to the old manufacturing system in *The Principles of Success in Literature*: The Principle of Vision (Chapter II), The Principle of Sincerity (Chapter IV) and The Principle of Beauty (Chapter V). Chapter VI deals with The Laws of Style, of which there are five: Economy, Simplicity, Sequence, Climax and Variety. *Jude the Obscure* seems almost systematically to destroy all these. The fiction presents the transgressive and antithetical experience Dickens suppresses, a working-class young man's gradual comprehension of bourgeois material and ideological structures. His ultimate inheritance of class is as immutable as Nicholas Nickleby's. Contemporary representations of working-class life like Arthur Morrison's *A Child of the Jago* (1896) seems to do this; but without the overthrow of Lewes's rules, or similar unstated rules, and the larger structures behind them, these 'realistic' fictional accounts are merely tokens, new travelogues of class. They are necessarily subsumed into a 'literature' which supports the larger structure by stealing working class experience (precisely the nature of Hardy's early trade in Dorset workfolk) and colonizing it. Lewes also suggests that the writer must be 'steadfastly imperial' in his approach, an unconsciously revealing formulation.

Havelock Ellis, Margaret Oliphant and an anonymous reviewer in the *Atheneum* all accused *Jude the Obscure* of coming 'dangerously near to farce'.[1] This begins to identify, through its *verfremdungseffekt*, the novel's articulated self-destruction. The process of Jude and Sue's self-education, the rationalization of almost every event in intellectual-ideological terms, as they interpret their world through their imaginary relation to real relations, becomes often pathetically ludicrous. They adopt an alien, allusive cultural language which grossly mismaps their world. Ingham cites a particularly clear example of this:

The two quotations introducing the Christminster section seem to capture the emergent optimism of Jude, now embarking on his academic course – 'Save his own soul, he hath no star' – and the joy of his incipient love for Sue – 'Nearness led to awareness . . . love grew with time.' Both fragments are torn out of context: Swinburne's eulogy on self-reliance is woefully inapt for Jude; and Ovid is beginning not a joyous love-affair but the tragic story of the doomed lovers, Pyramus and Thisbe.

Even more cruelly irrelevant are the snatches from Sappho . . . 'There was no other girl, O bridegroom, like her!' fixes Jude's growing delight in Sue at Melchester; but what Sappho in context was promising the bridegroom was that erotic joy, the gift of Aphrodite, that Sue, for all her painful worship of the goddess whose image she buys, painfully fails to deliver.[2]

This creates a structure of experience as artificial, and to a bourgeois reader as grotesque and improbable, as Ethelberta's. As Goode puts it:

The novel not only ruins the prospects of interpretation by explicit discussion but also offers its own system of literary allegiances, which makes it difficult for the critic to determine influences or place it in a tradition . . . *Jude the Obscure* does not even acknowledge the reader as a self-defined and separate object. It is simply not fit for consumption.[3]

Jude and Sue are both specifically made orphans of Gaia's death. The biological essentialism which casts Tess as fertile woman and Angel as intellect is reversed, now that Gaia has been killed by the governing patriarchal male structure, a structure celebrated by Christminster and everything it stands for. What is now a *sexus sequior*, unprotected by any counter-textual old religion, is turned ultimately to new religion; Sue Bridehead as christianity, and Arabella Donn as its ironic counterpart, the pub (where men are consumers and women supplicatory barmaids). This is the legacy of Gaia's judicial murder. Woman becomes the complaisant victim of culturally empowered superstitions which suppress both identity and sexuality, as opposed to Gaia's deification of fertility. These are the new containing structures. Tess's series of red and white images turning to black in the flag at Wintoncester gaol is reprised grotesquely in the image of the pig dying in the snow. This is the sum total of Tess's life and death in the face of the forces imperatives which made her the scapegoat and killed her.

However unworkmanlike the deed, it has been mercifully done. The blood flowed out in a torrent instead of in the trickling stream she had desired. The dying animal's cry assumed its third and final tone, the shriek of agony; his glazing eyes riveting themselves on Arabella with the eloquently keen reproach of a creature recognizing at last the treachery of those who had seemed his only friends.

'Make 'un stop that!' said Arabella. 'Such a noise will bring somebody or other up here, and I don't want people to know we are doing it ourselves.' Picking up the knife from the ground whereon Jude had flung it, she slipped it into the gash, and slit the wind-pipe. The pig was instantly silent, his dying breath coming through the hole.

'That's better,' she said.

'It is a hateful business!' said he.

'Pigs must be killed.'

The animal heaved in a final convulsion, and, despite the rope, kicked out with all his last strength. A tablespoonful of black clot came forth, the trickling of red blood having ceased for some seconds. (*JO*, p. 85)

The knife slipped into the gash is Tess killing Alec, spreading red into the white ceiling at Sandbourne; the rope around the pig is the hangman's noose at Wintoncester (the ultimate sign of male power over a woman).

Jude has been expelled from the land by Farmer Troutham but he retains vestigial Wild Man qualities which accelerate his destruction. His overt sexualization (as opposed, for instance, to Gabriel Oak's covert sexualization; a counter-text in 1874 is a traded text in 1895; in a wider sense this is the change from Applegarth and the Junta to Burns and the dockers' strike) is the Wild Man's satyrean quality; his drinking, which produces the Nicene Creed recited in a pub, is the Wild Man's failing of telling the truth when he is drunk. This produces the novel's satirical centre, the source of its high farce, the story of Christ coming to Christminster. Jude is an orphan Christ-figure, fatherless (or motherless) after the *Götterdämmerung* of *Tess of the d'Urbervilles*. As Norman Holland shows,[4] the comparison of Jude and Christ is extensive. Jude starts out for Christminster from Marygreen, summoned by the conjured magic of a self-written sign saying 'Thither J. F.' and propelled by the agency of Vilbert, a rural quack-doctor whose origins are in the doctor who saves the Wild Man in the mummers' play. This salvation is less efficacious (except, finally, for Vilbert himself, who survives to marry Arabella). Marygreen is Mary for the Virgin Mary and green for Calvary, as in Mrs C. F. Alexander's enormously popular Victorian hymn lyric 'There is a green hill far away'. The surrogate birth from Gaia (remember that the 'real' Jude of the novel is motherless) thus inherently contains Christ's birth and martyrdom. Jude's physical appearance, dark, bearded and Levantine, is Christ-like and he plans to start his mission, like Christ, at thirty.

Jude begins by seeking the destructive transmutation of class by language which the centralized education system also prescribed for Tess:

> Ever since his first ecstasy or vision of Christminster and its possibilities, Jude had mediated much and curiously on the probable sort of process that was involved in turning the expressions of one language into those of another. He concluded that a grammar of the required tongue would contain, primarily, a rule, prescription, or clue of the nature of a secret cipher, which, once known, would enable him, by merely applying it, to change at will all words of his own speech into those of a foreign one. His childish idea was, in fact, a pushing to the extremity of mathematical precision what is everywhere known as Grimm's Law – an aggrandizement of rough rules to ideal completeness. Thus he assumed that the words of the required language were always to be found somewhere latent in the words of the given language by those who had the art to uncover them, such art being furnished by the books aforesaid.
>
> When, therefore, having noted that the packet bore the postmark of Christminster, he cut the string, opened the volumes, and turned to the Latin grammar, which chanced to come uppermost, he could hardly believe his eyes.

The book was an old one – thirty years old, soiled, scribbled wantonly over with a strange name in every variety of enmity to the letterpress, and marked at random with dates twenty years earlier than his own day. But this was not the cause of Jude's amazement. He learnt for the first time that there was no law of transmutation, as in his innocence he had supposed (there was, in some degree, but the grammarian did not recognize it), but that every word in both Latin and Greek was to be individually committed to memory at the cost of years of plodding. (*JO*, pp. 49–50)

Jude dies of ossification before he reaches the book's age. The work he needs to do in order to earn a living leads eventually to his death, turning his lungs to the stone which builds that structure. This is the true 'christian' revelation: each stone is, in effect, a working-class individual who has been worked to death to produce Christminster's ideological, as well as its physical, superstructure. Jude has tried to transmute language by learning the Latin and Greek irrelevances which constitute Christminster's runic symbols and freemasonry of education and which have really become the millionaires' sons' class indicators by a process of transmutation by money. A working-class man's attempt at transmutation (or christian transubstantiation) must necessarily be a trangression, and Jude's trangressions of the governing marriage contract indicate this. He transmutes marriage by separating from his wife and living with, and having children by, a woman to whom he is not married. This produces the death of his children, Sue's madness, and remarriage to Arabella while he is too drunk to know what is happening. When Jude dies, listening to the cheers that accompany honorary degrees being given to aristocrats because they are aristocrats, the physiological transmutation (once again a 'naturalization' of power relations) has taken place; Jude is transmuted not by money but the lack of it. Air has been changed to stone and he can no longer breathe. Structure takes in Man and survives; Man takes in Structure and dies. (It is impossible to ignore the implicit pun: 'taking in' is simultaneously a matter of deception and inhalation, the act of the reader consuming a naturalized fiction.)

Jude's education and his fictional life begin in the novel's very first sentence when Richard Phillotson leaves Marygreen and Jude, watching the ceremony, is cast as Christ in the temple: 'The schoolmaster was leaving the village, and everybody seemed sorry' (*JO*, p. 28). This is effectively an authorial self-valediction. Everything that follows is a dismantling of the didactic mode and narrative omniscience which Trollope celebrates in *An Autobiography* when he talks about his 'profound conviction' of his responsibilities as a teacher and the 'high character which [novelists] may claim to have earned by their grace, their honesty, and good teaching'.[5] For Trollope this is a 'natural' part of a world in which the values of the gentleman, *déclassé* or not, create a secure hegemonic discourse. In *The Last Chronicle of Barset*, as elsewhere, this is specifically linked to the hierarchy of the christian church. Here Archdeacon Grantly is speaking to Mr Crawley, the impoverished perpetual curate of Hogglestock:

> 'We stand,' said he, 'on the only perfect level on which such men can meet each other. We are both gentlemen.' 'Sir,' I said, rising also, 'from the bottom of my heart I agree with you. I could not have spoken such words; but coming from you who are rich to me who am poor, they are honourable to the one and comfortable to the other.'[6]

This behavioural code, which is (just about) the behavioural code of the novel as Hardy trades it (until now), makes an artificial synthesis of the economic determinants of class, blessed by the superstitious precepts of a religion which encourages just this deference and acceptance of hierarchical order. Christianity and the notion of the 'gentleman' overcome Crawley's poverty because Grantly invokes a code Crawley has 'chosen' to subscribe to because it somehow justifies his identity as a poor and marginal individual. This is the Master of Bibliol's language when he rejects Jude; Jude aspires to it but he can never speak it because christian belief can never overturn his immutable class position, just as it can never overturn the Master of Bibliol's class position. But it is the code Jude aspires to when he dreams of what is, for a working-class man, an impossible trespass into the world of the clerical gentleman, an implausible synthesis of clerical-spiritual and worldly success.

> And then he continued to dream, and thought he might become even a bishop by leading a pure, energetic, wise, Christian life. And what an example he would set! If his income were £5000

a year, he would give away £4500 in one form and other, and live sumptuously (for him) on the remainder. Well, on second thoughts, a bishop was absurd. He would draw the line at an archdeacon. Perhaps a man could be as good and as learned and as useful in the capacity of archdeacon as in that of bishop. Yet he thought of the bishop again.

'Meanwhile I will read, as soon as I am settled in Christminster, the books I have not been able to get hold of here: Livy, Tacitus, Herodotus, Aeschylus, Sophocles, Aristophanes –'

'Ha, ha, ha! Hoity-toity!' The sounds were expressed in light voices on the other side of the hedge, but he did not notice them. His thoughts went on:

' – Euripides, Plato, Aristotle, Lucretius, Epictetus, Seneca, Antoninus. Then I must master other things: the Fathers thoroughly; Bede and ecclesiastical history generally; a smattering of Hebrew – I only know the letters as yet – '

'Hoity-toity!'

' – but I can work hard. I have staying power in abundance, thank God! and it is that which tells. . . . Yes, Christminster shall be my Alma Mater; and I'll be her beloved 'son, in whom she shall be well pleased.'

In his deep concentration on these transactions of the future Jude's walk had slackened, and he was now standing quite still, looking at the ground as though the future were thrown thereon by a magic lantern. On a sudden something smacked him sharply in the ear, and he became aware that a soft cold substance had been flung at him, and had fallen at his feet.

A glance told him what it was – a piece of flesh, the characteristic part of a barrow-pig, which the countrymen used for greasing their boots, it being useless for any other purpose. Pigs were rather plentiful hereabout, being bred and fattened in large numbers in certain parts of North Wessex. (*JO*, pp. 57–8)

The pig's prick is a smack in the ear for the whole Arnoldian enterprise of ideological invention which Jude subscribes to so enthusiastically. It represents economic reality and the exploitation of biological essentialism which the remade culture of Jude's absurd name-dropping seeks to silence, the business of fattening pigs according to demand (remember that Little Father Time becomes a neo-Malthusian; labour requirements and the availability of somewhere to live can change, and there is nothing Jude and his family can do about it). But subscription to these values does not make Jude a gentleman and so it does not admit him to the Christminster structure which would supply meaning to the classical writers and their works. Consequently they remain virtually meaningless, simply a list of names which make up a shopping list for someone who will never have the money to go to the shop. This illustrates the context in which the text's hierarchy of discourses become (or rather, wilfully fail to become) meaningful. The supply of stable meaning to the reader becomes subject to the destabilizing volatility of Jude's life, to the simultaneous imperatives of a culture which does not acknowledge the material facts of Jude's life and a material life which cannot afford the culture. In building Christminster, Jude builds an incomprehensible château of text around himself, becoming trapped and eventually stifled by the structure Cytherea Graye was able to escape by fictional convention a quarter of a century earlier.

As a result the most consistent harmonizing discourse of *Jude the Obscure*'s narrative is (often extreme and grotesque) satire, which magnifies what Ingham describes as 'the ironic irrelevance of the literary text'.[7] This narrative distance seems almost to reflect the way Jude and Sue distance themselves from the world they have to live in by trying to enact bourgeois myths of autonomy without bourgeois money and power. A typical example of this comes in their discussion about visiting Wardour Castle:

> 'To-morrow is our grand day, you know. Where shall we go?'
> 'I have leave from three till nine. Wherever can we get to and come back from in that time. Not ruins, Jude – I don't care for them.'
> 'Well – Wardour Castle. And then we can do Fonthill if we like – all in the same afternoon.'
> 'Wardour is Gothic ruins – and I hate Gothic!'
> 'No. Quite otherwise. It is a classic building – Corinthian, I think; with a lot of pictures.'
> 'Ah – that will do, I like the sound of Corinthian. We'll go.'
> (*JO*, p. 156)

All Jude and Sue can 'choose' to 'see' are old buildings or ruins, precisely the structures and the history (whether physical or ideological) they are trying to escape. This is also all they can create. The transgressive image of the fair remains, but only as a pathetic travesty. Now Jude and Sue go there to exhibit miniatures of Christminster: at the Great Wessex Agricultural Show at Stoke-Barehills, a 'Model of Cardinal College, Christminster; by J. Fawley and S. F. M. Bridehead' (*JO*, p. 314), and three years later at Kennetbridge Christminster cakes.

Perhaps the most abrasive example of a satiric edge attacking both consumer and protagonist comes when the children are killed.

> On reaching the place and going upstairs [Sue] found that all was quiet in the children's room, and called to the landlady in timorous tones to please bring up the tea-kettle and something for their breakfast. This was perfunctorily done, and producing a couple of eggs she had brought with her she put them into the boiling kettle, and summoned Jude to watch them for the youngsters, while she went to call them, it being now about half-past eight o'clock.
>
> Jude stood bending over the kettle, with his watch in his hand, timing the eggs so that his back was turned to the little inner ·chamber where the children lay. A shriek from Sue suddenly caused him to start round. He saw that the door of the room, or rather closet – which had seemed to go heavily upon its hinges as she pushed it back – was open, and that Sue had sunk to the floor just within it. Hastening forward to pick her up he turned his eyes to the little bed spread on the boards; no children were there. He looked in bewilderment round the room. At the back of the door were fixed two hooks for hanging garments, and from these the forms of the two youngest children were suspended, by a piece of box-cord round each of their necks, while from a nail a few yards off the body of little Jude was hanging in a similar manner. An overturned chair was near the elder boy, and his glazed eyes were slanted into the room; but those of the girl and the baby boy were closed . . .
>
> The nearest surgeon came in, but, as Jude had inferred, his presence was superfluous. The children were past saving, for though their bodies were still barely cold it was conjectured that they had been hanging more than an hour. (*JO*, pp. 354–5)

The deaths are prefigured by the eggs: Jude is asked 'to watch them for the youngsters'. In the overthrown hierarchy of meaning now available in a text which has repudiated its own authority this is literally what happens. The conjuring narrator gives Jude an evil eye, as if his aspirations to be a christian priest were indications of black magic. This is the future thrown down on the ground at Marygreen by the narrator's apparently metaphorical magic lantern. As Hole shows,[8] a witch boiling eggs dedicated to a specific individual becomes a magical killing, a less common version of Susan Nunsuch's pin-sticking in *The Return of the Native*. A 1583 entry in the parish register at Wells-next-the-Sea blames the death of fourteen sailors on Mother Gabley, 'an execrable witch of Kings Lynn' because she was found to have been boiling eggs in a pail of water at the time. Then we see the eggs hatched and grown as we see the children, the 'triplet of little corpses', hung up like fowls in a shop. This 'grotesque prestidigitation' shows the essential difference between this and an early 'traded' satire like *The Hand of Ethelberta*. In *The Hand of Ethelberta* the victims are patently artificial figures like Neigh and Lord Mountclere. Here the narrative acts against its realistic central protagonists, cheating on them as the early countertexts cheat on the 'traded' texts, so that the elements of blatant artifice and satire are equally blatantly the product of a misperception of power relations by the reader expecting the text to conform to the 'rules' of 'classic realism'.

Principally the satire is directed at christianity. On its most pervasive level this accounts for *Jude the Obscure*'s quality of light. Christian iconography, revived in Victorian images like Holman Hunt's 'The Light of the World', makes Christ a source of light. Bullen argues[9] that Jude's obscurity is essentially visual, located in the darkness of his arrival at Christminster and the preponderance of naturally and artificially underlit scenes. In this sense the reader is forced to experience Jude's marginality and the incomplete vision Christminster allows him when he comes within its walls. Goode locates the obscurity in an allegorical comparison, from Gibbon, of the growth of an obscure religion which comes to threaten the Roman Empire:

> in this world, to be educated (led out) is to cease to be proletarian. It is a way out of the field to which there is no return. *Jude the Obscure* rallies the avant-garde in the name of the excluded, and it remains an event because that means it poses the question of knowledge and its ideology, knowledge as education and carnality, the wall and the garden of bourgeois order. For to open them out is to admit the obscure, and that is the decline and fall of an empire.[10]

The foundation of Rome was used to subvert the traded text of *Desperate Remedies*: now the counter-text, *de facto* in control of a traded text which has rendered itself unfit for consumption, has come full circle and Rome's decline is used to present an allegorized destruction of the non-obscure structures (Christminster is a bright, beatific vision until Jude gets there) of the obscure religion which superseded its paganism.

The two readings are, of course, complementary. In Hardy's ironic/ counter-textual iconography, taking christianity as a corrupt successor of sun and earth worship, Christ brings to the Christminster which rejects him the darkness and obscurity which follow the sunset of *Götterdämmerung* in *Tess of the d'Urbervilles*. In the antinomian hierarchy of discourses which now structure, or de-structure, the text, this allusive, non-realistic proposition supplies the meaning which anchors the 'traded' story of Jude trying to make his way in the world.

This is the basis on which Hardy uses the christian notion of transubstantiation, the translation of god to man to bread and wine placed at the centre of the cultural-linguistic transmutation Jude aspires to, as a destructive vehicle in his magical-material transmutation of man into stone. At Marygreen Jude is bread, living at his Aunt Drusilla's bakery and driving her delivery cart. Then he becomes wine in a satirically disruptive passage in which the decision to get drunk is presented as an abstract, intellectual proposition:

It was curious, he thought. What was he reserved for? He supposed he was not a sufficiently dignified person for suicide. Peaceful death abhorred him as a subject, and would not take him.

What could he do of a lower kind than self-extermination; what was there less noble, more in keeping with his present degraded position? He could get drunk. Of course that was it; he had forgotten. Drinking was the regular, stereotyped response of the despairing worthless. He began to see now why some men boozed at inns. (*JO*, p. 91)

When Jude meets Arabella again after her return from Australia he finds her working in a pub with a bar made up of confessional booths; the barmaid-priest dispenses sacraments and absolution behind what becomes a communion-rail. On a direct polemical level the statement is that getting drunk is a cheaper and less destructive way than christianity of seeing Christminster through an ecstatic haze. When Jude goes all the way to Kennetbridge to find the composer of a hymn, 'The Foot of the Cross,' the man is about to become a wine-merchant. He even tries to sell wine to Jude. It is pointed out that the composer 'was brought up and educated in Christminster traditions' (*JO*, p. 214). Christminster traditions turn out to mean that the fiction of christianity does not produce a christian transubstantiation; Jude goes to the foot of the cross and finds simply the wine of the communion service, not Christ's blood. For Jude transubstantiation has the opposite effect, which is perhaps the central tenet of the text's self-destruction. When he gets drunk and recites the creed in a pub his employers take away his 'character' in Christminster, removing his identity as they remove his capacity to earn a living. Here again the barmaid becomes a priest blessing communion wine, with the ill grace of a bourgeois clergyman ministering to a working class flock:

> The barmaid concocted the mixture with the bearing of a person compelled to live among animals of an inferior species, and the glass was handed across to Jude, who, having drunk the contents, stood up and began rhetorically, without hesitation:
> 'Credo in unum Deum, Patrem onmipotentem, Factorem coeli et terrae, visibilium omnium et invisibilium.'
> 'Good, excellent Latin!' cried one of the undergraduates, who, however, had not the slightest conception of a single word. (*JO*, p. 141)

The agency which takes Christ to Christminster is 'liberal humanist' education. He learns by experience (and so do Sue and Phillotson) the extent to which this is simply an ideological pretext. The acquisition of knowledge seems to order the traded text but in this case learning is obscuring, as the darkness when Jude comes to Christminster also indicates. Education appears to be the route to a discourse which will give coherence to Jude's 'series of seemings', but it turns out to be a conjuring process, a mechanical narrative strategy which creates Jude according to its precepts.

When Phillotson leaves Marygreen he leaves his piano behind in Aunt Drusilla's fuel-house. Jude has been his voluntary pupil at night school. Unplayed, the piano remains the icon of Jude's hero-worship and it poses the question: is it, and is Phillotson's plan of study and Christminster followed by ordination, a part-automaton which can be played by an aspirant; or is it just potential firewood? The departing pianist (who never learned to play properly, as he never learns to in life) leaves Jude a scholastic machine he does not himself understand. Jude learns, but without the organized structure of a day school he effectively teaches himself a pretext without the context of power relations which might otherwise rob his knowledge of its 'inherent' value. Instead his context for learning is a beatific vision of Christminster. Consequently his reading lists assume the bizarre quality of the meaningless names he recites just before Arabella throws the pig's prick at him. Eventually, inexorably, this brings him into a direct personal conflict with Christminster's power structures. Phillotson, by contrast, is brought into lesser conflict with the lesser structures of institutionalized education and eventually sent back to his class and place of origin (with christian permission, naturally; the new parson at Marygreen lets him return to his old job after his expulsion from Shaston) to carry on the process. Again this is presented in terms of anti-christian satire, perhaps most clearly in the image of the churchwarden's head going through Samaria when he is hit with a map of Palestine in the fight scene at Phillotson's resignation.

Jude's decision to learn a building trade in order to go to Christminster is again part of the fatalistic conjuring which begins with his family curse. Here he meets a witch in church:

> As another outcome of this change of groove he visited on Sundays all the churches within a walk, and deciphered the Latin inscriptions on fifteenth-century brasses and tombs. On one of these pilgrimages he met with a hunchbacked old woman of great intelligence, who read everything she could lay her hands on, and she told him more yet of the romantic charms of the city of light and lore. Thither he resolved as firmly as ever to go.
>
> But how live in that city? At present he had no income at all. He had no trade or calling of any dignity or stability whatever on which he could subsist while carrying out an intellectual labour which might spread over many years.
>
> What was most required by citizens? Food, clothing, and shelter. An income from any work in preparing the first would be too meagre; for making the second he felt a distaste; the preparation of the third requisite he felt inclined to. They built in a city; therefore he would learn to build. He thought of his unknown uncle, his cousin Susanna's father, an ecclesiastical worker in

metal, and somehow medieval art in any material was a trade for which he had rather a fancy. He could not go far wrong in following his uncle's footsteps, and engaging himself awhile with the carcasses that contained the scholar souls. (*JO*, p. 54)

His reasoning is flawed by the narrative 'spell'. The work of an ecclesiastical mason working on the scholar souls' mausoleum has nothing to do with building shelters for the living. Instead he will be renovating shelters for the ideological structure which values these dead bodies more than the living workfolk and small traders, who remain unsheltered. Ultimately this reproduces the lack of shelter which gives Jude the chill that accelerates his last illness. It also runs counter to, and renders almost pointless, the sense of solidarity which leads him to join the Artizan's Mutual Improvement Society at Aldbrickham. Although he is a general tradesman by comparison to Christminster's specialists, Jude's skills are essentially decorative rather than structural. Nothing he does is of real use to anyone (except the dead). Neither his art nor Sue's father's is medieval because this is the late nineteenth century. Even if the buildings he works on are originally medieval, his work is still part of a Victorian impersonation, the specious appeal of a culture of economic conquest to an architectural model of 'natural' historical authority also employed by the new church builders at Marygreen. Jude's lungs show the real exchange: man is denatured to maintain the mausoleum's semblance of 'natural' authority. This failure to tell the living from the dead, or to seek a future life only in a hierarchical past, leads to a death in which Jude almost turns into one of the statues he saw when he first came to Christminster.

It is significant also that Jude's religious ambitions seem to lack any appetite for spiritual experience. As a grown man he is principally seeking an ethical context for altruism and mutual self-improvement. But he continues to do this in terms of the theological structure which militates against his progress and so the narrator satirically undercuts him. In the first chapter of 'At Melchester' his 'new idea' is presented in these terms:

It was a new idea – the ecclesiastical and altruistic life as distinct from the intellectual and emulative life. A man could preach and do good to his fellow-creatures without taking double-firsts in the schools of Christminster, or having anything but ordinary knowledge. The old fancy which had led to the culminating vision of the bishopric had not been an ethical or theological enthusiasm at all, but a mundane ambition masquerading in a surplice. (*JO*, p. 148)

And the chapter ends with another satiric flourish at Jude's expense. Again we have names and texts sanctified and made fit for consumption by Christminster, now those of the Tractarian revivalists:

The lodgings he took near the Close Gate would not have disgraced a curate, the rent representing a higher percentage on his wages than mechanics of any sort usually care to pay. His combined bed and sitting room was furnished with framed photographs of the rectories and deaneries at which his landlady had lived as trusted servant in her time, and the parlour downstairs bore a clock on the mantelpiece inscribed to the effect that it was presented to the same serious-minded woman by her fellow-servants on the occasion of her marriage. Jude added to the furniture of his room by unpacking photographs of the ecclesiastical carvings and monuments that he had executed with his own hands; and he was deemed a satisfactory acquisition as tenant of the vacant apartment.

He found an ample supply of theological books in the city bookshops, and with these his studies were recommenced in a different spirit and direction from his former course. As a relaxation from the Fathers and such stock works as Paley and Butler, he read Newman, Pusey, and many other modern lights. He hired a harmonium, set it up in his lodging, and practised chants thereon, single and double. (*JO*, pp. 154–5)

In effect he takes his own mausoleum around with him. This is also a piece of sharp social comment on the Victorian bourgeois commoditization of death and the pre-purchasing of memorials in new necropoli like Kensal Green and Highgate. Gaia's religion celebrated fertility, renewal and life; Christ's celebrates death and suffering, so in this sense it is the only appropriate religion for a working-class man or woman faced with a life lived in the face of exploitative work practices and a divisive social structure. Sue and Phillotson talk about Mill and the Utilitarian ideal, but Jude's life makes it very clear that this is the false indulgence of a myth of autonomy. The only utility which bears on these characters is their utility to Christminster's material-ideological structure.

Jude the Obscure's topographical structure, in which the characters wander in urban wildernesses as Tess has been sent to wander in a rural one (again the transition from 'field' to 'ville'), represents a distributive chain in the industrial process of reproducing and trading ideology. It is very much an imperial model. The allusive threat to the Roman empire by Jude's obscurity is thus equally a threat to the buoyant British empire, at this historical moment keeping Christminster in place economically and producing a jingoistic, anti-socialist popular culture by the military and economic rape of foreign countries. Christminster is obviously the centre of the empire. Marygreen is the furthest outpost we see, like Hintock an intaking from the wilderness. The rebuilt church there represents a re-imposition of order, but the village is sufficiently marginal to allow a renegade like Phillotson to teach there, like one of Kipling's casualties of empire. Shaston, Aldbrickham and Alfredston are ranged between. Melchester is the main distributive centre, the place where missionaries and imperial civil servants get their training.

In *Jude the Obscure* it becomes possible for the first time for the marriage contract to be legally broken. Partly, as I have already pointed out, this makes the novel part of a general trend in which the easing of divorce law and the Woman Question become central. Because the authority of marriage as the structure that maintains the Structure is broken, or at least seen as breakable, a governing fictional discourse which previously gave crucial support to the bourgeois novel's pretext of 'naturalness' and textual authority becomes openly discursive. In *Jude the Obscure* this change is enacted at the most fundamental level; in Hardy's fictional revolution the introduction of divorce follows the elemental breaking of the earth's bond to the sun. This is not the transgression, however dangerous, of a safe mode which Hardy offers in the traded accounts of Aeneas Manston's bigamy or Sergeant Troy's philandering. Women's potential for pseudo-active choice in *Jude the Obscure* is less, not more, liberated as a result of woman's new ostensible freedom to choose. But this freedom, like Jude's 'freedom' to choose a trade and sell his wage-labour, consists of being forced to face determining definitions of gender without the 'naturalizing' mediation of an indissoluble marriage contract.

When Jude and Sue live as man and wife outside contract, they are still forced by rules of propriety (really by the exigencies of their unstable class position, which enforces propriety on them) to 'pass' as man and wife, so that their life together increasingly becomes an alien, and alienating, impersonation. Each character's false liberation, one in terms of class and the other of gender, is inherently part of the other's in this novel, as the conjuror's determination of their mutual fascination shows. As Boumelha points out, '*Jude the Obscure* is unique in its siting of Jude and Sue at the conjuncture of class and sexual oppression'.[11] She goes on to say:

> For Sue, mind and body, intellect and sexuality, are in a complex and disturbing interdependence, given iconic representation in her twin deities. Apollo and Venus, which she transmutes for Miss Fontover – prefiguring the later collapse of her intellect and repudiation of her sexuality – into the representative of religious orthodoxy, St Peter, and the repentant sexual sinner, St Mary Magdalen.[12]

The women in the dormitory at Melchester no longer have the instinctual sexuality of the women in the sleeping-room at Talbothays dairy. Instead they are being trained in a new, discursive ideology of womanhood. The modal security (or imprisonment) of Cytherea Graye and Bathsheba Everdene's learning femininity by aspiring to marriageability is no longer subverted by the location of sexuality in a part-concealed counter-text; now the removal of the security of the château means that female identity becomes the sum of its parts. Arabella protects herself from this by creating her own narrative of feminine deception (falsifying dimples and pregnancy, getting a man to marry her by getting him too drunk to resist), accepting from the first her powerlessness and adopting strategies which ultimately reinforce the power relations acting on her but which at least retain a limited autonomy for her own lifetime. This narrative, or this language, necessarily exploits Jude simply because he is a man. But Sue's language of identity is at least in part revealed to Jude, as they attempt an 'honest' and 'open' relationship between the sexes. In this sense Sue becomes something to be construed, ultimately another part of the impossible transmutation process. As Ingham argues:

> because of its contradictions and ambiguities [*Jude the Obscure*] interrogates traditional images of women by allowing new read-

ings of them to conflict with the old. Blatantly the individual
subject is not an entity, as the kaleidoscope of critical Sue
(mis)construing indicates.[13]

But these new readings are all determined by the un-overthrown
power relations under which they are created; and so eventually
Sue's bid for autonomy and intellectual-emotional honesty collapses
and she is driven, through the narrative château Jude has unwittingly built around both of them, to the greater château of
Christminster's exploded christianity. In the end autonomy, or
any liberation which leaves Christminster standing, offers only the
'voluntary' sanctuary of an acceptance of ideological structure; or
death. Little Father Time (another Jude, of course) is the magical-
emblematic image of the future which lies beyond this, 'the coming
universal wish not to live' (*JO*, p. 356).

This conclusion is equally an authorial admission of the impossibility of the necessary revolution coming from any bid at 'autonomy'
by the writer of a bourgeois fiction. Why bother? The 'near thirty
years' of Jude's life also measure the period of Hardy's making of
prose fictions; and so the subversive enterprise ends.

He had slipped down, and lay flat. A second glance caused her to
start, and she went to the bed. His face was quite white, and
gradually becoming rigid. She touched his fingers; they were
cold, though his body was still warm. She listened at his chest.
All was still within. The bumping of near thirty years had ceased.
(*JO*, p. 425)

Notes

INTRODUCTION

1. Penny Boumelha, *Thomas Hardy and Women: Sexual Ideology and Narrative Form*, (Brighton, 1982).
2. George Wotton, *Thomas Hardy: Towards a Materialist Criticism*, (Totowa, New Jersey, 1985).
3. John Goode, *Thomas Hardy: The Offensive Truth*, (Oxford, 1988).
4. Patricia Ingham, *Thomas Hardy*, (Hemel Hempstead, 1989).
5. Peter Widdowson, *Hardy in History: A Study in Literary Sociology*, (London, 1989).
6. Wotton, p. 213.
7. Widdowson, p. 196.
8. Widdowson, p. 44.
9. Pierre Macherey, *A Theory of Literary Production*, (tr. Geoffrey Wall), (London, 1978), pp. 56–7).
10. R. G. Cox (ed.), *Thomas Hardy: The Critical Heritage*, (London, 1970), p. 92.
11. George Moore, Introduction to Emile Zola, *Piping Hot*, (London, 1885), p. xvi.
12. N. N. Feltes, *Modes of Production of Victorian Novels*, (Chicago and London, 1986), p. 63.
13. See Widdowson, p. 138 et al.
14. Guinevere L. Griest, *Mudie's Circulating Library and the Victorian Novel*, (Newton Abbot, 1970), p. 208.
15. Goode, p. 65.
16. Roger Ebbatson, *Hardy: The Margin of the Unexpressed*, (forthcoming), MS p. 145.
17. Ebbatson MS, pp. 158–9.
18. George Henry Lewes, *The Principles of Success in Literature*, (London, 1865), p. 1.
19. Henry James, 'Far From the Madding Crowd', *Nation*, XIX, (December 24, 1874), p. 423 in Griest, pp. 117–8.
20. Evelyn Waugh, *Work Suspended and Other Stories*, (London, 1982), p. 128.
21. Roy Morrell, *Thomas Hardy: The Will and the Way*, (Kuala Lumpur, 1965), p. 38.
22. Ingham, *Thomas Hardy*, p. 27.
23. Widdowson, pp. 38–9, 197 et al.
24. Dorothy E. Smith, 'Femininity as Discourse', in Leslie G. Roman, Linda K. Christian Smith with Elizabeth Ellsworth (eds), *Becoming Feminine: The Politics of Popular Culture*, (Lewes, East Sussex and Philadelphia, 1988), pp. 41–2.

25. William Makepeace Thackeray, *The Letters and Private Papers of William Makepeace Thackeray*, (coll. and ed. Gordon Ray), (London, 1946), IV, p. 161 in Griest, p. 140.
26. Ingham, *Thomas Hardy*, p. 12.
27. Patricia Stubbs, *Women and Fiction: Feminism and the Novel 1880–1920*, (Brighton, 1979), p. xi.
28. John Lucas, *The Literature of Change: Studies in the Nineteenth-Century Provincial Novel*, (Brighton and New York, 1977), p. 147.
29. Tony Tanner, *Adultery in the Novel*, (Baltimore and London, 1979), p. 15.
30. Susan M. Blake, *Law of Marriage*, (Chichester, 1982), p. 3.
31. Ingham, *Thomas Hardy*, p. 61.
32. Edmund Gosse, 'The Tyranny of the Novel', *National Review*, XIX, (April 1892), p. 164.
33. See Lucas, pp. 192–207.
34. Timothy Hands, *Thomas Hardy: Distracted Preacher?*, (London, 1989), p. 66.
35. Peter Stallybrass and Allon White, *The Politics and Poetics of Transgression*, (London, 1986).
36. Lionel Johnson, *The Art of Thomas Hardy*, (London, 1894), p. 56.
37. Ebbatson, p. 105.
38. Barbara Kerr, *Bound to the Soil: A Social History of Dorset 1750–1918*, (Wakefield, 1975), p. 11.
39. Marlene Springer, *Hardy's Use of Allusion*, (London, 1983), pp. 16–17.
40. Gillian Beer, *Darwin's Plots: Evolutionary Narrative in Darwin, George Eliot and Nineteenth Century Fiction*, (London, 1983), p. 257.
41. J. B. Bullen, *The Expressive Eye: Fiction and Perception in the Work of Thomas Hardy*, (Oxford, 1986), p. 192 et al.
42. J. Hillis Miller, *Fiction and Repetition: Seven English Novels*, (Oxford, 1982), p. 152.
43. Anthony Trollope, *Doctor Thorne*, (London, 1981), p. 12.
44. See Basil F. L. Clarke, *Church Builders of the Nineteenth Century*, (Newton Abbot, 1969), p. 32.
45. Louis Althusser, 'Ideology and Ideological State Apparatuses', in *Lenin and Philosophy and Other Essays*, (tr. Ben Brewster), (London, 1972), p. 155.

1   DESPERATE REMEDIES

1. Robert Gittings, *Young Thomas Hardy*, (London, 1975), p. 205.
2. Guinevere L. Griest, *Mudie's Circulating Library and the Victorian Novel*, (Newton Abbot, 1970), p. 61.
3. Peter Widdowson, *Hardy in History: A Study of Literary Sociology*, (London, 1989), p. 219.
4. Anthony Trollope, *An Autobiography*, (Oxford and New York, 1980).
5. T. S. Eliot, *After Strange Gods: A Primer of Modern Heresy*, (London, 1934), p. 55.
6. Pierre Macherey, *A Theory of Literary Production*, (tr. Geoffrey Wall), (London, 1978), p. 31.

7. Patricia Stubbs, *Woman and Fiction: Feminism and the Novel 1880–1920*, (Brighton, 1979), p. 6.
8. Roger Ebbatson, *Hardy: The Margin of the Unexpressed*, (forthcoming), MS p. 10.
9. Patricia Ingham, *Thomas Hardy*, (Hemel Hempstead, 1989), p. 33.
10. Roy Morrell, *Thomas Hardy: The Will and the Way*, (Kuala Lumpur, 1965), p. 46.
11. Griest, p. 121, refers to comments to this effect in Geraldine Jewsbury's reader's reports for Bentley between 1860 and 1875.
12. Ebbatson, p. 16.
13. Marlene Springer, *Hardy's Use of Allusion*, (London, 1983), p. 26.
14. Geoffrey of Monmouth, *Historia Britonum*, Bk I, Ch. xvi.
15. C. J. P. Beatty, Introduction, Thomas Hardy, *Desperate Remedies*, (London, 1975), p. 19.
16. I am grateful to Adrian Poole for suggesting this connection.

2 FAR FROM THE MADDING CROWD

1. Quoted by Rosalind Coward, *Patriarchal Precedents: Sexuality and Social Relations*, (London, 1983), p. 97.
2. Peter Widdowson, *Hardy in History: A Study of Literary Sociology*, (London, 1989), p. 49.
3. Terry Eagleton, *Walter Benjamin or Towards a Revolutionary Criticism*, (London, 1981), p. 127.
4. T. S. Eliot, *After Strange Gods: a Primer of Modern Heresy*, (London, 1934), p. 56.
5. Penny Boumelha, *Thomas Hardy and Women: Sexual Ideology and Narrative Form*, (Brighton, 1982), p. 41.
6. Widdowson, p. 136.
7. Patricia Ingham, *Thomas Hardy*, (Hemel Hempstead, 1989), p. 18.
8. Christina Hole, *English Folklore*, (London, 1941), p. 32.
9. Merryn Williams, *Thomas Hardy and Rural England*, (London, 1972), p. 17.
10. John Goode, *Thomas Hardy: The Offensive Truth*, (Oxford, 1988), pp. 24–5.
11. J. B. Bullen, *The Expressive Eye: Fiction and Perception in the Work of Thomas Hardy*, (Oxford, 1986), p. 68.
12. George Wotton, *Thomas Hardy: Towards a Materialist Criticism*, (Totowa, New Jersey, 1985), p. 130.
13. Edward Waring, *Ghosts and Legends of the Dorset Countryside*, (Tisbury, Wilts., 1977), pp. 12–13.
14. Alex Helm, *The English Mummers' Play*, (Woodbridge, Suffolk, 1981), p. 6.
15. Richard Bernheimer, *Wild Men in the Middle Ages*, (Cambridge, Mass., 1952), p. 42.
16. A. S. Parke, 'The Folklore of Sixpenny Handley', *Folklore*, 74, (1963).
17. Bernheimer, pp. 19–20.
18. Helm, p. 19.

19. 'A Conversation Between Thomas Hardy and William Archer', *The Critic*, (New York, 1901).
20. Barbara Kerr, *Bound to the Soil: A Social History of Dorset 1750–1918*, (Wakefield, 1975), pp. 207–24.
21. *Brewer's Dictionary of Phrase and Fable*, (London, 1981), p. 1139.
22. Ingham, *Thomas Hardy*, p. 34.

3   THE HAND OF ETHELBERTA

1. John Goode, *Thomas Hardy: The Offensive Truth*, (Oxford, 1988), p. 34.
2. Goode, p. 33.
3. Goode, p. 37.
4. Patricia Ingham, *Thomas Hardy* (Hemel Hempstead, 1989), p. 59.
5. Peter Widdowson, *Hardy in History: A Study in Literary Sociology*, (London, 1989), p. 176.
6. Merryn Williams, *Thomas Hardy and Rural England*, (London, 1972), pp. 51–2.
7. Richard D. Altick, *The English Common Reader: A Social History of the Mass Reading Public 1800–1900*, (Chicago, 1957), p. 83.
8. Peter Stallybrass and Allon White, *The Politics and Poetics of Transgression*, (London, 1986), p. 152.
9. Stallybrass and White, p. 155; see D. Hudson, *Munby, Man of Two Worlds: The Life and Diaries of Arthur J. Munby*, (London, 1972).
10. Penny Boumelha, *Thomas Hardy and Women: Sexual Ideology and Narrative Form*, (Brighton, 1982), pp. 41–2.
11. Widdowson, p. 151.

4   THE RETURN OF THE NATIVE

1. D. H. Lawrence, 'Study of Thomas Hardy', in *Phoenix*, (London, 1936), p. 413.
2. John Paterson, 'An Attempt at Grand Tragedy', in R. P. Draper (ed.), *Hardy: The Tragic Novels*, (London, 1975), p. 209.
3. Lawrence, p. 415.
4. Mikhail Bakhtin, quoted in Peter Stallybrass and Allon White, *The Politics and Poetics of Transgression*, (London, 1986), p. 209.
5. Christina Hole, *English Folklore*, (London, 1940), p. 67.
6. Hole, *English Folklore*, pp. 112–3.
7. George Wotton, *Thomas Hardy: Towards a Materialist Criticism* (Totowa, New Jersey, 1985), p. 112.
8. John Goode, *Thomas Hardy: The Offensive Truth*, (Oxford, 1988), p. 59.
9. Robert W. Malcolmson, *Popular Recreations in English Society 1700–1850*, (Cambridge, 1973), p. 31.
10. Wotton, p. 118.
11. Catherine Belsey, *Critical Practice*, (London, 1980), p. 70.
12. George Henry Lewes, 'The Course of Modern Thought', *Fortnightly Review*, 27, (1877), p. 321.

13. Wotton, p. 115.
14. Penny Boumelha, *Thomas Hardy and Women: Sexual Ideology and Narrative Form*, (Brighton, 1982), p. 48.
15. Rosalind Coward, *Patriarchal Precedents: Sexuality and Social Relations*, (London, 1983), p. 67.
16. Christina Hole, *Witchcraft in England*, (London, 1945), pp. 31–2.
17. Hole, p. 34.
18. Patricia Stubbs, *Women and Fiction: Feminism and the Novel 1880–1920*, (Brighton, 1979), pp. 58–87.

5 A LAODICEAN

1. Alfred Jarry, *Ubu Roi, Ubu Cocu, Ubu Enchaîné*, (Paris, 1978), p. 187.
2. J. I. M. Stewart, *Thomas Hardy*, (London, 1971), p. 157.
3. William Lyon Phelps, *Autobiography, with Letters*, (New York, 1939), p. 391.
4. Michael Millgate, *Thomas Hardy: His Career as a Novelist*, (London, 1971), p. 216.
5. The Revelation of St John the Divine, Ch. 3, vs 14–19.
6. Timothy Hands, *Thomas Hardy: Distracted Preacher?*, (London, 1989), p. 57.
7. Barbara Kerr, *Bound to the Soil: A Social History of Dorset 1750–1918*, (Wakefield, 1975), p. 233.
8. Valentine Cunningham, *Everywhere Spoken Against: Dissent in the Victorian Novel*, (Oxford, 1975), p. 39.

6 THE MAYOR OF CASTERBRIDGE

1. John Goode, *Thomas Hardy: The Offensive Truth*, (Oxford, 1988), p. 79.
2. Barbara Kerr, *Bound to the Soil: A Social History of Dorset 1750–1918*, (Wakefield, 1975), p. 243.
3. Kerr, pp. 188–191.
4. Richard Bernheimer, *The Wild Man in the Middle Ages*, (Cambridge, Mass., 1952), pp. 73–4.
5. Peter Stallybrass and Allon White, *The Politics and Poetics of Transgression*, (London, 1986), pp. 28–9.
6. Robert Malcolmson, *Popular Recreations in English Society, 1700–1850*, (Cambridge, 1973), p. 151.
7. Roger Ebbatson, *Hardy: The Margin of the Unexpressed*, (forthcoming), MS pp. 85–6.
8. Bernheimer, p. 71.
9. Bernheimer, p. 25.
10. George Wotton, *Thomas Hardy: Towards a Materialist Criticism*, (Totowa, New Jersey, 1985), pp. 63–4.
11. John Vernon, *Money and Fiction: Literary Realism in the Nineteenth and Early Twentieth Centuries*, (Ithaca, 1984), p. 7.
12. Christina Hole, *Witchcraft in England*, (London, 1945), p. 98.

13. Edward Waring, *Ghosts and Legends of the Dorset Countryside*, (Tisbury, Wilts., 1977), pp. 38–9.
14. Waring, p. 47.
15. Hole, *Witchcraft in England*, p. 151.
16. John Lucas, *The Literature of Change: Studies in the Nineteenth-Century Provincial Novel*, (Brighton and New York, 1977), p. 159.
17. Christina Hole, *English Folklore*, (London, 1940), p. 24.
18. Bernheimer, p. 120.

7   THE WOODLANDERS

1. Michael Millgate, *Thomas Hardy: His Career as a Novelist*, (London, 1971), p. 249.
2. John Lucas, *The Literature of Change: Studies in the Nineteenth-Century Provincial Novel*, (Brighton and New York, 1977), p. 168.
3. Barbara Kerr, *Bound to the Soil: A Social History of Dorset, 1750–1918*, (Wakefield, 1975), p. 13.
4. Kerr, p. 14.
5. J. S. Mill, 'On Liberty', *Collected Works*, XVIII, (London, 1977), p. 262; see John Goode, *Thomas Hardy: The Offensive Truth*, (Oxford, 1988), p. 151.
6. Christina Hole, *English Folklore*, (London, 1940), p. 86.
7. Hole: *English Folklore*, p. 89.
8. Richard Bernheimer, *The Wild Man in the Middle Ages*, (Cambridge, Mass., 1952), p. 14.
9. Alex Helm, *The English Mummers' Play*, (Woodbridge, Suffolk, 1981), p. 45.
10. Mary Jacobus, 'Tree and Machine: *The Woodlanders*', in Dale Kramer (ed.), *Critical Approaches to the Fiction of Thomas Hardy*, (London, 1979), p. 119.
11. Gillian Beer, *Darwin's Plots: Evolutionary Narrative in Darwin, George Eliot and Nineteenth Century Fiction*, (London, 1983), p. 240.
12. Jacobus, p. 117.
13. Kerr, p. 153.

8   TESS OF THE D'URBERVILLES

1. Penny Boumelha, *Thomas Hardy and Women: Sexual Ideology and Narrative Form*, (Brighton, 1982), p. 132.
2. Mary Jacobus, 'Tess: The Making of a Pure Woman', in Susan Lipshitz (ed.), *Tearing the Veil: Essays of Femininity*, (London, 1978), pp. 79–80.
3. Richard Bernheimer, *The Wild Man in the Middle Ages*, (Cambridge, Mass., 1952), p. 129.
4. Merryn Williams, *Thomas Hardy and Rural England*, (London, 1972), p. 25.
5. Edward Waring, *Ghosts and Legends of the Dorset Countryside*, (Tisbury, Wilts., 1977), p. 49.

6. John Aubrey, *Aubrey's Brief Lives*, (ed. Oliver Lawson Dick), (London, 1972), p. 90.
7. Tony Tanner, 'Colour and Movement in *Tess of the d'Urbervilles*', Critical Quarterly, 10, (Autumn 1968).
8. See particularly Friederich Max Müller, *An Introduction to the Science of Religion*, (London, 1873).
9. Barbara Kerr, *Bound to the Soil: A Social History of Dorset 1750–1918*, (Wakefield, 1975), p. 184.
10. Bernheimer, p. 157.
11. Roger Ebbatson, *Hardy: The Margin Unexpressed*, (forthcoming), MS p. 150.
12. George Wotton, *Thomas Hardy: Towards a Materialist Criticism*, (Totowa, New Jersey, 1985), p. 199.
13. John Goode, *Thomas Hardy: The Offensive Truth*, (Oxford, 1988), p. 117.
14. Kerr, p. 57.
15. J. B. Bullen, *The Expressive Eye: Fiction and Perception in the Work of Thomas Hardy*, (Oxford, 1986), p. 192.
16. Williams, p. 59.
17. Peter Stallybrass and Allon White, *The Politics and Poetics of Transgression*, (London, 1986), p. 179.
18. See Daniel P. Mannix, *Freaks: We Who Are Not as Others*, (San Francisco, 1990), pp. 83–93.
19. Bullen, p. 219.

9 JUDE THE OBSCURE

1. R. G. Cox (ed.) *Thomas Hardy: The Critical Heritage* (London, 1970), pp. 251–61.
2. Patricia Ingham, Introduction, Thomas Hardy, *Jude the Obscure*, (Oxford, 1985), p. xv.
3. John Goode, *Thomas Hardy: The Offensive Truth*, (Oxford, 1988), p. 140.
4. Norman Holland, '*Jude the Obscure*: Hardy's Symbolic Indictment of Christianity', *Nineteenth Century Fiction*, (June 1954).
5. Anthony Trollope, *An Autobiography*, (Oxford and New York, 1980), p. 217.
6. Anthony Trollope, *The Last Chronicle of Barset*, (London, 1977).
7. Patricia Ingham, Introduction, *Thomas Hardy, Jude the Obscure*, (Oxford, 1985), pp. xvi/ii.
8. Christina Hole, *Witchcraft in England*, (London, 1940), pp. 41–2.
9. J. B. Bullen, *The Expressive Eye: Fiction and Perception in the Work of Thomas Hardy*, (Oxford, 1986), p. 234.
10. Goode, p. 145.
11. Penny Boumelha, *Thomas Hardy and Women: Sexual Ideology and Narrative Form*, (Brighton, 1982), p. 137.
12. Boumelha, pp. 146–7.
13. Patricia Ingham, *Thomas Hardy*, (Hemel Hempstead, 1989), p. 78.

Bibliography

Althusser, Louis. *Lenin and Philosophy and Other Essays*, (tr. Ben Brewster), (London, 1972).

Altick, Richard D. *The English Common Reader: A Social History of the Mass Reading Public 1800–1900*, (Chicago, 1957).

Aubrey, John. *Aubrey's Brief Lives*, (ed. Oliver Lawson Dick), (London, 1972).

Beer, Gillian. *Darwin's Plots: Evolutionary Narrative in Darwin, George Eliot and Nineteenth Century Fiction*, (London, 1983).

Belsey, Catherine. *Critical Practice*, (London, 1980).

Bernheimer, Richard. *The Wild Man in the Middle Ages*, (Cambridge, Mass., 1952).

Blake, Susan M. *Law of Marriage*, (Chichester, 1982).

Boumelha, Penny. *Thomas Hardy and Women: Sexual Ideology and Narrative Form*, (Brighton, 1982).

Bullen, J.B. *The Expressive Eye: Fiction and Perception in the Work of Thomas Hardy*, (Oxford, 1986).

Chambers, E. K. *The English Folk Play*, (Oxford, 1933).

Clarke, Basil F. L. *Church Builders of the Nineteenth Century*, (Newton Abbot, 1969).

Coward, Rosalind. *Patriarchal Precedents*: Sexuality and Social Relations, (London, Boston and Melbourne, 1983).

Cox, R. G. (ed.). *Thomas Hardy: The Critical Heritage*, (London and New York, 1970).

Cunningham, Valentine. *Everywhere Spoken Against: Dissent in the Victorian Novel*, (Oxford, 1975).

Draper, R. P. (ed.). *Hardy: The Tragic Novels*, (London, 1975).

Draper, R. P. and Ray, Martin S. *An Annotated Critical Bibliography of Thomas Hardy*, (New York and London, 1989).

Eagleton, Terry. Introduction, Thomas Hardy, *Jude the Obscure*, (London, 1974).

_____ *Walter Benjamin or Towards a Revolutionary Criticism*, (London, 1981).

Ebbatson, Roger. *Hardy: The Margin of the Unexpressed*, (forthcoming).

Eliot, T. S. *After Strange Gods: A Primer of Modern Heresy*, (London, 1934).

Feltes, Norman N. *Modes of Production of Victorian Novels*, (Chicago and London, 1986).

Gittings, Robert. *Young Thomas Hardy*, (London, 1975).

_____ Introduction, Thomas Hardy, *The Hand of Ethelberta*, (London, 1975).

_____ *The Older Hardy*, (London, 1978).

Goode, John. *Thomas Hardy: The Offensive Truth*, (Oxford, 1988).

Griest, Guinevere L. *Mudie's Circulating Library and the Victorian Novel*, (Newton Abbot, 1970).

Hands, Timothy. *Thomas Hardy: Distracted Preacher?*, (London, 1989).

Hardy, Barbara. Introduction, Thomas Hardy, *A Laodicean*, (London, 1975).

Hardy, Thomas. *Desperate Remedies*, (London, 1975).
_____ *Far From the Madding Crowd*, (London, 1965).
_____ *The Hand of Ethelberta*, (London, 1975).
_____ *The Return of the Native*, (London, 1974).
_____ *A Laodicean*, (London, 1975).
_____ *The Mayor of Casterbridge*, (Oxford, 1987).
_____ *The Woodlanders*, (London, 1967).
_____ *Tess of the d'Urbervilles*, (London, 1978).
_____ *Jude the Obscure*, (London, 1974).
_____ *The Life of Thomas Hardy, 1840–1928 by Florence Emily Hardy*, (London, 1965).
_____ *Selected Poems*, (ed. David Wright), (London, 1978).
_____ 'The Dorsetshire Labourer', *Longman's Magazine*, (vol. II, 1883).
_____ 'A Conversation Between Thomas Hardy and William Archer', *The Critic*, (New York, 1901).
Helm, Alex. *The English Mummers' Play*, (Woodbridge, Suffolk, 1981).
Hole, Christina. *English Folklore*, (London, 1940).
_____ *Witchcraft in England*, (London, 1945).
Holland, Norman. *'Jude the Obscure*: Hardy's Symbolic Indictment of Christianity', *Nineteenth Century Fiction*, (1954).
Hudson, D. *Munby, Man of Two Worlds: The Life and Diaries of Arthur J. Munby*, (London, 1972).
Hutchins, J. *The History and Antiquities of Dorset*, (London, 1870).
Ingham, Patricia. Introduction, Thomas Hardy, *Jude the Obscure*, (Oxford, 1985).
_____ *Thomas Hardy*, (Hemel Hempstead, 1989).
Jacobus, Mary. 'Tess: The Making of a Pure Woman', Susan Lipshitz (ed.), *Tearing the Veil: Essays on Femininity*, (London, 1978).
_____ 'Tree and Machine: The Woodlanders' in Kramer (ed.), *Critical Approaches to the Fiction of Thomas Hardy*.
Johnson, Lionel. *The Art of Thomas Hardy*, (London, 1894).
Kerr, Barbara. *Bound to the Soil: A Social History of Dorset 1750–1918*, (Wakefield, 1975).
Lawrence, D. H. 'A Study of Thomas Hardy', *Phoenix*, (London, 1936).
Lewes, George Henry. *The Principles of Success in Literature*, (London, 1865).
_____ 'The Course of Modern Thought', *Fortnightly Review*, 27, (1877).
Lucas, John. *The Literature of Change: Studies in the Nineteenth-Century Provincial Novel*, (Brighton and New York, 1977).
Macherey, Pierre. *A Theory of Literary Production*, (tr. Geoffrey Wall), (London, 1978).
Malcolmson, Robert W. *Popular Recreations in English Society, 1700–1850*, (Cambridge, 1973).
Mannix, Daniel P. *Freaks: We Who Are Not as Others*, (San Francisco, 1990).
Mill, J. S. *Collected Works*, (London, 1977).
Miller, J. Hillis. *Fiction and Repetition: Seven English Novels*, (Oxford, 1982).
Millgate, Michael. *Thomas Hardy: His Career as a Novelist*, (London, 1971).
_____ *Thomas Hardy: A Critical Biography*, (London, 1982).
Morrell, Roy. *Thomas Hardy: The Will and the Way*, (Kuala Lumpur, 1965).

Müller, Friedrich Max. *Introduction to the Science of Religion*, (London, 1873).

Parke, A. S. 'The Folklore of Sixpenny Handley', *Folklore*, 74, (1963).

Paterson, John. 'An Attempt at Grand Tragedy' in *Hardy: The Tragic Novels*, (ed. R. P. Draper).

Phelps, William Lyon. *Autobiography, with Letters*, (New York, 1939).

Roman, Leslie G., Christian Smith, Linda K., with Ellsworth, Elizabeth (eds). *Becoming Feminine: The Politics of Popular Culture*, (Lewes, East Sussex and Philadelphia, 1988).

Springer, Marlene. *Hardy's Use of Allusion*, (London, 1983).

Stallybrass, Peter and White, Allon. *The Politics and Poetics of Transgression*, (London, 1986).

Stewart, J. I. M. *Thomas Hardy*, (London, 1971).

Stubbs, Patricia. *Women and Fiction: Feminism and the Novel 1880–1920*, (Brighton, 1979).

Tanner, Tony. 'Colour and Movement in *Tess of the d'Urbervilles*', *Critical Quarterly*, 10, (1968).

_____ *Adultery in the Novel*, (Baltimore and London, 1979).

Taylor, Richard H. *The Neglected Hardy: Thomas Hardy's Lesser Novels*, (London, 1982).

Trollope, Anthony. *An Autobiography*, (Oxford and New York, 1980).

_____ *Doctor Thorne*, (London, 1981).

Vernon, John. *Money and Fiction: Literary Realism in the Nineteenth and Early Twentieth Centuries*, (Ithaca, N.Y., 1984).

Waring, Edward. *Ghosts and Legends of the Dorset Countryside*, (Tisbury, Wilts., 1977).

Waugh, Evelyn. *Work Suspended and Other Stories*, (London, 1982).

Widdowson, Peter. *Hardy in History: A Study in Literary Sociology*, (London, 1989).

Williams, Merryn. *Thomas Hardy and Rural England*, (London, 1972).

Wotton, George. *Thomas Hardy: Towards a Materialist Criticism*, (Totowa, New Jersey, 1985).

Index